"A chilling story well told. The pace never slows in this noir thriller, taking readers on a stark trail of fear."

Carolyn G. Hart, N.Y. Times and USA Today Bestselling Author

Praise For The Author

"I love the way this man writes! I adore his style. There is something about it that makes me feel as if I'm someplace I'm not supposed to be, seeing things I'm not supposed to see and that is so delicious."
Rebecca Forster, USA Today Bestselling Author

This book "is creative and captivating. It features bold characters, witty dialogue, exotic locations, and non-stop action. The pacing is spot-on, a solid combination of intrigue, suspense, and eroticism. A first-rate thriller, this book is damnably hard to put down. It's a tremendous read."
ForeWord Reviews

"A terrifying, gripping cross between James Patterson and John Grisham. Jagger has created a truly killer thriller."
J.A. Konrath, International Bestselling Author

"As engaging as the debut, this exciting blend of police procedural and legal thriller recalls the early works of Scott Turow and Lisa Scottoline."
Library Journal

"The well-crafted storyline makes this a worthwhile read. Stuffed with gratuitous sex and over-the-top violence, this novel has a riveting plot."
Kirkus Reviews

"Verdict: The pacing is relentless in this debut, a hard-boiled novel with a shocking ending. The supershort chapters will please those who enjoy a James Patterson–style

page-turner"
Library Journal

A "clever and engrossing mystery tale involving gorgeous women, lustful men and scintillating suspense."
ForeWord Reviews

"Part of what makes this thriller thrilling is that you sense there to be connections among all the various subplots; the anticipation of their coming together keeps the pages turning."
Booklist

"This is one of the best thrillers I've read yet."
New Mystery Reader Magazine

"A superb thriller and an exceptional read."
Midwest Book Review

"Verdict: This fast-paced book offers fans of commercial thrillers a twisty, action-packed thrill ride."
Library Journal

"Another masterpiece of action and suspense."
New Mystery Reader Magazine

"Fast paced and well plotted . . . While comparisons will be made with Turow, Grisham and Connelly, Jagger is a new voice on the legal/thriller scene. I recommend you check out this debut book, but be warned . . . you are not going to be able to put it down."
Crimespree Magazine

WOMAN
ON THE
RUN

THRILLER PUBLISHING GROUP, INC.

WOMAN
ON THE
RUN

JIM MICHAEL HANSEN

R.J. JAGGER

THRILLER PUBLISHING GROUP, INC.

WOMAN ON THE RUN

Thriller Publishing Group, Inc.
Golden, Colorado

ISBN 978-1-954518-43-8

Printed in the United States of America

DAY ONE

May 17

Monday

1

Nick Teffinger got pulled out of a deep sleep by a heavy pounding at the front door. It was the middle of the night. There on the porch, under the rage of a ferocious storm, he found a woman he'd never seen before, a black woman to be precise, drenched as much as a human being could possibly be. She brought her face closer to where he could see it and said, "My name is Kimona. I have a message for you."

Her voice was foreign, Jamaican, maybe.

"Hold on."

He looked past her to see if anyone else was there, grabbed a quick towel to wrap around his waist, then took off the chain and pulled the door open. The woman wore jean shorts and a sleeveless T-shirt that rode high and let her navel show. Down below were flip-flops. She looked to be about twenty-five and in very good shape. Around her neck hung several gold chains and a cross. Tattoos covered her left arm.

No car was parked in the street.

She must have either walked or got dropped off.

"Come in," he said.

The woman shifted her feet and stayed where she was. "This will only take a second. The message I have is from Janjak. She wants you to come to Haiti. When you get there, she's going to arrange a meeting between you and Jori-Ray Rose."

Jori-Ray Rose.

The name was a sucker punch to Teffinger's gut.

She murdered Senator John Stone's daughter five years ago.

Teffinger put her away.

She'd become nothing more than a distant memory until just a few months ago, when she escaped.

"You have twenty-four hours. If you're not physically in Haiti by then, don't bother," the woman added.

"Is that where Jori-Ray's hiding? In Haiti? With Janjak?"

"Yes."

"Does she know you're here telling me this?"

"Of course. She wants to talk to you. That's why I'm here."

She smiled.

Then she leaned in and gave him a long soft kiss on the lips.

"That's from Janjak. She told me to be absolutely sure you got it. Come alone. If you bring anyone, all bets are off."

Then she turned and disappeared into the storm.

Janjak.

Teffinger had shoved her into the furthest corners of his psyche, never to be remembered or thought of again. Now, just like that, hearing her name out loud was all it took to bring it all back to the surface—her powers, her sexy ways, and most of all that horrific night on the forbidden island when Johnny Rail met his fate with a machete, either at Teffinger's hand, or Janjak's—it still wasn't clear.

He headed back to bed, closed his eyes and listened to the rage of the storm.

Sleep didn't come.

Instead his mind twisted this way and that, eventually taking him to that crazy moonlit night on the beach last year when the only two people in the world were him and Janjak.

* * *

Janjak was dancing in the sand with her top off and her arms up, as if not having a care in the world.

Teffinger took a seat and watched.

Although he fought it, her movements resonated in the deep recesses of his brain. He was wired for them. His eyes were always on the hunt for them. His loins were always ready for them. His tongue was always ready to taste them.

"Do you like me?" she said.

"No."

She laughed.

"Liar."

To prove herself right, she unwrapped her skirt and threw it at him. Under it, she wore nothing. Her body gyrated under the moonlight and her hands played in the air above her head.

"How about now? Do you like me now?"

"This won't work," he said.

A minute passed.

"Take me," she said. "Take me and after you do, I'll make that call you want. You can have your precious little princess back. I'll leave her alone."

He knew a trick when he saw one.

"No thanks."

"Do it now, right now, otherwise I'm going to close my

eyes and kill her."

He grunted.

"That's not possible."

"Mark the time," she said.

Then she laid down on her back on the sand, got her body perfectly still, and closed her eyes.

A second passed, then another and another and another. Teffinger's brain exploded with uncertainty. Could the woman really do it? Was there any chance she actually had powers?

He went over and kneeled at her side.

"Stop," he said.

She opened her eyes.

"Take me. Do it slowly," she said. "Take your time."

"If I do you'll set her free?"

"Yes. There are no tricks."

"I want you to stay away from Rail, too," he said.

"He's not part of the deal. Take me or don't, your choice."

She raised her arms above her head.

Against his will, almost as if being pulled by a force, Teffinger put a hand on the woman's stomach. It was warm. It trembled under his touch.

"You love me," she said.

"Yes."

"Show me how much."

His hands went to her breasts, her tiny but oh-so-compelling breasts. He could feel his touch go straight through the woman's body and into her brain.

"You love me," she said.

"I love you."

Those were words he hadn't said in a long, long time. When

they came out, he at first thought he was playing along, placating her, saying and doing whatever it took to get what he'd come all this way to get.

Then he realized that he meant them.

He meant them with every molecule in his body.

He loved her with everything he had and then ten times more.

She kissed him on the mouth.

"We'll be together forever," she said.

"Yes."

"This is our beginning."

"Yes."

"We'll never end."

"No, never."

His hands explored her body, her erotic little body, memorizing her curves and her reactions and her skin. He had never wanted a woman so badly in his life.

Kovi-Ke had been a mistake.

Evil Angel had been a mistake.

Every woman he'd ever met had been a mistake.

He realized that now, only too clearly.

He'd been born for her.

She'd been born for him.

He kissed her stomach.

Sand worked its way into his mouth and he didn't care. She was so right. There was nothing else left in the world, only this, only right here, only right now, only her and him, so perfect together, reinventing time and everything else in the universe.

2

M id-morning on Monday, Teffinger pulled the Tundra up to the gated portion of the ritzy Cherry Creek enclave, rang the buzzer for Senator John Stone's residence, and motored up the street when the gate swung open. Here the houses weren't houses, they were a lot more, and now, like five years ago, Teffinger got an uncomfortable hollowness in the pit of his gut as he entered. At the end of the road, backing to open space, was a stately structure straight out of a modern architectural magazine, replete with a circular driveway, water features and designer landscaping. The house itself had to be at least eight or ten thousand square feet, and the grounds went on forever. Teffinger parked on the street, walked to the front door and rang the bell.

The Senator himself answered.

He shook Teffinger's hand with an iron grip, all business, and said, "Thanks for coming. This means a lot."

"No problem."

The man had Teffinger's six-two beat by at least an inch, maybe two, and had the girth and muscle to match. His hair was blond and still thick, even at middle age. He looked like the kind of guy who could hold his own in a bare knuckles fistfight if someone got stupid enough to bring it on.

They ended up out back next to the swimming pool with glasses of lemonade. There, the man leaned in and got straight to the point. "I already talked to Chief Tanner and he filled me in on all the little details of that woman who showed up at your door last night. The reason I wanted to meet with you is to let you know face to face that I want this bitch Jori-Ray Rose back in prison. Do you understand what I'm saying?"

Teffinger nodded.

"Completely."

"I'm still in shock that she even escaped. How the hell does something like that happen in this day and age? She murders my daughter and now five years later she's out walking around in the sunshine, Haiti, I guess?"

"That's the assumption."

"Well, tell me something. Do we have a extradition treaty with Haiti?"

"Yes."

"So, all we have to do is catch her, and they'll ship her ass back?"

"That's the plan, on paper."

"On paper . . . what does that mean, exactly?"

"It means extradition can get tricky sometimes," Teffinger said. "But let's not get ahead of ourselves. The first thing we have to do is catch her."

"And you're going there to do that, right?"

"Exactly."

"Good. Who are you taking?"

"No one. The plan is to meet with Jori-Ray by myself and get whatever intel I can to catch her."

Stone shook his head.

"That's what bugs me. Why does she want to meet with you?"

Teffinger shrugged.

"I haven't a clue."

"You must have an inkling."

"I should but I don't. I'm the enemy. I'm the last person she should want in her face."

The man took a long sip of lemonade and locked eyes with Teffinger. "She's insanely beautiful, that Jori-Ray Rose. You already know that but remember to be careful of her. Even now, after all these years, she's still only twenty-eight. She can ruin your life. She already did it to me." He paused and added, "Don't take that the wrong way. I'm taking a hundred percent responsibility for my part of it. I made mistakes and I'm not too proud to own them. I'm just saying that she has a way to make a man do things. Be careful of her. Don't ever let her in, not even an inch."

Teffinger nodded.

"How's your wife holding up?"

"Catherine? She's fine, so far. The worst part was three months ago when that little bitch escaped. Things have settled down since then. But it's going to get harder if the press catches whiff of this Haiti connection and starts running with it. Catherine's not wired for wave after wave of memory lane. Neither am I to tell you the truth. So the faster we can get this closed, the better it will be on everyone." He tapped his fingers and added, "Tell me about this Haitian woman, Janjak. You know her, apparently."

"That's true. I had a case that took me to Haiti. I crossed paths with her during that."

"And?"

"And, the people over there think she's got powers, voodoo powers or whatever. They believe she can steal souls."

Stone laughed.

"You're kidding, right?"

Teffinger shook his head.

"I'm not. It's a different world over there. People don't mess with her. They don't take the chance."

"Yeah, well, I'm pretty sure no one can steal anyone's soul, no matter where in the world you are, even assuming that there are such things as souls, which, between you and me, I don't believe for a second. But the more pertinent issue is this: how do this voodoo woman and Jori-Ray even know each other?"

"Unknown."

Stone leaned in.

"If Ms. Voodoo had something to do with Jori-Ray escaping, I want her heart ripped out and acid sprayed into the hole."

"I get it."

The man studied Teffinger.

"Jori-Ray was your biggest case," he said. "It was high profile and you had it at the tender age of 29. You did a good job, gathering the evidence, making sure there were no chain-of-custody issues, and all the rest of it. It's probably the thing that eventually launched you to the head of the homicide department. Wouldn't you agree?"

Teffinger nodded.

"I would."

"So button it back up," Stone said. "Things that can pull you up can also drag you back down. You don't want that to happen and neither do I. Do we understand each other?"

"If you're threatening me, I think we do."

Stone smiled and slapped Teffinger on the arm.

"I am, but only lightly. I know you'll do good."

Then he got serious, pulled a photo out of his wallet and handed it to Teffinger. He'd seen it before. It was September

Stone, age fifteen, tenth grade, taken a month before Jori-Ray Rose shot her in the face and killed her.

"Keep that with you," Stone said. "If you lose your way, take it out and give it a good hard look."

Teffinger dropped it in his shirt pocket and said, "Does that work for you?'

Stone nodded.

"Every damn day. I want it back when you're done."

3

It took Teffinger all day and three different airplanes to get to Port-au-Prince International Airport in Haiti, arriving late evening just as the sun was going down. Near the airport he rented an overpriced motorcycle, followed crappy roads filled with crazy drivers and wayward pedestrians into the guts of the city, and eventually checked into a budget hotel called the Villa Blue, located on an edgy street filled with neon bars and clubs. Lots of people were out milling around and doing whatever it was that they were doing. The hot water was lukewarm, and so was the cold water, but the room itself was spacious and the sheets appeared to be fresh enough that he probably wouldn't catch anything. There was no TV or radio. The air conditioner hanging in the window surprised him by actually working when he flipped it on.

With nothing to do in the room, and the hour too early to sleep, he wandered out into the streets. Most of the faces were black but no one paid him much mind on account of his not being the same.

Up the street, the sultry beats of a live Cuban band spilled out the open door of a club called Cadillac Joe's. The place was packed to the rafters. Teffinger weaved through the bodies to the bar, got a beer—something called a Prestige—and made his way up a set of stairs to a balcony area that overlooked the band and the dance floor. Sin and sex and pot wove through the air.

Something rubbed against his ass.

He turned to find a black woman twerking on him. Bent over at the waist with her face pointed away, he couldn't tell what she looked like, but the part he could see was clothed in the shortest Daisy Dukes he'd ever seen.

She gyrated into him like a maniac vibrator, second after second after beautiful second, and, just like that, nothing else existed in the universe, only her.

She was a drug.

He was already addicted.

After an eternity that seemed like it would never end, it suddenly did; the woman pulled away, right in the middle of a song, and wove straight into the crowd, not turning around or looking back.

Her hair was long, straight and pitch-black.

Down below she was barefoot.

Up top she wore a short white cotton shirt that barely covered her breasts, putting a taut stomach and back on full display. Her skin was mocha brown and glistened with moisture from the workout she'd just given him. Her left arm was heavily tattooed.

Just like that, she was gone.

Teffinger's instinct was to follow, but if she was done, she was done. He'd wait until he spotted her again and see if she did the same thing to someone else. If she did, then Teffinger was nothing special. He'd chalk it up to a few good moments and let it go.

It took ten minutes to finally spot her.

She was on the lower level at the side of the stage looking

directly at him. As he spotted her, she curled her finger, indicating for him to come to her.

He swallowed what was left in the bottle, set it on the floor and headed down.

When he got to her, she put her arms around his neck and whispered in his ear, "You don't recognize me, do you?"

He studied her face.

It was beautiful and did in fact look familiar but too vague to place.

She smiled and said, "Think."

He did.

It did no good.

"Do we know each other?"

She nodded.

"Picture me wet."

He tried.

It did no good.

"Let's try this,' she said.

Then she gave him a long slow kiss.

He recognized it immediately.

It was the same as the one he got last night at 3:30 in the morning from the mysterious girl at her door; the kiss that was purportedly from Janjak.

"You're her," he said.

"Very good. Do you remember my name?"

"Kimona," he said.

"Look at you with all the memory cells. I'm impressed."

He'd only been in this part of the universe for less than thirty minutes. The hotel he checked into, he didn't even know that would be the one until he drove by and spotted it.

"This isn't an accident, you being here," he said.

"No."

"So, how'd you know I was here? Did you follow me from the airport?"

"No. Janjak told me."

"She told you I was here? Janjak did?"

She nodded.

"Yes."

"And how did she know?"

The woman shrugged. "I don't know. She knows everything. You know that. Here's the important thing. She wants to be sure you have company tonight. She wants to be sure that anything you want, you get."

"Including you?"

"Especially me."

"And why is that?"

"In case you die tomorrow," she said. "I'm sort of like a last meal."

Teffinger smiled.

"Well, I'll be honest, I am a bit hungry. So I'm going to die tomorrow? Is that what this is? Janjak brought me here to kill me?"

The woman shrugged.

"I don't know what's going on, exactly. I'm just following orders." She rubbed her stomach against his and said, "Why don't we go to your place and get to know each other better?"

Teffinger didn't doubt for a minute that Janjak could and would kill him if there were a legitimate reason. He couldn't pinpoint one though. They hadn't seen each other in over a year. They'd parted as friends, sort of. He didn't see how anything could have changed since then. He had no dark secrets she could have discovered, and he hadn't crossed her, other than in the ways she already knew of.

Kimona tugged at his arm.

"Come on, let's go."

They left the club but instead of taking her to the hotel, Teffinger took the woman for a walk. She turned out to be Kimona Delva, a 26-year-old surfing instructor from Santo Domingo in the Dominican Republic, who came to Janjak for help three years ago when her brother, Crosley, fell into a trance and no doctor could figure out what was wrong. Janjak travelled all the way to his bedside and, although it took the entire night and half the morning alone with him in his room, she pulled him out of it. Kimona, in return, became indebted to her for five years. She was now three years into it with two years remaining.

"It's not like jail or anything bad," she said. "I know a lot of people are scared of her and, to tell the truth, they should be. I've seen stuff nobody should ever have to. But she also does a lot of good things that a lot of people don't know about. I get to help her mostly with that stuff. It's almost like a blessing. I'm thinking about staying on after my five years are done."

"What about the other things? The ugly ones?"

The woman shrugged.

"If you talking about stealing souls and the curses and stuff like that, she usually doesn't involve me in it, at least not directly. She's got two sides. She basically keeps me on the good one, maybe because it suits my personality better and she doesn't have to worry about me running." The woman hesitated and then said, "Do you love her?"

Teffinger considered it.

It actually took him longer than he thought to come up with the answer.

"No."

The woman put an expression on her face, doubtful.

"How about in the past? Have you loved her in the past?"

He wrinkled his brow.

"That's a complicated question. There were some, what I'd call, moments," he said. "I'm not sure exactly what they were and I'm not sure they were all that voluntary on my part. They were something, though; and there was the sex, we did have that. I've never taken the time to sort out what it all was. When I left Haiti I put it all in the rearview mirror." He kicked a can and said, "How about you? Do you love someone?"

She linked her arm through his and drew him tight.

"You," she said.

He chuckled.

"Me?"

"Yes; at least for tonight. Come on. Let's go to the hotel. You don't have to do anything with me if you don't want to but I at least have to get naked and give you a full opportunity. I got some pot we can smoke."

DAY TWO

May 18
Tuesday

4

When Teffinger woke up Tuesday morning, he was alone, on the couch instead of the bed. Kimona had apparently slipped out sometime during the night. She'd done her job well last night, namely got naked, danced for him and offered herself, but he couldn't accept. It was at the orders of Janjak as opposed to her own volition, and that was a deal-breaker. Instead of sex, they smoked pot, cuddled on the couch with their clothes on and told each other stories from their past until they couldn't keep their eyes open any longer.

Teffinger checked around for a note and found none.

He headed outside for a jog through the streets of Port-au-Prince. Last night, awash in the neon and the buzz, the place had been pure magic. Now in the light of day it was achy and hung over.

A mile clicked off.

He was strong, in spite of being up late.

The breathing was a lot easier down here at sea level.

He picked up the pace.

Kimona.

She was in Teffinger's blood.

She filled every pore of his being.

He needed more.

He needed a thousand more nights exactly like last night.

He needed walks on the beach with her.

He needed to get lost with her in a secret place where no one had ever been.

He needed it all, everything, a hundred percent, right now.

Three miles later, he got back to his room. He showered, grabbed some much-needed coffee and a plateful of breakfast, then fired up the Indian and pointed it towards Janjak's lair, reminding himself one last time that he was here to do a job, namely get that murderer Jori-Ray Rose back to prison.

He also needed to be careful doing it.

All that talk from Kimona last night about Teffinger possibly getting killed tomorrow, it was drumming louder and louder inside his gray matter, even more so than last night given that tomorrow was now today. He needed to be careful to not turn his back on Janjak, not for a second. The talk was that she could steal your soul from a distance and you wouldn't even know it until she started to carve it up with a razor blade. She could break you from the inside just because it amused her. Death was no escape. In fact, when you died it got worse. At least while you were alive you had worldly elements in your life. In death there was nothing except Janjak. Once she had you, she had you forever, unless she decided to let you go.

That was the talk.

The first time Teffinger heard it, he laughed.

He didn't do that any more.

That's not to say that he believed it a hundred percent. But there was something going on with the woman; he'd have to admit that a thousand times over if it ever came to it.

Teffinger rode the Indian until he ended up miles and miles

south of the city, on a beaten single-lane dirt road that went on forever before it finally dead-ended at the ocean. He stopped just short of Janjak's place, which was up around the bend, and hid the motorcycle in the foliage as an escape precaution.

No one was around.

He took a deep breath, wiped sweat off his brow with the back of his hand, and proceeded on foot.

This was it.

This is what he'd come for.

Around the bend, aqua waters came into view, lapping softly at a silky sand beach. A jeep and several other vehicles were stationary near a couple of thatched structures that looked like garages or outposts. A barefoot man sitting on the ground in the shade had his back against a wall. His head was bent forward and a hat dipped over his face, in siesta mode. His shirt was off and his chest was thick with muscles. Next to him, leaning against the structure, was a rifle.

Other than him, there was no sign of life.

He'd hoped to see Kimona but she was nowhere in sight.

A rowboat was pulled up on the sand, just out of the water's grip.

Three or four hundred yards offshore a small island made of sand and palms rose out of the water. The thatched roofs of three or four structures were visible on the far side. On the beach were a handful of rowboats.

Teffinger walked over to the siesta guy and nudged him awake with his foot. The man moved like lightning, already up with the rifle in hand, backed up a safe distance, with murder in his eyes. He pointed the barrel at Teffinger's chest just waiting for a reason.

Teffinger held his hands up in a calming manner and said,

"I'm here to see Janjak."

The man surveyed him.

"Are you the one from Denver?"

Teffinger nodded.

"Yeah."

"You're nothing special."

The man nudged the rifle towards the rowboat, indicating for Teffinger to head that way, which he did, as the man followed with the barrel pointed at his back.

Teffinger rowed.

The man sat in the front with the rifle pointed.

Halfway across the inlet, something bumped against the bottom of the hull.

It was a shark, undeniably, a small one, maybe only four feet or so, but definitely enough to rip flesh and crush bones if its prehistoric brain told it to.

Mr. Rifle paid it no mind.

When they made it to shore, the man led Teffinger across the island, winding through the palms and brush, to the opposite side where there was a large structure surrounded by several thatched outbuildings. They made their way past the structures to the beach. Out in the water forty or fifty yards distant was yet another small island, a circular satellite of sand not much more than fifty yards across, holding a few trees and breaking the water's surface by only a marginal amount. The sand between here and there was submersed under the water only a few feet.

The rifle pushed into Teffinger's back.

"Move!"

He turned, saw poison in the man's eyes, and stepped into the water, which was incredibly warm and rose only to his waist as he headed across.

At the island he found what he expected.

On the far side, lying face down on a blanket near the water's edge, was a woman; a woman with very dark skin, wearing a white bikini bottom and no top—Janjak, to be precise. She turned her face briefly towards Teffinger as he approached, too fast for him to make out her mood. When he got to her she said, "Rub my back."

Her voice was deep, as he remembered.

Her back wasn't normal.

It was covered with scars, a hundred or more, each about two inches long, carved in with the tip of a blade, not stitched, and allowed to close on their own, resulting in wounds that were slightly raised and visibly lighter than her skin tone.

One of those had been put there by Teffinger last year. He had no idea where she got the others.

"Thanks for Kimona, last night," he said.

The woman didn't raise her head or show her face, which was hidden against her arm and under long, black dread-locks.

"You wasted her," she said. "That was a mistake."

Teffinger shrugged.

"I was hoping to see her again."

Janjak rolled onto her back, blocked the sun with her hand, and studied him. Her face wasn't pretty but it wasn't ugly either, it was somewhere there in the middle. Her lips were large and her teeth had a slight, almost imperceptible, touch of gray. Her breasts, on full uninhibited display, were small, almost boyish, but her chest and arms and stomach were strong and in their prime. About thirty or so, she didn't look any older than when Teffinger had last seen her, a year ago. She said nothing, rolled back onto her stomach and said, "Rub my back."

Teffinger knelt down in the sand and complied.

The woman's muscles were taut.

Her body was strong and shapely.

Her skin glistened with heat.

"When do I see Jori-Ray?"

"We'll get to all that in due time. Right now, the only thing you need to worry about is my back."

Teffinger had questions but kept his mouth shut.

He worked at the woman's back for a good five minutes. Then she spread her feet apart ever so slightly and said, "Do my ass and my legs."

"Is she here somewhere?"

"We'll get to that," she said. "Just keep rubbing."

Teffinger complied, working from her lower back down to her feet and then up again.

Suddenly another person was there with them, appearing from out of nowhere, walking in knee-deep surf at the edge of the sand. It was Kimona, topless, wearing only a pink bi-kini bottom that played so well against her delicious mocha skin. Teffinger had never seen anything so beautiful in his life.

Janjak got up, grabbed Teffinger's hand and said, "Come on. Let's join her."

5

Teffinger came to consciousness in the bow of a Boston Whaler that was cruising on plane into open turquoise waters. He had no recollection of how he got in that condition but assumed he was either drugged or Janjak had done something to him. The last thing he remembered was making love to Kimona at the edge of the water while Janjak sat in a yoga position on the sand and watched.

At the wheel of the vessel was the rifle guy who detected Teffinger's movement and said, "Stay down." Neither Janjak nor Kimona were present.

Teffinger's pants pockets were empty.

His cell phone was gone.

His wallet was gone.

The keys for the motorcycle were gone.

There was nothing there, nothing.

The sky above was clear and filled with sunshine. The water rose and fell calmly with easy swells as the Whaler cut through it. Above, three seagulls flew in the opposite direction, back towards land.

They continued for forty-five minutes or more, finally arriving at a string of three small islands or cays, none bigger than five or six acres, all within a few hundred yards of one another. They circled around and through, seeing hypnotic pristine beaches and swaying palms but not a single sign of human life, not now or from the past, stretching all the way back to the beginning of time.

Teffinger had been here before.

This is where Johnny Rail was murdered.

He knew the rumors, namely, the waters here were cursed. The islands used to be rocky crags. No one ever came here. Something—some called them Dyab—slowly transformed them over time, turning them into paradises. No sailor could pass by without stopping.

People disappeared.

Boats disappeared.

There were stories of bad things, supernatural things, things where souls got dragged under the water and were made to live forever with no air.

Whether the rumors were true or not didn't matter.

The reality was that no one ever came here.

It wasn't worth taking the chance.

The rifle guy maneuvered the Whaler between the three islands, out of sight of open waters, and trimmed the engine up as he drifted into a beach. The bow nestled into the sand. He pickled up the rifle, pointed it at Teffinger's face and said, "Out, cowboy."

Teffinger complied, dropping over the side into waist-high lukewarm waters, and making his way to the dry sand of the beach.

The rifle guy backed up, gave Teffinger the finger, and disappeared.

The beach was pristine and under other circumstances Teffinger could have spent the rest of his life right there with no regrets. The opposite side of the island was no more than a couple of hundred yards over.

He cut across.

Halfway there he came across a human skull lying in the sand and picked up it. It was bone dry and brittle. Thirty feet away was a pile of bones, a large pile, human skeletons, with twenty or thirty easily identified skulls. None contained flesh. It looked like a body dump of some kind. Not recently though. They have been here for years, maybe decades.

He dropped the skull and kept going.

What he found for the rest of the island was nature uninterrupted, nature strutting her stuff with all the passion and mystery and eroticism she could command.

There were no signs of human activity.

There were no footprints.

There was no trash.

So, what was going on?

Had Janjak dropped him here to rot to death?

Is this the death Kimona had been talking about last night?

His heart pounded.

No one ever came here.

He knew that.

Janjak knew that he knew it.

She knew that he already had to be worried about rotting to death. Was that her plan? To kill him slowly so he could watch every minute of it until he went crazy and his throat and lungs turned to dust?

Would Kimona come to save him?

Or was she just a temporary meaningless mirage offered up by Janjak?

Teffinger waded across the inlet to the second island and explored it, finding nothing but nature. Then he headed to the third island and got more of the same.

Over an hour had passed.

He was alone.

He hadn't spotted anything that could be eaten. There were no bananas or fruits or berries. Likewise, fresh water was absent. There were no streams or ponds. The sky held no indications of wet weather in the near future.

In an effort to conserve his strength, he made his way into the shade of a palm tree where he leaned against it and watched the waters lap gently against the sands.

He should have never trusted Janjak.

She'd set the easiest trap in the world and he'd walked right into it, not just with eager feet, but with a giant stupid grin on his face.

He was pathetic.

The hours passed. With each one, Teffinger wanted—no, needed—for something to happen, anything, but nothing ever did; no one came, no boats appeared on the horizon, no planes flew overhead. The pure beauty of the island was quickly dimming. Instead of a tropical paradise it was now a place that could not and would not give him water or food. The white pristine beaches were now barbwire fences that he couldn't go past. The sun-drenched aqua waters mocked his inability to quench his thirst. The gentle sounds of the lapping waves were reminders that there was no music.

The side of the island that faced the open waters was covered in palms. Among them, Teffinger was all but invisible to any ships that might pass.

Plus, he had no fire.

He had no mirrors.

He had arms that could wave.

That was it.

Late afternoon came. He hadn't eaten since this morning. If a thick juicy cheeseburger with a side of fries and a beer suddenly dropped out of the heavens and landed on a table in front of him, he could easily wolf it all down in a matter of minutes. Then he could do it again.

None dropped, though.

He walked in the shallows of the waters, looking for anything that might be edible. There were starfish. He threw a couple up on the sand to dry out. Later, he'd crack them open with a rock and see if there was anything inside. There was an occasional small fish but far too wary and quick to be caught with bare hands.

Then he had an idea.

He made his way back to the body dump where he broke bones until one splintered with a sharp pointed end. He tore off part of his shirt and tied that bone to a stick.

There; he had a spear of sorts.

He went back to the shallows to try his luck only to find out that his luck was bad. The small fish were too small and too quick to spear. If there were larger fish, they must be out farther and deeper down.

He did, however, find crabs hidden under rocks.

He pulled one apart and squeezed out the guts. They stank like rotten fish and couldn't have been grosser looking. Maybe, if things got really bad, he'd come to a point where he'd put something like that in his mouth. That time hadn't come yet, though. He put it down to dry in the sun, marking the location so he could get back to it later.

He tasted the saltwater, rinsing it around in his mouth but not swallowing.

Who wrote that poem about the ancient mariner—water,

water, every where, nor any drop to drink—?

Coleridge, maybe?

He hadn't thought of it for more than a decade.

The afternoon morphed into evening.

With his spear, Teffinger hunted for snakes or frogs or any-thing else potentially edible, but found nothing.

Then he laid palm leaves on the beach in a makeshift bed and waited for the darkness to come.

When it did, he laid on his back, using his shoes as a pil-low, and stared up at the stars.

Kimona hadn't come for him.

If she cared for him at all, she would have found a way.

He curled up on his side and closed his eyes, expecting sleep to take him quickly, as it always did.

It didn't though, not tonight.

His throat was sandpaper.

Tomorrow morning it would be even worse.

He needed to make something happen as soon as he woke up.

He'd start with the crab. He'd get one down into his stom-ach and see if he could hold it there without throwing up.

The time for being comfortable had passed.

The time to do what was necessary had come.

DAY THREE

May 19
Wednesday

6

Teffinger woke Wednesday morning stiff and sore and alone on the beach. The first rays of dawn were just beginning to lift the blackness out of the sky. Sand was on his face, under his fingernails and in his clothes. A dip in the lapping waters cleaned him off and woke him up. Too wet to put his clothes back on, he flipped over rocks until he found a crab that scampered the wrong way and ended up in his other hand. He killed it with a rock, cracked it open and worked some of the innards out with the spear. Before he could chicken out, he shoved them in his mouth and swallowed. He let some time pass to see how his body reacted.

He didn't get queasy.

He didn't vomit.

So he held back his gags and got the rest of it down.

The deep hunger in his stomach softened.

So did the dark thoughts in his brain.

He could live on crabs if he had to. As for water, it would rain sooner or later. When it did, he'd catch it with palm leaves and drink until he was ready to explode. Before then, he also needed to think of a way to store it.

Maybe he could build a bowl out of leaves.

Or maybe he could fill his shoes.

At a minimum, he could take off his clothes and drench them, then wrap them in leaves and keep them in the shade.

He should be able to ring water out of them out for at least a day, maybe even longer.

There was a chance he could actually survive.

All he had to do was last long enough for someone to show up. When Denver didn't hear from him, sooner or later they'd send someone. They knew he was going to meet with Janjak. They would be able to track her down. After that, though, it would be tough going. She'd never tell them anything, not in a million years; and she'd keep Kimona hidden away. They wouldn't have cause to arrest her and, even if they did, the locals would have to do it, and they'd never cross her. It was doubtful that Denver would ever hear about the islands, much less connect Janjak to them.

Denver was a chance but it was a slim one at best.

He had to face it.

He might be here a long, long time.

If he ran into a stretch where it didn't rain for five or six or seven days, he'd be dead. He'd end up drinking seawater and bouncing off to crazy-land.

Calm down.

Just take it one minute at a time.

There had to be a source of moisture other than rain. Maybe there were leaves he could chew; and, although he hadn't seen any yet, maybe there was some kind of fruit, mangoes or coconuts or whatever.

He'd seen something living in small shells, possibly snails.

They looked slimy but juicy.

Somewhere in the back of his mind, though, he remembered something bad about them—that they gave you a stomach bug or diarrhea or a fever or whatever. Relatively inconsequential in civilization, something like that could be fatal in a place like this. He'd stay away from them, at least for a while.

He got better at catching crabs, netting two more by late afternoon. He also got better at eating them. That, in turn, gave him energy to explore. He found some kind of thorny plant that had small green berries but when he tasted one it was bitter and acidy; maybe a warning. He decided to hold off on them until and unless things got desperate.

His better bet was the sea.

Late afternoon, he spotted a giant turtle paddling slowly close to shore, six feet or so under the surface. He dived for it but it took off like a rocket.

The sun beat down all day, producing a few high thin clouds in the afternoon but nothing that would even remotely turn to rain. Late evening, he took one more slow walk around, finding no footprints in the sand or evidence of civilization, and, more to the point, no indications of water.

As soon as it got dark enough to lie down on the beach and close his eyes for the night, he did.

Thoughts were difficult to form.

The exhausting dryness in his mouth and throat had begun to creep into his entire body.

His eyes were dry.

His skin was dry.

Every organ inside him was dry.

His brain wasn't working right.

He'd trade his house, his '67 Corvette and everything he owned for a gallon of water. Hell, he'd even trade his soul to Janjak.

Was that what she wanted?

Was that the design behind all this?

Tomorrow morning he had to be strong. He had to resist the temptation to fill his body with seawater. It would give him a brief measure of relief, then it would leave him with a body and brain full of salt. It would leave him with a thirst ten times what it was now. It would drive him crazy, fast.

He closed his eyes.

The darkness felt like whisky.

He smiled, briefly.

Then everything turned black.

DAY FOUR

May 20
Thursday

7

When Teffinger woke with the sun high, he realized he'd slept well into the morning. He knew why; sleep was better than life. In sleep there were crazy demon dreams but no real pain. He muscled to his feet, unsteady, got out of his clothes, shook the sand out of them, and then laid down in the shallow aqua waters at the edge of the sand.

The waves lapped gently over his legs and chest.

He took a mouthful of water, swirled it around and then spit it out.

That helped, a lot, actually.

He did it again.

Should he swallow some, just a little, to see what happened?

The sky was blue and full of sunshine; in other circumstances, a paradise.

No rain was coming, not an ounce.

Seagulls flew overhead.

Where did they get their water?

Did they drink the sea?

He laid there for some time. The movement of the waves across his body was like a massage from a beautiful woman. For a while, it even masked the hunger in his stomach. Then the hunger broke free like a sudden maniac demon.

He waded over to the rocky area where the crabs were. He

turned over a lot of rocks before he finally got a hit. It was too fast for him, though. He was a lot slower than yesterday. His coordination wasn't as good either. He worked at it for over an hour and never got close to catching one. Exhausted to the point of desperation, he made his way into the shade of the palms, got dressed and closed his eyes.

Today may well be the day.

It had come a lot faster than he thought it would.

He fell into a fitful, desperate sleep, the kind you might never wake up from.

Nightmares filled his psyche.

They twitched his body and tugged at his breath.

Then, he was drowning. His mouth and face and lungs were filling with water. He choked with a violence so strong that it brought him to sudden consciousness and jerked his torso into an upright position. What he saw, if he could believe it, was someone standing above him, pouring water over his face.

It was a female, but he couldn't make out her features given the blinding glare of the sun above her.

She wasn't Janjak.

She wasn't Kimona.

She was white.

She had long, flowing blond hair.

She said nothing, turned and walked down the beach. Teffinger watched her for a few moments, too exhausted to give chase, before realizing that something was on the sand next to him, namely three plastic jugs filled with water.

There was also a Styrofoam cooler filled with food.

8

Late afternoon, on the beach at surf's edge, Teffinger spotted someone walking towards him from the opposite direction, still some distance off but definitely someone real. It was a female with long blond hair. This time, he knew who she was.

She was Jori-Ray Rose, the killer.

She was the one he was here to capture.

His chest pounded.

His body was strong again. It had recovered quickly. He could subdue her easily if he could get his hands on her.

As she got closer, he saw something in her right hand.

It was a gun.

He looked around for a rock or stick or anything that might serve as a weapon. There was nothing, only sand and water. He kept walking towards her. When he got close enough, he'd remain calm and show he wasn't a threat. He'd close the gap, nonchalantly, inch by inch.

Then he'd pounce.

Twenty feet away, she shouted "Stop right there!"

Teffinger complied.

The woman was in surprisingly good shape considering she'd been eating prison food for the last five years. Her body was strong and solid. The last time he saw her was in court, back when she was 23. Now she was 28 and even more beautiful than she'd been before. Her skin was golden. Obviously, she'd been hiding out down here in Haiti for some time.

"No food, no water," the woman said. "How did that feel?"

Teffinger raked his hair back with his fingers.

It immediately flopped back down over his forehead.

"Whatever you're doing, it isn't going to work," he said. "Why don't we sit down and figure this out."

She smiled.

"I wanted you to suffer," she said. "I wanted you to remember what suffering is. That's what I've gone through for five years. Five years!"

A small wave lapped at Teffinger's feet, swirling the sand. He shifted to maintain his balance, working a half step closer to her in the process.

"Look, we can work this out," he said. "What you're doing now, you're only making things worse."

The woman fired the gun into the water next to Teffinger's feet and shouted, "Back up!"

He complied.

Then he waited.

"I'm going to say something and I want you to listen very, very carefully," the woman said. "Can you do that?"

Teffinger shrugged.

"Sure."

"Good," she said. "I did not kill September Stone."

She paused to let the words sink in.

Teffinger frowned.

"You're talking to the wrong person," he said. "You had a trial. You were convicted. You had an appeal. The conviction was upheld. There's nothing I can do about any of that."

The woman scowled.

Then she fired the gun into the air.

"You're not listening to what I'm saying! I did not kill September Stone. I didn't do it! I shouldn't be in jail!" She shook her head in disgust and said, "It's your fault."

Teffinger wrinkled his brow in confusion.

"My fault?"

"Yes, exactly."

"And how is that?"

"Because you didn't go after the evidence," she said. "All you did was go after me. You didn't do your job; and because of that, I've been rotting in prison for the last five years. Now, things are going to change. You're going to go back and do your job. Because until you do, the person who killed September is out there somewhere running around ass-fuck free. And I'm not going back to jail; you better believe that. I'll die first."

Teffinger shook his head.

"The case is closed," he said. "It's been closed for over five years."

"Re-open it," the woman said.

Teffinger frowned.

"That's not how it works," he said.

"Do it or die, your choice."

She gave him one last look, then turned and walked off down the beach.

Teffinger followed at a safe distance.

She waded to the next sand-spit, got into a beached Boston Whaler guarded by three men, and took off.

Her hair blew.

The boat threw clean white spray into the air.

He headed back, took a swallow of water just because he

could, and sat in the shade of a palm tree.

It's your fault.

You didn't go after the evidence.

All you did was go after me.

The words had come out of the woman's mouth as if they were the stone-cold truth. She believed them, that was apparent; Teffinger had seen no lies. That didn't mean they were true, though. He did go after the evidence. It was the evidence that went after her, not him. Everything had pointed to her.

Every damn thing.

9

Early evening, a woman appeared from out of nowhere, a beautiful woman with long straight hair dyed blue, walking up the beach barefoot towards Teffinger carrying a box, a heavy one, judging by her posture. She was in her early thirties, with a fit body moving like a symphony under a green hippie-like sundress.

She smiled, set the box down in the sand, and said, "Do you remember me?"

Teffinger focused.

She did look familiar, he had to admit, but from where he didn't know.

"Picture a short brunette weave and conservative gray suit. And white glasses."

White glasses.

He suddenly knew who she was, namely Alabama Avery, Esq., Jori-Ray's attorney from the murder trial. The woman smiled and shook his hand.

"Nice to see you again," she said.

"Alabama Avery," he said.

"That's right. Call me 'Bama, please. Jori-Ray has given me full permission to talk to you. She's waived any and all rights to the attorney-client privilege." She took the top off the box, which was full of documents, and handed him a piece of paper. It was a release signed by Jori-Ray, dated over a month ago.

Teffinger frowned.

"You need to be real careful," he said. "You need to be real sure you're not doing anything to aid and abet a fugitive."

She patted his arm.

"Thanks for your concern but it's not necessary. Jori-Ray didn't kill September Stone. That's what I'm here to talk about."

Teffinger raked his hair back with his fingers.

"You already talked about that, to the jury if I remember right," he said.

She shrugged.

"That's correct, but the jury didn't get the whole story."

"And why not?"

"Lots of reasons, actually," she said. "The rules of evidence, as I'm sure you're aware, don't allow everything in, for starters. But more to the point, I didn't let Jori-Ray testify. If I did—and put her credibility at issue—the prosecution would have been able to bring up everything in her past. That would have fried her." She got a distant look, exhaled and added, "That was my thinking at the time. Now, reflecting back on it, that was probably a critical mistake."

"Yeah, well, you make your calls and you live with the results."

The woman nodded.

"Yeah, I know how it works. Let me ask you something, though. Did you ever wonder how I ended up with the case?"

"Not really. You were someone in the public defender's office. She was accused of a crime. I never really thought about it past that."

"I'd never had a homicide trial. Ten other people in our office had. Robert Baxter had had seven. So why was I chosen?"

He shrugged.

"Everyone starts somewhere at some time."

"True, but in this case, I was chosen to fail," she said. "I was the least likely to give her a good defense. Someone wanted her in jail and somehow, some way, put pressure on our office to make sure it happened."

Teffinger wrinkled his brow.

"What evidence do you have to support that?"

"Just the fact that it happened."

He shook his head.

"If you're saying there was corruption or some kind of conspiracy, you need a whole lot more than suspicion to make something like that fly. And here's the worst part. Even if you're right, even if you got the case because you were the least likely to succeed, the fact is that you're still a lawyer, and Jori-Ray got legal representation. She had her trial. That's the bottom line." He added, "If you weren't qualified, or if you screwed up, the appellate attorney needs to raise an issue of ineffective assistance of counsel on the appeal. Was that done?"

She nodded.

"That issue is always raised in a murder case."

"And?"

"And, the appellate court found that it had no merit," she said. "But the issue of a conspiracy within our own office obviously was never raised. The issue of outside pressure on our office was never raised."

"Because there was no proof," Teffinger said.

"That's correct," she said. "But that doesn't mean it didn't happen."

He shook his head.

"Okay, I'll play, just for argument's sake. Who put the pressure on your office?"

"My guess? John Stone."

"Why?"

"Because he's the only person in the mix who has the influence and the connections. And he's the father of the victim."

"So, he wanted to be sure Jori-Ray went down? Is that what you're saying?"

The woman nodded.

"He didn't want anybody good at her side. He didn't want anyone who could wiggle her off the hook."

Teffinger considered it.

"Maybe he did place a call. Who knows? Let's suppose he did. The bottom line is still the bottom line. Jori-Ray had an attorney. She had a trial. She had an appeal. The system went through all its steps."

"You're not getting it," the woman said. "You're assuming that John Stone wanted Jori-Ray to go down because he believed she was guilty. But there's a flip side to that. Maybe he knew she didn't do it. Maybe he arranged for her to go down so that he could protect someone."

"Who?"

"I don't know."

"Himself?"

"I don't know."

"Let's see if I have this right," Teffinger said. "Are you saying that John Stone killed his daughter?"

"I don't know. All I know is that you never looked into it. You never even considered him as a suspect. You never looked into anyone except Jori-Ray."

"Why would he kill his own daughter?"

"I don't know. Look through this box. There's a lot of stuff in here that no one has ever seen. I'll be back tomorrow to talk some more."

He followed her to a boat guarded by two men with rifles and watched as they motored away.

10

Shortly before dark, something happened that Teffinger didn't expect, namely, another visitor showed up from out of nowhere. This time is was Kimona; up above, topless, except for the straps of a backpack; and down below, wearing a short blue wraparound skirt. She had a big smile on her face as she approached. Just like that, all the addictions came flooding back. Whatever the reason she didn't bring him food or water, she was forgiven. The only thing he wanted was to melt into her.

She dropped the backpack to the ground, wrapped her arms around his neck and gave him a long, deep kiss.

"Before we play, we need to take care of a tiny bit of business first."

"Play?"

She turned around, wiggled her ass into him and said, "I'm here until the morning."

"On you own? Or because Janjak sent you?"

She ran a finger down his nose.

"Both. I need you to take a selfie video. Make it to Sydney. Tell her you're fine. Tell her you're working on a plan to capture Jori-Ray. Tell her that you don't want anyone coming to Haiti. Tell her your phone is compromised so you're sending this from a friend. Tell her you'll try to contact her again in another three or four days."

Teffinger didn't mind the idea.

Most of it was true.

Plus, he didn't want Sydney showing up and possibly getting herself in danger.

So he did it.

Kimona said, "Hold on. I'm going to text it to Janjak and she'll forward it on." Ten seconds later she said, "Done." She pulled a bottle of red wine out of the backpack, grabbed Teffinger's hand and said, "I'm going to dance for you later."

"Oh, yeah?"

"Yeah. First let's take a walk and get drunk."

They walked on the wet sand at the water's edge, passing the bottle back and forth as the sun set. It was picture perfect except for in Teffinger's gut, which sensed something to be wrong, so much so that he finally grabbed Kimona's arm, jerked her to a stop and said, "Something's on your mind."

She studied him, almost as if trying to figure out if she could trust him.

Then she said, "Janjak's men abducted a woman this afternoon."

Teffinger pictured it.

That's exactly what happened to Kovi-Ke.

It's how he ended up here in Haiti in the first place.

"Who?"

"I don't know. Janjak's going to do a big voodoo ritual with her at midnight tonight. They've been preparing all day. She knew it was upsetting me and told me to go and spend the night with you." She paused and added, "I know I was telling you before about how I was thinking about signing up for more time with her after my five years were done. That wasn't true. I think I was saying it because she can read my thoughts. The truth is, I'm scared, Nick. I'm scared to death. I need to break away from her and do it quick."

"Before your five years are up?"

The woman nodded, almost as if afraid to mouth Yes out loud.

Then she said, "Will you help me?"

A chill ran up his spine, straight into his brain, almost as if a warning by Janjak to be very careful about how he answered.

To his amazement, he said, "Sure. Why not?"

She looked at him, incredulous.

"You will? Really?"

He took a long swallow from the bottle.

"We'll have to be careful," he said. "Let me see if I can think of a plan. Until then, just keep everything normal."

"Nick, she has to think I died, otherwise she'll go after my brother. That's what the plan has to be. We need to fake my death and it needs to be perfect. She has to really believe it, way down deep inside. How do we do that? She knows everything."

"Let me think about it."

11

eading back on the beach with the sun almost down, Kimona told Teffinger that she'd met Jori-Ray and didn't believe she was a killer. "She's a little wild, I'll give her that. You were the detective on the case, right?"

"That's right."

"So what happened?"

Teffinger flashed back, not really too sure how much he wanted to volunteer. Then the words started coming out.

"It was actually one of my first cases," he said. "I'd only been in homicide for a year at that point. A guy named John Stone was a big-shot attorney in a big-shot law firm that was based out of New York but had branches all over the world, including Denver. Stone had come out of New York to start and grow the Denver operation, which was up to about six-ty-five lawyers at the time of the murder. He had a wife he'd been married to for a long time, by the name of Catherine. They had one daughter named September who everyone called Nine. One night John Stone made a frantic 911 call to the effect that his daughter had just been shot and looked like she was dead. The paramedics and local police responded. I was the detective on duty that night and got called in. And that's how it all started."

"How does Jori-Ray fit in?"

"Ah, good question. She was a call girl who operated out

of a local escort service called Ladies in Waiting. She specialized in the richer clients who had more off-beaten kinkier requests and could afford what it took to pay someone to fulfill them."

"Meaning what?"

"Meaning whatever the guy's kink was; bondage, threesomes, watching, whatever. Jori-Ray really had no limits so long as the money was right. John Stone was the kind of guy who could always make the money right. To cut to the chase, they ended up spending a lot of time together. Stone fell for her and she fell for him. He was going to leave his wife and they were going to get formally married."

"What about the wife? She knew nothing?"

Teffinger shook his head.

"Wives never have a clue," he said. "Here's the twist. Stone had thrown his hat into the ring for Senator. His name was on the ballot for the upcoming election in November."

"When did September get shot?"

"Actually, in September, same as her name."

Kimona chuckled.

"That's a little weird."

"Everything's a little weird," Teffinger said. "Anyway, Stone had changed his mind about Jori-Ray and started to try to buy her off and make her go away. The money thing should have worked but didn't because she was too emotionally invested. Things got ugly. She wanted him. She wanted to be a Senator's wife."

"You got to feel for her, a little."

"Yeah, well, anything on the come is just that, something on the come. Time goes on and Stone cuts off communications with her, stops taking her calls and whatnot. She shows up after dark one night when Catherine was going to be in

Boston at a philanthropy event. She breaks into the house with a gun to confront Stone and bring him to his senses. Inside the house, she encounters September in the kitchen. They end up in a fight, Jori-Ray shoots her, and then runs off."

"So, the father, Stone, was he home, or what?"

"Oh, he was home alright, but he was way at the far end of the residence, asleep. He takes pills. He didn't even hear the fighting. It wasn't until the gun went off that he woke up. Anyway, the story I just told you is backed up by tons of hard evidence, galore. A security camera picked up Jori-Ray approaching the residence and breaking in. You can see the gun in her hand. It was a 9mm SIG. It turned out to be registered to a real estate developer named Bradley Lee. Lee testified at trial that he had Jori-Ray over to his loft one night two months earlier for sex. The next morning, he found the gun, two Rolexes and ten thousand dollars in cash missing. The two Rolexes were later recovered from Jori-Ray's safe. The SIG was recovered two hundred yards away from John Stone's house, in the open space. That's the route Jori-Ray took when she ran off."

"Were her fingerprints on it?"

"No. She wore gloves the whole time. You can see them in the security footage. Oh, I almost forgot the most important part. Jori-Ray's blood was at the scene from her fight with September. It was in September's clothes, on the kitchen floor, all over. September had only been fifteen at the time but she put up an awfully good fight. Jori-Ray's skin was under her fingernails."

"Damn," Kimona said. "That's sad."

"The press was all over everything, and when Stone's connection with a call-girl came to light, he bowed out of the race. Over the next four years though he mended fences with both the public and his wife Catherine and gave it another try."

"And got elected?"

"Yep."

"Wow. You wouldn't think so."

"He's a persuasive guy," Teffinger said. "And he's as good looking as hell."

"You know, I hear the story, and I appreciate all the evidence, but I still can't picture Jori-Ray shooting someone dead; maybe by accident, but not on purpose."

Teffinger grunted.

"That's where the law comes in," he said. "Jori-Ray had intentionally broken into and entered a private residence, armed with a stolen gun, and was in the middle of committing a felony. While committing that felony she shot and killed someone who was lawfully inside that home and defending her property and life. Even if the shot happened by accident during a fight, it's still a homicide." He exhaled and added, "What I don't get is how Janjak and Jori-Ray are connected. How do they even know each other? Do you know?"

"No."

"No?"

"No. I don't have a clue." She squeezed his hand. "Nick, are you going to re-open the case?"

He didn't hesitate.

"No."

"But—"

"It's not even mine to re-open," he said. "It's something the district attorney would have to do and that never, ever happens, except in exceptional cases, like someone being cleared by DNA evidence obtained after the fact. I was just the detective. All I did was collect the evidence and present it to the D.A. It's their call at that point. If Jori-Ray wants me to go out hunting for new evidence just because she proclaims her innocence, it's not going to happen. I have lots of bad guys out there I still haven't caught. I have unsolved cases sitting on my desk. Two of them involve drive-by shootings where children were killed. The last thing I have time for is to go back and second-guess a case that's already closed, especially where the evidence is overwhelming. If Jori-Ray thinks there's evidence out there to prove her innocence, what she needs to do is hire a private investigator to go find it. At this point, the burden is on her, not on the D.A. and certainly not on me."

Kimona frowned.

"Nick, you need to re-open the case. If you don't, I think Janjak is going to kill you."

DAY FIVE

May 21
Friday

12

ick, you need to re-open the case. If you don't, I think Janjak is going to kill you.

That's what Kimona had said last evening. It was a simple enough statement but it had gnawed at Teffinger all night. Maybe she said it because she was actually looking out for his best interests. But there was a flip side. Maybe she'd said it because she was doing Janjak's work.

Maybe she was just attempting to manipulate him.

Maybe she was playing him for a sucker.

Teffinger had hoped to look into Kimona's eyes in the morning and get some clarity, one way or the other, as to whether she was true or was a trick. When he woke, though, she was already gone; the second time she'd done that. He hadn't heard her leave. He hadn't heard a boat start up. She'd just disappeared like a ghost. The whole thing shook him. He needed to know without doubt that she was real. He needed to know that now, this minute. Without that, he wasn't sure whether to move forwards or backwards with her. He was stuck in limbo until he saw her again, and there was no telling when that would be.

Drawn in the sand was a large heart.

That's what a lover would do.

It was also what someone pretending to be a lover would do.

He stripped down to his shorts and set off on a barefoot jog down the beach, trying to see if he could logically swing his brain one way or the other. Kimona had asked for his help to escape Janjak. That could be real. It could also be a trick. That's how you could ingratiate yourself to someone else and form a bond—pretend you were in danger; have them save you; rely on them, be indebted to them just for the very thought.

You know what?

Screw it.

Don't over-think it.

Just go with it until the wheels fall of, and if they do, they do.

The island looked different this morning. Gone was the place that would shrivel his stomach and dry his throat to the point where he couldn't even swallow. The insane beauty of the sand and the sea and the sky was back.

Seagulls flew.

The breeze blew.

The lapping of the waters was an endless song.

The swaying of the palms was an erotic dance from a lover, just for him.

He was going to live; he knew that for certain, even if he had to lie about re-opening a case to make it happen. All was fair at this point.

He ran back and forth on the beach for over an hour, not allowing himself to slow down until the last hundred yards, which he walked. He ate and drank, but not overly because he didn't know how long the rations would have to last, then he opened the box of documents that the blue-haired lawyer, Alabama Avery, Esq., had left behind for his perusal.

What he found inside were several reports from a private investigator that Alabama—'Bama—had apparently hired prior to the trial, a guy by the name of Jack Flamingo, who Teffinger had never heard of before, and who appeared to have an office in the crumbling low-rent district out by the rail yard.

The files seemed to be ramblings of preliminary, half-baked investigations that had been started and then abandoned. Most of them contained brief notes regarding persons Flamingo had been following, proving information as to who, but no actual notes as to what he saw or learned, or why he was following the person in the first place. Some of the files contained handwritten notes of telephone conversations that Flamingo apparently had with someone. A first initial and a last name, but no address or phone number, usually identified the person on the other end of the line. The time and date of the conversation were indicated for a few but not many.

Nothing was typed.

The handwriting was terrible, like something a first-grader might do; the words were almost impossible to decipher. There were no complete sentences. Rather, there were only jumbles of words and strings of unconnected phrases, many followed with a question mark as it might be a question or possible lead that had popped into Flamingo's mind. A good number of the pages had been marred with runny stains from having set a wet glass on top; possibly a whiskey glass or the like.

They made Teffinger's brain hurt.

He turned them off after a half hour or so and then took a swim.

The water was sane and warm.

The sky was alive with brilliant sunshine.

The lawyer said she'd be back today to talk to him. What Teffinger needed to do was grab her boat when she arrived. He needed to get back to the mainland and out of Janjak's grasp. Then he needed to somehow get some private time with Kimona. He had a plan to help her escape—if she was serious about it—although it wasn't what she'd be expecting.

He stuffed food and water into the backpack that Kimona had left behind, and then waded over to the next adjacent island. Then he went to where the boat marks and footprints filled the sand, where Alabama would most likely land when she showed up today, whenever that might be.

There he hid in the palms and waited.

It was time to stop being the puppet and start taking control.

13

Jori-Ray's lawyer, Alabama, didn't show up until close to noon, and when she did it was with two of Janjak's men, each armed with a rifle. Teffinger waited in the hidden recesses of the palms, on the hopes that at least one of them would wander off. Neither one did. They sat down on the beach, passed a flask back and forth, shuffled around a little, relieved themselves in the water, and shot at seagulls, smattering their fair share to smithereens, but they never ventured far. Grabbing the boat wasn't going to happen, not today.

Under cover, he headed back to where Alabama would be waiting for him and found her wandering around, shouting his name.

He appeared as if he'd just be out doing a little exploring.

The woman had nothing in her hands.

She hadn't brought him any food or water.

She got right to the point.

"Did you read those documents I left you?"

"Read? No. I looked at them long enough to tell they were gibberish."

The woman smiled.

"Point taken," she said. "Let me give you a little background. Like I said before, Jori-Ray didn't kill September. She did, I'll readily admit, break in. She had a stolen gun with her. She was going to confront John Stone and there was a possibility if things didn't go right that she was going to kill him."

Teffinger tilted his head.

"You're admitting that?"

The woman nodded.

"I have to. It's true. She didn't know September was home. She thought she was going out of town with the mother like she usually did. Anyway, it's true that September showed up in the kitchen and saw Jori-Ray. We think she came down for a snack at the exact wrong time, but the reason she was there really doesn't matter at this point. She was there and that's that. She told Jori-Ray to leave but Jori-Ray had gone way too far for that to happen. They were both freaked out and ended up getting into a fight."

"Quite a fight, the way I see it."

Alabama nodded.

"It was brutal. I'm not sure exactly who was winning but what happened is that Jori-Ray got a serious blow to the back of the head. It knocked her unconscious. Looking back at it, she doesn't think it came from September. She thinks someone else was present and clobbered her from behind."

"But it could have come from September, possibly?"

"Yes, possibly. She can't swear a hundred percent that it didn't come from September, but, like I said, she's almost positive it didn't. Either way, though, she is positive—a hundred percent positive—that at that point the gun was no longer in her hand, and hadn't been for some time. More to the point, she's positive that that when she got unconscious, it hadn't gone off yet. She would have definitely heard it if it had."

Teffinger didn't disagree.

You can hear a gun when it fires close to you, no matter

what you're doing, even fighting for your life. The weapon at issue didn't have any type of a silencer.

"Here's the bottom line," Alabama said. "At some point, Jori-Ray regained consciousness. She doesn't know how long she was out but doesn't think it was very long. The important thing is this, when she came to, September was lying on the floor, dead. She'd been shot in the face."

"So, Jori-Ray didn't shoot September, that's what you're saying—"

"That's exactly what I'm saying," Alabama said. "She absolutely freaked out at that point. She looked around for just a second to see if the gun was there and she didn't see it. That doesn't mean it wasn't there on the floor somewhere or whatnot, it just means that she was moving so fast at that point that she didn't see it. She ran out the back door and headed into the open space and escaped. She did not have the gun with her when she did that."

Teffinger raked his hair back with his fingers.

"We know she went out the back door," Teffinger said. "Her blood was on the handle. There's no security camera back there, but we also know the exact route that she took when she left. The dogs followed her scent. We found the gun off in the terrain within easy throwing distance—not more than thirty feet, actually—from where she had been running. That points to her leaving with the gun and then discarding it, before she got around people and someone saw her with it, wouldn't you say?"

Alabama nodded.

"I would, unquestionably."

Teffinger raised an eyebrow.

"So?"

"So, it's great evidence, except what actually happened is

that she didn't leave with the gun. She didn't have it. She didn't throw it."

"So what's your explanation?"

"Whoever killed September ended up tossing it there."

Teffinger scrunched his face as if trying to make sense of it. Then he said, "That's a great story. The only thing wrong with it is that all the evidence points to Jori-Ray. There's no evidence of anyone else being there, other than John Stone."

"That's my point," Alabama said. "That's why you need to re-open the case, to get the rest of the evidence."

"To catch the real killer—"

"Exactly."

"Because Jori-Ray didn't do it—"

"Exactly."

Teffinger shook his head.

"If that's the true story, why didn't she testify to it at trial?"

"You know why."

Teffinger raised an eyebrow.

"Because no one would have believed her?"

"That's right," Alabama said. "But the other part—the bigger part, actually—is that if she testified, her credibility would automatically be an issue in the case. The prosecution would be able to cross-examine her on all those types of nasty things that juries love to hear and love to hold against you."

She was a whore.

She was a liar.

She was a cheat.

She drove drunk and slept with girlfriends.

She'd had an abortion; twice, actually.

And on and on and on.

"The jury would have convicted her based on just that stuff alone. The damage of Jori-Ray testifying far, far outweighed any good that might have come from it. The jury already didn't like her because she was pretty. Let's not forget about that. They were ready to take her down from the minute she walked into the courtroom; before that, actually. Let's not forget about all the crazy negative pre-trial publicity; all the talking-heads referring to her as a cold-blooded killer, a danger to society, a monster, and whatnot." Alabama shook her head. "No, her testifying was never an option. Not in a million years. It was my call. It was my advice. I told her not to testify and she didn't."

Teffinger exhaled.

Then he said, "I'm sorry, Alabama, you seem like a dedicated and capable attorney, but you're wasting your time with me. I'm not going to re-open the case. I'm not going to look around for more evidence. Jori-Ray is an escaped felon. What I'm going to do, if I'm able, is catch her and take her back to jail. I'm sorry that's the way it is, but that's the way it is. I'm sorry I'm being honest with you but that's the only way I can operate. Whatever Janjak ends up doing to me because of it, that's just what's going to have to happen. The games are over. The talk is over. The chest-beating is over. It's time to move on to whatever it is that's going to happen next."

The woman didn't react.

She didn't slap him.

She didn't insult him.

She didn't accuse him of not caring about catching the real killer.

She didn't get up and leave.

Instead, she picked up one of water bottles, unscrewed the cap and said, "May I?"

"Yes. Of course."

She took a long swallow, screwed the cap back, and set the jug down carefully in the sand. Then she looked him in the eyes and said, "Can I finish the rest of the story now?"

14

Teffinger wasn't sure what he expected once he told Alabama that he definitely wouldn't re-open the case, but he was pretty sure he didn't expect more story.

"Like I've told you time and time again, Jori-Ray didn't shoot September," Alabama said. "I've know that from the first day I represented her. So my goal, as her lawyer, was to find the real killer and expose him, or her. Unfortunately, that turned out to be easier said than done. At first, I hired a private investigator by the name of Michael Cortland."

Teffinger knew the man.

He was one of the best.

He'd been a homicide detective of some renown in Atlanta before going private and establishing a national investigation agency called Cortland Investigations, Inc., with branches in over twenty states and several hundred employees.

"Him personally, or his agency?"

"Personally," Alabama said. "He came to Denver and personally worked the case with his own two hands day in and day out for over two months. We came up with a lot of theories as to who it might have been—someone September was involved with, like a jilted lover or a drug dealer or someone she'd witnessed doing something and was afraid she'd talk; or someone who just happened to be in the house at the same time as Jori-Ray, possibly someone planting surveillance devices on John Stone, political opponents for example, or someone he was somehow secretly involved with; or possibly even someone who was tailing Jori-Ray for whatever reason and saw a way to frame her for murder; or even someone who hated John Stone strong enough to kill his daughter just to make him suffer. Also, of course, we explored the theory that John Stone himself shot her, either on purpose or by accident. The theories go on and on and on. Nothing was too fanciful or too ridiculous for us to consider."

She exhaled.

"So what'd he come up with?"

"An insanely large bill," Alabama said.

"No real evidence?"

"A few oddities and things we didn't expect but, no; in the end, no real evidence that was strong enough to drag into court. At the end of the day, whoever killed September was still hidden way back in the shadows."

"So, Jori-Ray was lying to you. The proof was never there to find."

Alabama shook her head.

"No. We've always had a bond. I may not be the best lawyer in the world but I can look into someone's eyes and tell if they're lying to me or not. She wasn't."

"Well, Michael Cortland is quite the skilled investigator," Teffinger said. "If he couldn't find anything, neither could I, even if I re-opened the case, which like I said I'm not."

"Yes and no," Alabama said. "Cortland's a great investigator but he's also a big business and has to play by all the ethical and legal rules. He's a great mind but he always has to stay inside the lines. He'll never do anything to jeopardize his license. The system limits him. I decided to give him a rest and find someone, shall we say, a little more pragmatic;

a little more result-oriented." She tossed a handful of sand into the box of documents that she'd left with Teffinger yesterday and said, "Enter Jack Flamingo."

"Never head of him," Teffinger said.

"He wasn't licensed," Alabama said. "He'd been in the CIA for over twenty years and did great work, supposedly, but always had a weakness for the bottle, which ultimately lead to his separation. He spent his days lifting weights and his nights in the bars. I heard about him from a friend of a friend of a friend. His job was simple, namely, to figure out who killed September. All he had to do was get us pointed in the right direction. It was never my intent to bring him into trial to testify. Once he figured it out, I was going to bring Michael Cortland back in to flush out the details and then sit pretty before the jury."

"And?"

"And, I didn't care about the details," Alabama said. "I wasn't looking for weekly reports. I didn't care if he broke every law in the universe. All I wanted was the end result—the killer's identity and motive."

Teffinger frowned

"That's pretty risky, for a lawyer," he said. "He was your agent operating at your request. As the principal, you're responsible for his actions, including the illegal ones. You could have ended up disbarred."

Alabama hardened her face.

"I didn't give a flying fuck about any of that," she said. "I needed to get the job done. Anyway, I did distance myself somewhat. I didn't want any reports and he never sent any. Also, I paid him in cash. Time went on and then something strange happened. He told me that he thought he was being followed. He was also convinced that someone had broken into his place at least once, and maybe more. He had never found the door unlocked or jimmied, but he was pretty sure some things had been moved around, not a lot, but enough. He didn't want off the case or anything like that, but he was pretty sure he had hit a nerve and someone out there was getting scared enough to keep tabs on him."

"So, he was getting close."

Alabama nodded.

"That's what he thought," she said. "Anyway, we were getting closer and closer to trial. He kept rattling the bushes and was beginning to concentrate more and more on figuring out who was on his tail, the theory being that that was the person he was ultimately looking for. We were about thirty days out from trial and he called me on a Wednesday afternoon. He was really excited and wanted to talk to me immediately but not over the phone. I was out of town that day and wouldn't be back until the morning. We made plans to meet at the Civic Center Park at ten the next morning."

She stopped talking and looked Teffinger in the eyes.

"So, what happened when you met him?"

"I never did."

"Why not?"

"He died that night."

"How?"

"If you believe what they say, the cause of death was blunt trauma to the head resulting from an accidental fall," she said. "But that's wrong. It was murder."

15

Teffinger had been so wrapped up in Alabama's eyes as she told the story that he momentarily forgot where he was. Suddenly the island sprung to life and grabbed his senses.

The palms rustled.

The ocean lapped against the sand.

A seagull buzzed overhead, looking for food.

He refocused on Alabama and said, "So he was murdered, you say?"

"Yes."

"Based on what?"

"Okay, it goes like this," she said. "He was living in an old standalone brick building in the edgy part of northwest Denver, close to the tracks. He was off and on with this tattooed girl named Chesty."

"Because of the obvious?"

She smiled.

"Yes. She came over to see him Thursday morning and found him dead. From what she could tell, he had piled some phone books on a chair and was standing on them trying to change a light bulb in a ceiling fixture. He fell off, hit his head on the hardwood flooring, and died. The light bulb he'd been holding was shattered on the floor next to him. She called 911. The cops showed up, followed by a Denver homicide detective by the name Sophia Cruz."

"I know her, obviously," Teffinger said. "She's still in the department."

"Is she any good?"

"Absolutely," Teffinger said.

"Well, not this time," Alabama said. "She concluded the same thing that Chesty did, namely that it was an accident. The autopsy showed that Flamingo had a serious alcohol level at the time in question. If he had been driving, it would have been two times over. It was easy to conclude that he fell off the chair, drunk, and that was that."

Teffinger shook his head.

"I don't see any errors," he said.

"Well, that's what happens when you jump to the first conclusion that makes any sense," she said. "You always have to look deeper. You have to be sure there's nothing lurking there under the surface."

"Like what?"

"Well, like this. Detective Cruz concluded there was no homicide and released the scene in the mid-afternoon on Thursday. I went over to take a look afterwards. Mind you, I wasn't tampering with a crime scene at that point because it had been released. There was no tape on the door or anything like that."

"I understand."

"Anyway, the body had been removed, obviously, but nothing else had been cleaned up yet. The smashed light bulb was still on the floor. The cover for the light fixture was still removed and sitting on a couch. The fixture itself had only one bulb. Supposedly Flamingo was aiming to replace."

Teffinger nodded.

"Makes sense."

"Yeah, it does, until you look at it a little harder," Alabama said. "Have you ever replaced a bulb in a light fixture?"

"Of course."

"Good, tell me how you do it."

"Seriously?"

"Yeah. Just play along."

"This is a little crazy," Teffinger said.

"Agreed. But indulge me, just for a moment."

Teffinger exhaled.

"Okay," he said. "You get the cover off. You unscrew the dead bulb. You screw in the new one. Then you put the cover back on."

"Right."

"And?"

"And now, how many bulbs are now in the fixture."

"One."

"And how many burned out ones do you have?"

"One."

"And where does it go?"

"The trash, I assume."

"Right. So, you start with one burned out bulb. You end up with one new one, and the burned out bulb goes into the trash."

Teffinger wrinkled his face.

"Yeah."

"That's not how it ended up at Flamingo's scene," Alabama said. "The fixture was equipped for one bulb. Nothing was screwed in there. There was one bulb on the floor, smashed."

"So what?"

"So, this," she said. "While I was over there, I looked around for the burned out bulb. And low and behold, I found it. It was in the trash can in the kitchen."

"Okay, so what?"

"So, I screwed it into the fixture and flipped the switch on. Low and behold, it lit up just fine."

Teffinger scratched his head.

"You're starting to make my brain hurt."

"Well, put up with the pain because we're almost at the end. I checked the smashed bulb on the floor. The glass was broken to smithereens but the filaments were intact, meaning it wasn't a burned out bulb either." She ran her hand through her hair and added, "Here's what happened. Someone killed Flamingo by sneaking in while Flamingo was drunk and smashing him in the head with something. He then set up the scene to make it look like Flamingo fell, drunk, changing a light bulb. To make that scenario work, though, there had to be a burned out bulb. If the bulb was working, obviously Flamingo wouldn't be changing it. So, he took the bulb out and threw it in the trash, and then got a second bulb, ostensibly the new one that was getting put in, and staged it like it had been dropped while being installed. He never suspected that anyone would ever pay any attention to the bulb in thc trash. But it was working fine. So the whole thing was staged. It was a cover-up for murder."

Teffinger's heart raced.

"Jesus," he said.

"Yeah, you get it?"

"I do. Why didn't you tell this to Detective Cruz?"

"I did," Alabama said. "She said the scene had been released. At that point she really couldn't consider the bulb in the trash as evidence. Someone could have planted it there."

Teffinger chewed on it and said, "Technically she was right."

What he didn't say was, It should have raised a red flag, though. It should have at least given her cause to sniff around a little more, maybe even print the bulb.

"Technically, maybe," Alabama said. "But no one planted that bulb there. So here's the bottom line. Someone murdered Jack Flamingo; and it's the same person who murdered September Stone. It was the person who Flamingo was closing in on. What you need to do is re-open the Jack Flamingo case, which was hardly investigated at all. You need to get to the bottom of it. Not just for his sake, but for Jori-Ray's."

She threw another handful of sand in the box of documents.

"This is what Flamingo was working on," she said. "This is where you'll find his killer."

Teffinger stood up and paced.

Then he said, "Let me think it through. Let me look at the documents again."

"You do that. I'll be back tomorrow. Okay?"

He shook her hand.

"Yeah. Can you bring some water and food?"

She shrugged.

"I'll check with Janjak."

Then she was gone.

16

When Alabama left, Teffinger immediately got busy studying the documents again. Few of them had dates, so it was hard to tell which one the man had been working on last. By and large they still remained undecipherable. What Teffinger needed to do was identify some of the people Flamingo had interviewed and go talk to them; find out when the conversation happened and what Flamingo's focus had been.

One thing did stand out, however.

Whoever killed Flamingo—assuming he was actually murdered, not to mention murdered for this investigation as opposed to some other one, if he in fact had something else going on—may well have been someone for hire. There was one person in the mix who definitely had enough money for something like that, namely John Stone.

That didn't make an ounce of sense, though.

It was too stupid to even think about.

He put the box away and took a swim in the warm aqua waters, practicing his overhand technique and trying to keep his leg movement to a minimum. He went out a hundred yards, then another.

Suddenly a boat come into view at a distance, a Boston Whaler, on plane at high speed, coming directly at him and throwing spray like a madman. As it approached, the person at the helm came into better focus.

It was a woman, a black woman.

Janjak?

No, wait, it was Kimona.

She appeared to be alone.

No one else was visible.

She was waving an arm at him now.

He waved back and started swimming towards shore. Before he could get there, still fifty yards out, the vessel came off plane right next to him, throwing a wild wake.

Kimona screamed at him.

"Get in!"

The words were laced with panic. Her face was etched with fear. Some type of cloth was tied around her left arm, something in the nature of a makeshift bandage.

It looked bloody.

"Hurry! Get in!"

She extended her right arm.

He grabbed it and swung up.

The woman looked behind them.

Two boats were approaching at high speed.

She shouted, "Hold on!"

Then she hammered the throttle. The boat immediately responded with a thunder of engine, jumping up to plane in a matter of seconds. Teffinger got next to her to shout over the noise.

"What's going on?"

"Janjak. She tried to kill me!"

"When?"

"Just now. You need to help me!"

Teffinger turned his head to the back. The two boats were still in hot pursuit, maybe closing the gap and maybe not, it was hard to tell. One had two men in it. The other had three.

A rifle was pointed at them. The tip flashed with a silent but vivid orange explosion.

Teffinger jerked Kimona aside and took the wheel.

He pushed the throttle to full extension and then trimmed the motor up, too much, spinning the prop, then back down, just a touch, until the grip of the prop was perfect.

The roar of the water pounding against the hull was deafening.

The gas was at a quarter tank.

The waves were four-foot swells, raising and dropping the vessel in a rhythmic motion.

Kimona got next to him, holding onto to the helm, constantly jerking her head back to see if the gap was closing. Blood dripped out from under the bandaging, which Teffinger now realized was a ripped off piece of her dress.

"What happened?" he shouted.

"Just keep going!"

Suddenly a bullet hit the vessel, shattering a hole in the windshield right between them, so violently that Teffinger flinched.

He jerked the wheel to the left, not a lot because a lot would slow them down, but enough to change course.

A bullet flew past to their right.

"Nick!"

"Get on the floor and stay there!"

17

Teffinger raced ahead at full speed with Kimona on the floor next to the hull, bouncing wildly as she tried desperately to find something to hold onto. Blood poured from her arm.

"Nick!"

"Hold on!"

He took a frantic glance to the rear. Beautifully, the boat with three people was falling behind, a victim of the weight. The other one though was keeping up and possibly even closing the gap. The person at the wheel looked like Janjak, with her dreadlocks wildly flailing and her naked chest bounding up and down.

He pounded ahead, reading the swells as best he could and trying to cut into them to keep from bouncing too high, which would only bring him crashing down harder, slowing the momentum.

The next time he turned, the man with the rifle wasn't pointing it at them any longer.

He shouted to Kimona, "They ran out of bullets!"

"Are you sure?"

"No, but I'm hoping."

The boat was getting closer, but only slowly. The other boat—the one with the three—had dropped way back now, a half mile or more, although still in pursuit.

Teffinger shouted, "Take the wheel."

When she did, Teffinger made his way to the bow of the boat with a strong hold on the railing, to the anchor locker. No flare was there but an anchor was, an eight or ten pounder attached to fifty feet or so of half-inch rope. He tied the end of the rope to the front cleat and briefly questioned his sanity.

The gap was definitely closing.

In five minutes, maybe sooner, the other boat would be on them. There was no way they're reach shore before that happened. They were still miles off.

The gap closed.

The other boat was right behind them now, not more than a hundred yards back. No gun pointed in their direction however, meaning they'd stupidly wasted all their bullets. It was going to come down to a fistfight. The man, shirtless, was ripped with muscles. Teffinger might be able to hold his own for a while but not forever. Janjak was strong as hell. Kimona would be no match for her, not with a bloody left arm.

He told Kimona, "Hold on!"

She did.

"Tighter! Both hands!"

She complied.

"We're going to ram them!"

He trimmed the motor down, kept the throttle wide open, and jerked the wheel to the left. The boat fishtailed around. Teffinger aimed it directly at the other boat, which jerked at the last second and passed by within feet.

The driver was clearly Janjak.

Her eyes were filled with rage.

Both boats spun, each trying to get into position to ram into the side of the other one.

Janjak almost got him, actually making contact but at an

angle, deflecting off.

They circled, again and again, accelerating and decelerating, like two crazed madmen, with neither one able to make a clear hit. Off in the distance, the third boat was closing the gap fast.

Teffinger shouted, "Take the wheel!"

Kimona did.

"Go straight for them!"

"Nick—"

"Just do it! Hit them!"

Kimona pushed the throttle to full power, spun to the left and headed directly at the other boat, which also spun to the left at the last second, making things like two dogs chasing each other's tail. Teffinger threw the anchor into the other boat and shouted, "Go straight!"

Kimona did.

The rope tightened and then snagged abruptly.

The other boat's outboard motor ripped off.

Janjak and her crazy henchman flew through the air and splashed violently into the water. Teffinger shot to the front of the boat to get the line off the cleat but the cleat was no longer there. A large jagged hole had replaced it.

He grabbed the wheel, gunned it and took one last look backwards as he headed towards the distant shoreline.

The other boat was peacefully floating with no power.

Janjak and her henchman had already gotten to it and were climbing up. The other boat was almost at the scene, slowing down to pick them up.

Teffinger checked the gas gauge.

It was on empty, meaning they were on reserve.

He had no idea how long it had been like that.

Come on baby.

Be nice.

18

Teffinger and Kimona almost made it to shore, almost; to within a couple of hundred yards, give or take, where the outboard sipped its last fume, sputtered and died. The water was insanely calm. It would carry them into shore, eventually, but they didn't have the time. The other boat was a ways off but heading in their direction at full plane. Teffinger cast an eye on Kimona's bloody arm, assessing the situation.

"Can you swim with that thing?"

"I don't know."

He pulled her shoes off.

Then he grabbed her hand and pulled her with him as he jumped over the side. They swam as well as they could. Teffinger was fine, he could overhand it all the way to shore with no problem, but Kimona—even if she hadn't been injured—wasn't particularly strong, using some kind of side-swim motion where her head never went under the water.

Teffinger stayed with her.

Come on, baby.

Just keep doing what you're doing.

We're going to make it.

They made it but not by much. The other boat was almost to them. There was no time to rest, not a second's worth. They disappeared into the palm trees and ran parallel to the shore as fast as they could. The hope was to stay out of sight and make Janjak and her men split up and go at least two ways, and maybe three. It may have worked and it may not have. All they knew is that after thirty minutes of running no one was visible on their tail.

They slowed to a walk.

Teffinger unwrapped Kimona's bandaging to find that the wound was a nasty cut, a half-inch deep and stretching across most of the outside of her arm.

"Janjak threw a machete at me," Kimona said.

Teffinger pictured it as he ripped a four-inch strip off the bottom on Kimona's dress and wrapped it tight around the wound.

"That won't close without stitches," he said. "So why'd she do that? Throw the machete?"

"She went insane."

"Why?"

"Because Jori-Ray was staked out in the sand, drying. It was horrible. There were dead snakes with their heads cut off and all kinds of burned torches and in the middle of everything Jori-Ray was all alone, staked out spread-eagle in the sand. Her face and body were covered with blood, but not hers, not from wounds, more like from blood that had been dripped on her."

"A voodoo ritual."

"Yes. I went over to her. You could tell she'd been there a long time. Her eyes were closed and at first I thought she was dead but then they suddenly opened, which was freaky beyond belief. They were unfocused, desperate, and seriously surprised to see me. She said, Help me! Please help me!"

Kimona paused with the horror of it etched on her face.

"I was so horrible the way her voice sounded. I untied her," she said. "Her wrists and ankles were all bloody and torn from trying to pull free for however many hours she'd been like that. When I got her loose, she curled up in a ball, really slow as if her muscles were contracting and she had no power over them, and then she started making these strange noises, like a dog whimpering or something. The next thing I knew, Janjak and one of her men were charging at me. Janjak was shouting something. I don't know what it was but she was out of her freaking mind. She was absolutely crazy with hate. I took off and was outrunning them. That's when Janjak threw the machete. I heard it pass by with a horrible swooshing sound. I didn't even realize until later that I'd been hit. Anyway, I made it to one of the boats and headed out to sea. I wasn't sure where I was going to go, and then I remembered you."

Teffinger pulled Kimona to a stop, then dropped to the ground and checked the bottoms of his feet. He had nothing on other than the boxer shorts that he'd been swimming in when Kimona showed up. His skin was scratched and scraped in a hundred different places.

His throat was a desert.

Kimona dropped to the sand next to him and eased onto her back and closed her eyes. Her hand made contact with Teffinger's and they gripped each other tight.

Teffinger's mind spun.

They had no shoes, no money, no phone, no identification, no food, no water, and perhaps most importantly, no weapons. As far as he knew, there was no civilization in this part of the country, other than Janjak's lair.

He closed his eyes.

The darkness felt like a waterfall.

Suddenly Kimona said, "We got company!"

19

Teffinger opened his eyes to find two of Janjak's men right there, not more than a few steps away, dead in their tracks and pointing rifles at his chest. One of them shouted, Arriba!

Shit!

They were fucked.

This was his fault.

He should have never stopped, no matter how much hurt was creeping into his body and brain. He should have swung away from the coast and headed deeper into the terrain. He should have fought through the pain and did what needed to be done to keep Kimona out of danger.

Now it was too late.

Arriba!

He got jerked to his feet and then got his hands tied behind his back like some sissy bitch, with the same for Kimona. One of the men fired two shots into the air. Then with Teffinger and Kimona in the lead and the guns at their heads, they marched back to the beach, then west, walking in the wet sand at the surf's edge. Sweat poured down Teffinger's face and into his eyes. He tried to squint it out but only managed to blur his vision. Panicked, he tried to think of a way to escape—something, anything—but nothing came; not even close, not even a single ounce worth; unless, maybe, he could get a handful of sand and throw it into one of the men's eyes, and then kick the other one in the groin before he even knew something was in motion, and then—

Up ahead in the distance, Janjak walked towards them, alone, moving at an agitated pace with her chest bouncing up and down. She had something in her hand, not a rifle; a stick, maybe?

Teffinger fought for the right words to throw at her.

It was all he had at this point.

He and Janjak had history; they had a relationship, although whether it was one of hate or love or fear or voodoo or something in between at this point, it was impossible to say. As the woman approached, Teffinger made out what was in her hand.

It was a blow dart.

Twenty steps away, she brought it to her mouth and blew with every ounce of breath in her lungs.

A dart pierced Teffinger's chest.

He teetered for a second, trying to stay on his feet, as something irrevocably evil coursed through his veins and into his bones.

He dropped, and as he did, the sun turned from yellow to black.

20

Teffinger woke up on sand under a palm tree and knew immediately where he was, namely back at the island. Alabama's box of documents was sitting crooked next to him. His water and food had been restocked. The sun was low, in the first throes of evening. A rifle leaned up against a palm tree. He looked around, saw no one, and grabbed it tighter than his first true love.

It was loaded.

Yeah!

This changed everything.

Everything, baby!

That's right.

Down at water's edge was something he didn't expect, namely a Boston Whaler, nestled gently in the sand and secured with an anchor wedged into the beach. Water lapped gently against the hull. It looked like the one he and Kimona had escaped in.

Kimona.

Where was she?

The last thing he remembered was being marched down the beach with Kimona at his side and rifles at their backs. Then the blow dart came, followed by darkness and horrific nightmares, one after another after another as if straight out of hell. He checked his chest to find it bruised and swollen and tender but not bleeding or infected.

He took a long, deep, endless swallow of water, letting it pour down his throat for as long as he could hold his breath. Then he did it again and could already feel it bringing him back to life.

He wolfed down a banana and a granola bar. All the while he kept his eyes peeled on the beach in case one of Janjak's men was heading back and noticed that he was awake and armed.

An encounter would follow.

It would be to the death.

There was nothing in between at this point.

In the sand next to the food was a pile of folded clothes, not Teffinger's, but possibly his size; two pairs of khaki shorts, an aqua-colored T-shirt with palm trees and the words Haiti 1804, socks, tennis shoes, and a towel.

He got dressed.

Everything fit, even the shoes.

If he had to, he could run without his feet bleeding.

He headed to the Whaler, hopped in with the rifle, and found the tank almost full.

His instinct was to get while the getting was good, before bullets started flying at him.

Yeah.

That was the thing to do.

He'd head to Janjak's lair and find out what happened to Kimona.

If anyone hurt her, it would be their last living act.

He lowered the prop into the water, pulled the rope on the outboard and let it warm up as he freed the anchor from the sand and pushed the vessel out into the water. Then he took off, slowly, not wanting to bury the prop in a sandbar.

A hundred yards out, he turned.

There he saw the last thing he expected.

Janjak was on the beach, dancing with her arms up over her head.

He immediately shifted into neutral, deciding.

It didn't take long.

Two seconds later he got back into gear, swung the stern around in a one-eighty and headed for her at a slow speed. He needed to warn her not to hurt Kimona. If she did, he'd rain down a hell on her the likes of which even her crazy voodoo brain couldn't imagine. And, if she'd already hurt Kimona, or killed her, that hell would start immediately.

Right here.

Right now.

As he approached, the woman, so incredibly topless, came into better and better focus. The firmness of her stomach was a sight he'd seen many times before but had never tired of. The gyration of her hips was something few men would be able to resist, particularly at a time and place like this where a thousand years of animal genetics could rise to the surface and bring fire to your soul in the blink of an eye.

Don't fall under her spell.

Fight it with everything you have.

He drifted the boat into the sand, hopped over the side into knee-deep water and walked towards her.

She wrapped her arms around him and pulled in tight, letting him feel the infinite pleasures of her body. Then she licked his ear and whispered, "You love me."

It was crazy.

It wasn't true, not even close.

It was a voodoo trick.

He knew that.

He went to deny it.

Instead to his shock he said, "Yes."

"Say it."

"I love you," he said.

"You always will."

"That's true." He forced himself to untangle from her and added, "But this can't happen."

She laughed.

Then she spun around and went back into that dance, that erotic, hypnotic dance, swaying her body back and forth like a love-drunk schoolgirl finally getting ready to lose her virginity.

Teffinger closed his eyes.

Instead of protecting him, it turned everything black and made him alone in the universe. He opened them back up and all the colors sprang back to live. Janjak was naked now, lying face down on her stomach in the sand.

"Rub my back," she said.

He resisted.

"This isn't going to happen."

"You love Kimona—"

"That's right."

"You love me and her, both of us."

"That's right."

"Which one more?"

"I don't know."

"Well, that's interesting." She wiggled her ass and added, "She's not dead, that little fireball of yours. Not yet. Would you like to know how to save her?"

"Yes."

"There's one way, but only one way."

"Which is, what?"

"We'll get to all that in due time. For right now, just rub

my back." She sighed and added, "I hate it that you have a control on me. It makes me want to kill you."

21

Teffinger rubbed the she-devil's back, saying nothing, waiting for her to tell him what he needed to do to keep her from killing Kimona.

"You know I'm helping Jori-Ray," Janjak said. "For her, I brought you here to Haiti, I put you on this island, and I made you sit down and listen to what she and her attorney Alabama had to say. You had to take it seriously. You had to look at the evidence. You had to give it your full attention. That wouldn't have happened back in Denver. You're full attention would have been on capturing her."

Teffinger kept rubbing.

"You had her staked out to die," he said. "Is that how you help people?"

"You don't understand anything," she said. "You think you do but you never do; not when it's about Haiti, or me. There was a quid pro quo."

She flipped over and raised her arms.

"Do my front."

He complied.

Her skin was silken smooth.

Her stomach muscles quivered under his touch.

"In return for me helping Jori-Ray, she agreed to do something for me," Janjak said.

"What, exactly?"

"Exactly? Be an offering."

"An offering . . . I don't get it."

"An offering. Some say to the devil, some say to death, some say to the earth and sun; whatever you believe, they must be done when they're demanded."

"And how are they demanded?"

"Not relevant," Janjak said. "What is relevant, however, is that the person being offered—always a woman—must participate voluntarily. She can't be physically forced. It starts at midnight with a long voodoo ritual with the woman staked out. When the ritual is done, she must stay there for twenty-four hours. At the end, if she's alive, she is free to go; and she gets some limited powers. If she's dead, she gets a special burial ceremony equal to a queen."

She spread her legs.

"Do my thighs," she said. "Jori-Ray was more than half way through her offering when Kimona interfered. That ruined the entire thing. Now I have to start completely over."

"With Jori-Ray?"

"It could be, if she agreed," Janjak said. "But I won't even ask her. The one to go through it should be the one who ruined the first one."

"Kimona," Teffinger said.

"Exactly."

"But you can't force her."

"That's right," Janjak said. "I'm going to give her the option to do it voluntarily, of her own free volition. She can agree or not, her choice. But if she doesn't agree, she'll be put to death in a way that will be much more horrible than anything she would have experienced otherwise."

Teffinger stopped rubbing, straddled the woman's chest and grabbed her throat with both hands.

He squeezed.

The woman didn't resist.

Her eyes stared directly into his.

A second passed, then another and another and another, and then a sudden pain came to Teffinger's hands, something that felt worse than fire.

He rolled off.

The pain got crazy.

It spread up his arms and into his whole body, shaking him into convulsions.

Janjak said, "Rub me between my legs," and the pain suddenly disappeared, just like that, every single ounce of it.

Teffinger's chest pounded.

Whatever just happened, it was real.

It was as real as death.

He complied with the woman's request.

She tilted her head back, closed her eyes and rocked her body with his motion.

"You said there was a way I could save her," Teffinger said.

"There is. Jori-Ray fulfilled her obligation to me. She did the offering. It wasn't her fault it got ruined. So I want to fulfill my obligation to her. I want to be sure you re-open the case. I want you to find the real killer. I want all charges against Jori-Ray dropped and I want her freed, including any charges based on her escape. Here's the important part. Are you listening?"

"Yes."

"Good. I'm going to do the next offering in ten days, which is the last day of May," she said "Kimona will either do it at that time, and possibly live, or she'll have a different and very ugly fate that will one hundred percent kill her. If you have Jori-Ray freed by that time, I'll give Kimona to you for your hard work. That's how you can save her. And that's the only way."

She stood up and grabbed his hand.

"Come on. Let's take a walk on the beach. We're going to spend the night here, together. We're going make love and drink wine until the sun rises. Then you'll fly back to Denver and begin your work. Alabama will be at your disposal. You love me."

He squeezed her hand.

"I do."

"You'll always love me, even if I have to kill Kimona."

He tried to say nothing but words came out.

"I will. I'll always love you."

DAY SIX

May 22
Saturday

22

Saturday morning, flying out of Haiti, Teffinger's head slowly began to clear from all the crazy clutter that always came when he was around Janjak. It was like an evil fog lifting. He remembered mouthing the words that he loved her, and meaning them when he said them, but now had no idea why, because that was the furthest thing from the truth. He remembered their passionate sex on the beach last night and how, at the time, it felt like life itself pouring into his body. Now it seemed like a drunken and barren one-night stand with a stranger.

Kimona.

What were her conditions right now?

Did Janjak already confront her with the reality that she would either have to do the offering in ten days, or die by even worse means? Was she lying in the dirt right now with a cold metal cuff around her ankle so she couldn't escape?

Was she thinking of him?

Was her every waking thought a desperate hope that somehow he'd miraculously show up at the last second and save her?

He exhaled, fighting off a growing panic, and looked out the window to the world below. A freighter carved a path through flat endless waters, looking like a toy from this distance. Small islands rose above the waterline at the horizon; maybe uninhabited and forgotten by the world, or maybe some tropical paradise for someone who'd managed to get everyone else's money into his own pockets.

One thing was clear.

Jori-Ray had done an offering.

She'd put her life on the line.

It was her payment to Janjak.

A truly guilty person would have never gone that far. They would never have even tried to talk to Teffinger to begin with, much less gone to those kinds of extremes. They would have simply absconded to a country that had no extradition treaty with the U.S. and called it good.

Jori-Ray was innocent.

She actually was.

She wasn't the normal guilty person running around crying innocence.

If that was true—and it certainly seemed to be—that meant, gratefully, that there actually was another killer out there somewhere to catch. Teffinger would catch him, or her, sooner or later, he knew that, but he also knew that doing it within the next ten days had the same chances as a squirrel making it safely across a ten-lane freeway at rush hour. He needed a plan to save Kimona by stealth or force or trickery or whatever other means it took, fair or foul, when the witching hour came. He also needed to contact Kimona's brother and warn him to disappear now, today, right this minute, before it was too late.

At Miami International Airport, with a two-hour gap until a connecting flight to Denver, Teffinger grabbed a hotdog and diet Coke, made his way outside to the taxi area and sat on a bench in the middle of all the movement and shuffling.

Two minutes later a woman sat down next to him.

To his shock, it was Alabama, blue hair and all, looking nice, dressed in shorts and a Nirvana T-shirt.

"So, what's the verdict?" she asked.

"I believe you, I really do," he said. "But ten days? Come on."

She said, "There's a rule of criminal procedure, Rule 35(c), to be precise. It allows the court to overturn a conviction, even if all other appeals have expired or been unsuccessful, if there is evidence of material facts, not theretofore present and heard, which, by the exercise of reasonable diligence, could not have been known to or learned by the defendant or his attorney prior to the submission of the issues to the court of jury, and which requires vacation of the conviction or sentence in the interest of justice." She smiled. "I have it memorized."

"I can tell."

"You figure out who the real killer is and get the evidence," she said. "I'll file a Rule 35(c) motion on Jori-Ray's behalf and you'll have to get the district attorney to join in on the motion. That's what needs to be done within ten days. Obviously, the court will need to schedule a hearing down the road and consider the motion. But if the defense and prosecution are both in agreement, it will almost certainly be granted. The important thing is this: Janjak is not actually asking for a court order to be granted in ten days. That would be impossible. We all appreciate that. All she needs is for the motion to be filed and agreed to by both parties. If that's done within ten days, Kimona is free to go."

Teffinger shook his head.

"I would have to have real evidence," he said. "The D.A. would never concur in a motion like that unless it was truly legitimate; and, compelling, meaning way beyond speculation or maybe this or maybe that. I can't even imagine what it might be. It would almost need to have the same weight that would justify formally charging the person for the crime. That kind of evidence usually takes months and months to gather. It takes interviews and search warrants and lab analysis and document reviews and on and on and on."

The woman grabbed his arm and squeezed.

"We don't have months and months," she said. "We have ten days."

"That's what I don't get," he said. "What's the magic of ten days? Why not three months?"

"It has something to do with the offering. That's all I know." She sighed and added, "Look, Jori-Ray is innocent. I failed as her attorney the first time. I'm not going to do it a second time. I'm here to help you all I can. I'm a hundred percent in. You figure out what you want me to do and I'll do it; and I mean, anything. It doesn't have to be legal. If we have to break in somewhere, I'll do it. If we have to trick somebody, I'll do it. If we have to blackmail somebody, I'll do it. If I have to suck someone's cock, I'll do it."

Ordinarily, Teffinger would be telling her to stop talking for a minute so he could pull up the visual. This time, though, he skipped right over the joke and concentrated on the meaning behind the words.

She would do anything.

She was there to help.

They had ten days.

"We'll get started and see where things take us," he said.

"My advice, Teffinger?"

"Sure, why not?"

"Make it work," she said. "If you're thinking you can fail but then save Kimona by some kind of miracle attack, it won't work. Janjak's had her taken somewhere. She's not at Janjak's place any more. You'll never be able to find her much less save her. Janjak put her in a trance, too. So even if you find her, she won't be normal. Only Janjak can reverse what she did. You know her. You know what I'm saying is true."

23

The first thing Teffinger did when he got back in Denver was meet with the chief, Double-F Tanner, who listened quietly to the story as he creased every wrinkle in his 60-year-old face. The more he let Teffinger talk without interruption, the more nervous Teffinger got. He'd seen the pattern before. The man was giving him every opportunity to make his case because at the end he wasn't going to give him what he wanted.

"So that's it," Teffinger concluded.

"Okay," Tanner said.

"Okay, re-open the case?"

Tanner shook his head

"No, okay, I understand what you said." The man sighed and diverted his eyes briefly. "You're gifted at what you do, Teff. We both know that. If my daughter were missing, there would be nobody I'd want on the case besides you. That said, we're not going to re-open the Jori-Ray Rose case." He hardened his face and said, "Not in a million years. There's nothing there, other than speculation and innuendo. If the defense thinks there's compelling exculpatory evidence out there, it's their obligation to go get it. Not ours. We'll look at it, if they come up with something, but that's it. It undermines the whole concept of justice if we start second-guessing jury verdicts and start sniffing around back at square one. If makes us look like we don't know what we're doing. That has consequences that are bigger than just this one case."

Tanner snapped a pencil in two.

"That's that," he said. "Sorry."

Teffinger raked his hair back with his fingers.

"How about the PI, Jack Flamingo?"

Tanner frowned.

"There's nothing there," Tanner said. "All we have is this attorney, Alabama what's-her-name, saying that Flamingo thought—repeat, thought, with no proof—that someone might have broken into his apartment at some point. We have no proof that ever happened. Even if it did, lots of people have their place broken into."

"We also have the light bulb," Teffinger said.

"Again, Teff, I don't really care about some light bulb in the trash. We have no idea where it came from, who put it there, or anything else. The coroner's already ruled it an accident. The case is closed. Look, your whole department is busting at the seams with cases screaming for justice. We need to concentrate on them." He shook his head. "I got to be honest, Nick. You come back from Haiti with all the voodoo talk almost as if you believe it's true. You're starting to worry me a little. Do you need a break? A vacation, or whatever? Do you want to talk to somebody?"

Teffinger went to defend himself.

Instead he just shook his head and said, "No."

"Okay, then. Are we clear on everything?"

"How about this," Teffinger said. "Maybe I will take some vacation time and sniff around on my own."

Tanner replied immediately and forcefully.

"Absolutely not. Take vacation days if you want but don't even think about working either of these cases. What cases are opened or closed is my call, not yours. I'm sorry to be so blunt but I'm getting the feeling you're not hearing what I'm saying. My advice to you? Get back to your desk and concentrate on Mary-Ann White."

Mary-Ann White.

Six years old.

Disappeared from her bed on April 1st.

Never seen again.

Her file was sitting on the corner of Teffinger's desk.

"If you want to get some justice going, get it for her," Tanner added. "Her mother calls me every day. Did I ever tell you that?"

"No."

"She still cries every time we talk."

"I understand."

He stood up and headed for the door. As he opened it, Tanner said behind him, "Teff, don't go behind my back on this. I want to be real clear about that."

Teffinger said nothing.

Then he left.

24

Teffinger worked the Mary-Ann White case for the rest of Saturday afternoon, getting nowhere new, but at least re-familiarizing himself with what he already had and coming up with a few new things to run down. Then he headed home, ate two TV dinners washed down by a Bud light, showered, waited until night, and pedaled the Specialized down to Rodeo Nights, three miles from his house. He could have taken the Tundra but there was a good chance he was going to tie one on and didn't want to risk getting stupid at the end and slipping behind the wheel, even for a mere three miles.

The place was already in motion.

On stage was a county band with a female singer, belting out a cover of one of his favorite Gretchen Wilson songs.

Well, I ain't never been the Barbie doll type

No, I can't swig that sweet Champagne,

I'd rather drink beer all night

In a tavern or in a honky tonk

Or on a four-wheel drive tailgate

He claimed a seat at the bar, downed a quick Bud, and ordered a second. His scent was in the room. Women were already looking his way. Right now, he had too much in his brain to pay attention. That would no doubt change later when the beer took control.

Suddenly his phone rang.

He checked the caller.

It was Alabama.

She must have heard the band when he answered because she said, "Where are you?"

"Rodeo Nights. Why?"

"Rodeo Nights?"

"Yeah. It's a country bar on Alameda."

"Stay there. I'm coming down."

The line died.

He downed what was left of his beer and ordered a third. Everything was beginning to beautifully soften. His attention was on the dance floor and, in particular, a little cutie in a short white dress and matching cowboy hat who'd been smiling his way all night, and just now waved.

He waved back.

He'd flirt, but that was it.

The important part of him was reserved for Kimona. Someone tapped him on the shoulder and said, "Hey, cowboy."

He turned.

It was the girl behind the bar, flashing red lipstick, thick blond curls and a world-class smile. She slid a beer his way and said, "On the house."

"Well, aren't you the nice one?"

She leaned in, gave him a kiss on the cheek and said, "I get off early tonight—midnight—in case you were wondering."

He checked his watch—10:16—and slid her a twenty-dollar tip across the bar to her.

"Thanks."

She handed it back to him, leaned in and pulled her bra forward at the top, exposing a small but perky anatomy.

He slipped it in.

She fingered it, then rubbed her nipple and said, "I'm not going to lie. You're getting me hot, cowboy."

"Well, let me know when you're sizzling."

She laughed.

"That'll be about ten minutes."

"I'll set my alarm."

Two minutes later, Alabama appeared in front of him, with another woman at her side, one with a world-class chest. She got her face close to his to get over the music and said, "I want to show you something."

"Who's your friend?"

"Chesty."

He'd heard the name before but couldn't place it.

"She's Jack Flamingo's squeeze. Or was, to be more precise."

He remembered now.

She was the one who found Flamingo dead on the floor and called the police.

"Look at this," Alabama said.

With that, she reached for Chesty's phone, pulled up a photo and handed the device to him. The picture was a selfie of Chesty and Jack Flamingo, taken by Chesty. They were on the 16th Street mall in the heart of Denver, near the Daniel Fisher Tower, which Teffinger recognized.

They looked happy.

Alabama grabbed the phone and zoomed in until a face in the background came into focus.

"Look at this guy," she said.

It was a tanned man with a chiseled face, thirty or thereabouts, with long black hair and a five-o'clock shadow, wearing a black cap that had the word Beatles in white lettering. It seemed like he was looking directly at the camera, meaning at Chesty and Flamingo.

"See him?"

"Yes."

"Does he look like a Beatles fan to you?"

"Not really."

She took the phone back, pulled up a different photo, and handed the device back to Teffinger. It was a second selfie of Chesty and Flamingo, this time at a crowed place that looked like the People's Fair, down at Civic Center Park. There were lots of merchants selling T-shirts and art and knick-knacks, and you could see a band playing on a stage in the background.

"People's Fair?" he said.

"Yes, exactly. Find the guy."

"Huh? What do you mean?"

"Look at the faces in the background."

He zoomed in and scrolled around.

To his shock, there in the background, was the same face that was in the other picture, wearing the same black Beatles hat, and staring, as before, directly at Flamingo and Chesty, as if keeping them under surveillance.

Teffinger studied Alabama's face and said, "You think this is the guy who killed Flamingo?"

"I'd bet my left tit on it."

He looked at Chesty.

"Do you know who he is?"

She shook her head.

"I have no idea."

DAY SEVEN

May 23
Sunday

25

Sunday morning, Teffinger called the FBI profiler, Dr. Leigh Sandt, who actually answered. Her voice made him pull up the image of a classy lady, about fifty, with killer Tina Turner legs.

"It's me."

"Teffinger?"

"Guilty."

"It's Sunday morning."

"Yeah. This call never happened. This is way, way, way on the down low. Okay?"

A pause.

Then, "Okay, I'll play. What's up?"

"I'm going to send you a photo. I'm hoping you can tell me who he is."

"What'd he do?"

"Murder and murder, if I'm right."

"Two murders?"

"Yes."

"How soon do you need it?"

"Yesterday?"

"Of course."

An hour later she called back. "His name is Axel Chard. Do you know the actress Lulu Paige? She goes by the name Lupa?"

"Sounds familiar but—"

"She mostly did thrillers. Wake Up & Die was probably her biggest thing."

"I've seen that!"

"She was the bad guy's girlfriend, the one who helped him dig up the body when the police started closing in."

"I remember her," Teffinger said "Sexy as hell."

"Yeah, well, she got killed last year."

"You mean in real life?"

"Exactly," she said. "Your buddy Axel Chard was a suspect in her murder."

"He didn't go down for it, though?"

"Negative," Leigh said. "Lupa was married at the time to a hot-shot lawyer in L.A. by the name of Connor Huntington. He was out of town at a legal convention and Lupa was home alone at their house in Laurel Canyon, which was actually owned by David Crosby once upon a time. Someone broke in and robbed the place. In the process, Lupa got herself shot in the face."

The words were a train to Teffinger's chest.

Shot in the face.

That was the exact same way that September had been murdered.

"So, how did he get to be a suspect?"

"Just a slight thread," Leigh said. "This was big news out in L.A. and the police were asking everyone to call in with tips. One of the tips came from a waitress at a dive bar who thinks she saw Lupa's husband, Connor Huntington, meeting with a guy in the bar about two weeks before the murder happened. She saw Huntington give the guy a briefcase during that meeting. The tip turned out to be accurate. There was video footage of both men entering the bar. Huntington entered with the briefcase. The other guy left with it. The guy meeting Conner was subsequently identified as Axel Chard. He's a French guy who's way off the radar screen. But the belief is that he's a super-expensive hitman who travels the world and does jobs that need to be done right for people who can't afford to get caught. The suspicion was that Huntington hired him to kill his wife. But that was it, suspicion only. There was no evidence at the crime scene. There were no traceable communications between the two, by text or phone or email. There was no big withdrawal of money by Huntington around the time or any other time for that matter. The only thing the police had in the end was that one meeting. Huntington said the man was a private investigator who he was meeting off the grid and giving him information about an assignment. He wouldn't say any more than that and wouldn't give any particulars because it would violate the attorney-client privilege, since it was connected to one of his cases. Axel was never located to see if his story matched up. So, it didn't end up going anywhere."

"Did anyone else become a suspect?"

"Yeah, of course. Lupa was sleeping around, so there was all that type of drama, and she was hooked on cocaine, so there was that too. In the end, though, no one got charged. The case is still open."

"Do you have the name and number of the detective in charge?"

"I do. You got a pencil?"

26

The L.A. homicide detective in charge of Lupa's murder, a guy named Mateo Navarro, had some additional information when Teffinger finally managed to get him on the phone: "Axel was in town for two weeks before Lupa got murdered. Most guys, if they were in town to do a hit, they'd stay somewhere low, under the radar. Wouldn't you think?"

"I would," Teffinger said.

"Not Axel," Navarro said. "He's a 5-star guy all the way, the Waldorf Astoria Beverly Hills, to be precise. I will give the guy this, though. He at least used an alias."

"Such as?"

"Ethan Laurent."

"So he stayed French, then—"

"Exactly," Navarro said. "He speaks English very well but has an accent. He probably figured it would be weird if he was walking around with an American name. Anyway, the big thing about him is that he likes the ladies. He doesn't like to go out into the world and hunt for them though. He gets them the easy way."

"Money?"

"Bingo," Navarro said. "He had at least ten top-drawer escorts show up to his room and spend the night. They were our big hope. We were able to track eight of them down and bring them in for questioning. Axel never told any of them anything. He was polite and funny and filled them with co-caine, but he never discussed anything personal with them. He claimed he was a lawyer from New York in town for depositions, but other than that, he was all about the small talk and love-making."

"What about his clothes?"

"High class," Navarro said. "Expensive suits, silk ties, and the like. But he also had jeans and T-shirts."

"Did any of the girls see a gun?"

"Unfortunately, no."

"Did he order room service?"

"Yes. Lots of lobster; steak and lobster."

"Well that's distinctive. Go back to the cocaine for a minute," Teffinger said. "Did he take it too or did he just use it to juice up the girls?"

"He took it. He did his lines on their stomachs."

Teffinger pictured it.

"Sounds reasonable."

Navarro laughed.

"You want the file? I can email it to you if you want."

"Sweet. One more thing. Were you able to get any DNA for him?"

"I wish. By the time we dialed him in as a suspect, whatever might have been around was long gone."

"Yeah. Thought I'd ask anyway, just in case. Oh, one more thing—"

Navarro laughed.

"That's two last things."

"Math, it's not my strong point. Any idea where he was before he showed up in L.A., or any idea where he went when he left?"

"Again, negative," Navarro said. "We did check airline

manifests, but there was nothing for Axel Chard or Ethan Laurent. We ran down a couple of French names but they weren't him. He's a slippery guy. I've wrestled greased strippers who weren't as slippery as him."

Teffinger laughed.

"I'm going to use that one," he said.

27

Teffinger set out for a three-mile jog, letting his mind go free-style, and always coming back to the same thread, namely that September's father, the Senator, had the money and connections to hire a high-flying hitman like Axel Chard. At that point in the thought process, though, everything hit a brick wall.

Why would the Senator kill his own daughter?

And equally to the point, if he actually did hire a hitman to do the deed for whatever crazy reason, why would he be home at the time? Why wouldn't he be a hundred miles away in front of a thousand alibi witnesses?

The case was too cold.

That was the problem.

September's murder was six years ago.

Flamingo's was five.

Axel Chard was in town five years ago; that was established through Chesty's selfies. Was he here six years ago, though, when September was murdered? That might be something Teffinger could figure out through hotel registries, although the man certainly would have used an alias, so the tracking would be tedious at best. And, if the man brought escorts to his room, they would be scattered across the globe by now. He'd be lucky to find even one and, if the man's MO held true, she really wouldn't know anything anyway. It all seemed like a lot of work without any realistic hope of a reward. It would be like spending a thousand dollars to buy a mystery package, and finding a shiny new paperclip inside.

Great purchase, Teff!

Hey, clip my papers for me, will you?

Too bad you didn't start with a million!

You could have ended up with a new phone or something!

At best, if he followed the Axel Chard trail, he was staring at a grind.

Grinds took time.

Time wasn't his.

Suddenly his cell phone rang and the voice of the chief, Double-F Tanner, came through. "I talked to the Senator about your efforts to capture Jori-Ray. It didn't go over well. He wants to talk directly to you."

"Why? To throw blame?"

"He's pissed that the result didn't happen," Tanner said. "I think he wants details on the voodoo woman."

"Why?"

"He didn't say this directly, but I think he wants to know exactly where Jori-Ray is being kept. He might be wrestling with the idea of sending a vigilante party over there to grab her. I don't know. Anyway, I told him you'd give him a call. Do me a favor, will you? Don't talk about all that voodoo crap like it's real, okay? And be sure you tell him eye to eye that no one's going to be re-opening the case."

28

There hadn't been a single murder in Denver last night—a Saturday in May—which was as perfect as it was unlikely, because it meant that now on Sunday morning the department was a ghost town. Teffinger got there shortly after eleven, pulled the old Jori-Ray Rose files out of cold storage, carried all three boxes down to his Tundra one at a time, and got the hell out of there before anyone could ask what he was doing.

It had been over five years since he'd last looked at the case.

The dust had long since settled.

As with all things, it would look at least slightly different now because of nothing else but the passage of time. It might look a lot different if he didn't fixate on Jori-Ray as the only suspect and instead kept his mind open.

Was there anything in there that pointed to the Senator?

Teffinger had been the one to interview the man back at the time, which was routine given that he'd been in the house at the time of the murder. That interview had been saved in a number of ways, including a thumb drive. Teffinger made a fresh cup of coffee, plugged that thumb drive into his computer, and sat back and watched.

He was only two minutes into in when he had a terrible thought. The main reason he believed Jori-Ray to be innocent was because she did an offering for Janjak.

What if that was a lie?

What if it was just a made-up story that Alabama fed him?

He closed the computer and paced.

Was he being played?

Just the thought brought him to a standstill.

He didn't know how to figure it out, other than to confront the woman herself.

He called her.

"Tell me something," he said. "When Jori-Ray did that offering for Janjak, were you there?"

"Yes."

"So you saw it with your own two eyes?"

"Saw it? I was doing everything in my power to talk her out of it," Alabama said. "I didn't know what it would all entail but I had my concerns that she wouldn't survive it."

"Did you take any pictures or anything like that?"

The woman paused.

"Janjak doesn't allow that," she said. "She'd kill anyone who broke the secrets. You should already know that."

"So, how do I know it really happened?"

"What do you mean? I told you it happened, for starters. Plus you know that Kimona found Jori-Ray staked out the next morning. She released her and Janjak tried to kill her in return. You saw that blood with your own two eyes. What are you driving at?"

"What I'm driving at is that I got the story from two sources, you and Kimona. You represent Jori-Ray. Kimona works for Janjak. How do I know you're not all in cahoots?"

The woman exhaled.

Then she said, "Let's meet. I have a way to put all your concerns to rest."

"How?"

"You'll see."

Driving over, Teffinger's phone rang. It was the Senator, John Stone.

"Nick? Did the chief get a hold of you?"

"Yes. I was just about to call you."

"Swell. I was hoping you could drop over to my place so we could chat; the sooner the better from my end. I'm available right now."

Teffinger put him off until three.

He needed to get back into the file first.

This might be his only opportunity to shake the man's tree.

The Senator wasn't amused; he'd have to give up a tee-time at Cherry Hills Golf Club.

But three it was.

Alabama, it turned out, was living in a friend's sailboat at the Chatfield Marina while he was away for two months on business in Africa. She greeted Teffinger dressed in jeans down below and a bikini top up above and her blue hair flying loose, barefoot, with a bottle of water in one hand, half gone, and a full one in the other, which she handed to him.

He took it and said, "Like old times."

"Yeah. Close your eyes and add some voodoo and you're right there. Hold on."

She ducked down into the cabin and came out with the box of Jack Flamingo's notes.

"Take these when you leave. I made a digital copy of everything but figured you'd be better off with the originals."

He nodded.

"Thanks. So what's up? Why am I here?"

She looked around as if searching for anyone who might be watching them, then grabbed his hand and led him down into the cabin.

"What I'm going to show you doesn't exist. You never saw it. Promise me that."

He took a swallow of water.

"Sure. Okay."

"No one can ever know it exists."

With that, she picked up her phone, pulled up a video and handed it to him, then fell back on the bed and propped up on her elbows to watch him.

"Hit play," she said.

The scene was back in Haiti, in the black of a soulless night.

Jori-Ray Rose was walking slowly on the beach in a white sundress and a headdress of feathers, surrounded by a procession of nearly-naked men and women holding torches that threw bursts of eerie light. Lots of other people were in the shadows, largely out of sight except for hypnotic flashes that highlighted the agitated dancing and movements and tribal face paint. Somewhere out there in the night, drums beat out a frantic tempo, almost as if knocking at the devil's door.

Jori-Ray's face was motionless.

She was scared to death but trying not to show it.

The video ended.

"Scroll to the next one," Alabama said.

He did.

A new scene showed up. Jori-Ray and Janjak were standing toe to toe, surrounded by torches and bodies and all hell in motion. In Janjak's hand was a machete. Jori-Ray held her arms out and Janjak cut the woman's left wrist, then her right, not deep, in fact only enough to draw a trickle of blood. Then she handed the machete to Jori-Ray, who did the same to her, only deeper, much deeper in fact.

They put their wrists together, right to left, and left to right; blood to blood.

Janjak said something to Jori-Ray.

It wasn't audible in all the hysteria but Jori-Ray nodded.

Janjak then tied rope around the woman's wrists, then her ankles. At no time did Jori-Ray protest or try to break away.

The video ended.

"One more," Alabama said.

Teffinger scrolled to it.

Jori-Ray was staked out spread-eagle on the ground, with her sundress pulled down to her waist, exposing a heaving chest. A man was above her, in a crazy dance, dangling a large snake above her face. She was hysterical, pulling at the ropes and screaming. Terror filled her eyes.

The snake was mere inches above her.

She twisted her head to the side, frantic to keep it away from her eyes.

The man suddenly bounced it off her cheek, dropping it down and then pulling it up just as fast, before it could sink its fangs into her flesh. He did it again, and again, and again.

Janjak suddenly appeared.

She handed him a machete.

He twirled it around, over and over, and then suddenly swung it and chopped off the reptile's head, which landed on Jori-Rays face before it bounced off and landed in the sand just inches from her ear.

The hysteria pitched to an even higher level as the man let the blood and guts drip down onto Jori-Ray's face. When the flowing had nearly stopped, he flung it up into the sky and screamed.

Suddenly another person appeared above Jori-Ray, a woman this time, wearing nothing but a loincloth. A large white snake dangled from her right hand, twisting violently up in down in an effort to bite her, over and over and over again.

The drums pounded like wild banshees.

The woman went into a dance, a thing possessed, now swirling the snake like a rope.

Then the video ended.

29

By the time he got home, Teffinger only had an hour or so to look over the Jori-Ray Rose file before he would have to leave to meet with John Stone, and, more importantly, decide whether to officially reopen the case or not; and correspondingly fall victim to the wrath of hell raining down on him from the chief. Seeing the offering with his own eyes thoroughly convinced him that Jori-Ray was innocent. Old stiff-arms like the chief, though, would only see voodoo stupidity.

The notes reminded Teffinger that September had a boy-friend—Paul Bench.

He was a good-looking grunge type with long messy blond hair who wrote songs and sang in a garage band called Easy Chaos. Teffinger had interviewed him briefly back in the day but never viewed him as a suspect. The kid, fifteen at the time, was home at the time of the killing, verified by both of his parents. He rarely went over to the girl's house because of the dad, who hated him. He had never heard of anyone called Jori-Ray Rose.

Teffinger tracked him down and gave him a call.

"Man, you're going way back," Bench said. "It seems like forever ago. I thought everything was done."

"It is," Teffinger said. "You know, guys like me, we wake up in the middle of the night sometimes with stupid questions nagging at us. I was just wondering if anything weird was going on in September's life before she got killed."

"Weird? Like what . . ?

"I don't know," Teffinger said. "Just, whatever."

"No, not really. I mean, we were just high school kids. She was on the track team, you know, she was really strong, so it never surprised me that she'd physically go after someone who broke in. She sort of had this toughness about her. She wasn't always like that. But in the last year or so, yeah, she was."

"Okay."

"You know, now that we're talking about it, it was always a little strange to me how it all come on, the toughness, I mean. It was like a switch flipped on one day. We'd been going together about two years, which is forever at that age. In the beginning, she was just your average girl hanging out with her friends and working on her grades and coming to our band practices and whatnot. Then she—I don't know—got attitude. I don't mean that in a mean way; she didn't get mean. It was more like a defense thing."

"A defense thing?"

"Yeah, like no one was going to push her around. Maybe in hindsight she was building some kind of buffer from her dad, building up to eventually sever the tie. The guy was a jerk."

"How so?"

"You know. You've met him."

"Right."

"You know, there was one thing strange that she said one day. She said she wanted to get a gun."

"Did she say why?"

"No. As soon as she said it, she punched me in the arm and said, 'Had you going,' like it was just a joke. I don't think it was, though."

"Did she ever get one?"

"Not that I know of. It never came up again."

"Did you guys take drugs?"

"This is between us, right?"

"Absolutely," Teffinger said. "I'm not taking notes or anything. The file's closed."

"We smoked a little, and did acid a couple of times."

"Who got the stuff?"

"She did. It was always her. She had money; I didn't have anything. Her dad kept a lot of cash in a wall safe in the den, behind a painting. She figured out the combination and took a little here and there; maybe more, actually. She bought me a new Stratocaster for my birthday, American Standard edition. Those run over a grand. A month later she bought me a super-sweet Vox amp with twin speakers. Those ain't free either."

"Did her father ever find out?"

"About her taking the money? No, not that I know of. He put it in and took it out. It was more like a revolving door kind of thing with him. He didn't keep a ledger or anything, and it was a lot of cash, I'm talking about sixty or seventy or eighty grand, or maybe even more. It wasn't the kind of thing you'd count on a daily basis."

Teffinger knew what it was for.

It was for the escorts.

It was also used to try to keep Jori-Ray silent.

"Okay," Teffinger said. "What are you up to now, just for grins, life-wise?"

"I got a bachelor's degree from CSU. I work in a bank as an assistant manager."

"Ouch. Dry stuff. No more music?"

The man chuckled.

"No. That's all history. So is the long hair. Here's a funny thing. I ended up marrying Katie Black. Do you remember her?"

"No."

"She was September's best friend. We got married right out of high school and finally have a kid on the way, coming this October. If it's a girl we might even call her October, sort of as a tribute to September. We're not sure yet but it's a possibility."

Hanging up, Teffinger had one thought and one thought only, namely that September wasn't the cookies-and-cream girl he'd thought she was. She wanted a gun, and maybe even got one, still there in the house hidden away somewhere.

Was someone after her?

Who knew she had access to her father's safe?

Were they shaking her down for a cut?

Did they somehow get in trouble where they needed a lot of money and wanted September to give it to them?

Did she refuse?

Did they break into the house that night to force her open the safe? Did they want it all at that point? Were they in the house when Jori-Ray showed up?

Teffinger's phone rang.

It was John Stone, not happy.

"Are you coming or what?"

Teffinger checked his watch.

Shit.

3:15.

He was already fifteen minutes late and had at least a twenty-minute drive.

"On my way," he said.

"I hope so."

The line died.

30

The Senator was in the back yard between the pool and the fountain, working on his puts on the artificial green, when Teffinger arrived. The man's full set of clubs leaned against an abstract sculpture, no doubt a reminder to Teffinger that he was missing out on all his little tee-time fun just to have this meeting, which Teffinger was late for, by the way. Teffinger filled him in on Haiti, barely able to get two full sentences out in a row without the man's ego jumping in.

At the end, Stone said, "So, Jori-Ray's still at this Janjak place, as far as we know, and the Haitian authorities won't help because they're all scared of catching some stupid voodoo curse. Is that about right?"

Teffinger frowned.

"If you're thinking about sending a bounty hunter or vigilante group, don't," he said.

"Why not?"

"It won't end well."

Stone laughed.

"That's a risk I'm willing to take."

"Force won't work with Janjak."

"Fuck, they can sneak in. That little crazy bitch won't even know it's happening." The man hardened his face and added, "It's going to happen. I just made up my mind. Yeah, it's going to happen. It's definitely going to happen. I know exactly who to call." He smiled and added, "Maybe Janjak will die in the process, you never know. The world would be a better place, don't you think? Jori-Ray too, for that matter."

Teffinger raked his hair back with his fingers.

It immediately fell back down over his face.

"Let me ask you something," he said. "Did September have a gun?"

The man stopped breathing and stared.

"Huh? No, of course not. A gun?"

"Yeah. When you cleaned up all her stuff, did you find a gun?"

"No. Why would I find a gun?"

"Just curious," Teffinger said. "How about money?"

"What do you mean?"

"Did you know she was siphoning money out of your wall safe? She knew the combination. Did you know that?"

Stone slammed the putter onto the ground, so hard that the shaft snapped.

"Who's feeding you this bullshit?"

"Answer my question," Teffinger said. "When you cleaned up her things, did you find any large sums of money?"

"No, of course not. Are you actually reopening the case? I thought that was settled."

"Apparently it's not," Teffinger said.

"The chief said it was. Did he change his mind?"

"No."

The man sized Teffinger up and shook his head in wonder. "You're going rogue? I wonder how that's going to work out for you—"

Teffinger shrugged.

"I'm going to go wherever the evidence takes me." He stared the man directly in the eyes and added, "Wherever it takes me."

Stone stepped forward, close.

He face was full of bark and bite.

Then he punched Teffinger in the chest, so fast and hard that his head whiplashed and he crashed to the ground.

He got up, brushed off his pants and looked around.

A curtain in the house fell shut.

Then he left.

On the way, over his shoulder he said, "I'll see you around."

Stone's response was loud and quick and filled with finality.

"No you won't, asshole, because you're fired. Someone's setting you up and you're too dumb to even know it. Good luck in your new job as a security guard."

31

Teffinger wasn't even halfway home when his phone rang. He knew who it was—Double F—and let it go to voicemail. It might well be the conversation that ended his career and he didn't want to have it while dealing with tailgaters and road noise. He also wanted to give himself one more chance to come to his senses. It wasn't too late to just forget about the whole thing and concentrate on how to rescue Kimona.

Kimona.

She seemed so far away.

He didn't even have a picture of her.

He passed a McDonalds on Alameda, suddenly realized he was starved, and swung through for two cheeseburgers, large fries and a diet Coke, which he took to the Green Mountain trailhead and ate on the tailgate of the truck.

His phone rang.

It was Sydney, the newbie in the department, personally recruited by Teffinger out of Vice less than a year ago. He pulled up an image of her toned body and mocha African-American skin.

"Jesus, Teff, what the fuck's going on?"

"Stuff that you need to stay out of," he said. "I don't want it taking you down."

"Double-F called me," she said. "He has a message for you."

Teffinger cocked his head.

"Let me guess," he said. "He's giving me a raise."

"Teff, stop being you for a minute and get serious," she said. "Because that's what this is. Serious. I don't want to have to break in a new boss. You need to call him, right now."

Teffinger chuckled.

"You have me broken in?"

"Teff, the guy loves you, you know that. But he has his limits. Don't force him to do something he doesn't want to."

"I'll call him," he said. "It's about time I find out who he really is, and vice versa."

"Let me know how it goes."

"I will."

He finished what was left of the fries, washed it down with the last swallow of Coke, and went to dial the chief. Before he could punch the first digit, his phone rang and the voice of Katrina White came through. She was the mother of Mary-Ann White, the six-year-old who disappeared from her bed on April 1st. Teffinger had talked to her a lot when the case first developed; lately, not so much.

"I'm very sorry to bother you," she said. "I need you to tell me we're getting close to finding her."

Teffinger swallowed.

"I'm trying," he said.

"Is there anything I can do to help?"

"Yes."

"There is? What?"

"Call me every day," he said. "Call me just like you did right now."

Silence.

Then the woman said, "You're a good man, Mr. Teffinger. I know you'll find her. I have faith in you. You just need to understand; this is so, so hard for me. She's my baby. My soul has a hole in it ten miles deep. I need her back. I need her back or I'm going to die."

As soon as he hung up, Teffinger dialed the chief and said, "I didn't re-open the Jori-Ray case; it re-opened me." He outlined all the evidence he had so far, and how he got it, and added, "The bottom line is this. I have serious questions as to whether I might have made a big mistake. I honestly believe I narrowed the focus too much and caught the wrong person. If I don't dig down now that I've got fresh evidence slapping me in the face, I'm just rubber-stamping all my prior mistakes. Maybe I'll find nothing, in the end; but I have to look. I owe it to September to be sure I caught the right person. I owe it to Jori-Ray, too. If there's a real killer out there running loose, I need to bring him in."

The chief paused, deciding.

Teffinger was losing.

He could feel it.

"Look," he added. "We can do this two ways. The first way; the official line will be that Jori-Ray case is not back open but the Flamingo case is. We're pursuing a theory that his death was not an accident but was a homicide connected to the work he was doing on the Jori-Ray case, which justifies our looking around in both places. If we do it the that way, though, Stone will be on the horn to the mayor, and the governor and district attorney, too, most likely. They'll all be beating at your door with devils and pitchforks. I don't want you to be in that position. More to the point, I don't want you to have a conflict to where you always feel you have to rein me in. I need the freedom to work."

The chief exhaled.

"What's the other way?"

"The other way is that you suspend me without pay for insubordination."

"What's the third option?"

Teffinger smiled.

"I'm voting for two," he said. "I want you to suspend me. I won't contest it. I'll be honest with you. I might need to color outside the lines. I don't want to drag the department into a lawsuit. So, suspend me. That way you're protected, politically, and the department's protected, legally, and I can do what I need to do. Down the road, you can reinstate me when the time's right, if you want."

The chief groaned.

"The insubordination will always be on your record," he said. "Even if I withdraw it at some point, the stink will never go away. All we have in this game, in the end, is our record and our reputation."

"Record?" Teffinger said. "It's a piece of paper sitting in dark cabinet somewhere. Jori-Ray, being in prison for a crime that she might not have committed, that's real life."

The chief hesitated.

Then he said, "I'm not going to suspend you. Sorry. We're going with option one; the Jack Flamingo case is re-opened. No coloring outside the lines, though, Teffinger, and I mean it. If we're going to do this, we'll need something that will hold up in court. I'm not going to put my ass on the line for garbage we can't use."

The line died.

32

That evening after dark it rained; poured, is more like it; hissy-stormed like a drunken banshee is even more like it. The wind howled. The streetlights and trees shook. Teffinger watched it all from the garage, sitting behind the wheel of the '67 with a Bud light in his gut and a second in his hand, with his minds-eye on Kimona, wondering where she was, what condition she was in, whether she was thinking of him, and all the rest.

Finding September's real killer and convincing the district attorney to file a motion, all within the next few days, would be impossible.

Who was he kidding?

In the end, he'd have to return to Haiti and try to save her.

Maybe he should get that going in the morning and screw all this time-wasting crap.

Lightning flashed.

The world lit for the briefest split of a second.

Thunder cracked, so close that Teffinger recoiled.

Then the electricity went out.

The whole neighborhood defaulted to a state of primal darkness.

Teffinger flashed back to when he was ten, walking down by the South Platte with Mandy-Lou Freelander, suddenly stumbling on a giant twisty snake, then frantically searching for a branch to pick it up before it disappeared forever into the brush.

There were no branches.

It was getting away.

He bent down with a pounding heart, getting closer and closer, inch by inch, and then snatched it by the tail and dangled it for a split second before tossing it as far away as he could.

When he turned his head to Mandy-Lou, she was staring at him with a look that he'd never seen before.

She wanted to kiss him.

He could feel it.

He would do that, if she made a move.

He'd never done it before but he'd do it now, with her, right here.

Lightning arced across the sky, way up high, setting off a rolling wall of thundering bass, snapping Teffinger back. He downed what was left of the Bud in a long solid gulp and then grabbed another, a third, from the fridge. When he got back to the garage, headlights were splashing up the street, throwing eerie projector lights into horizontal rain. They went to the end of the street, three doors up, where the turned around in a one-eighty and pulled in front of his house, where they went out.

Teffinger flashed the lights of the '67, then left them on.

A woman emerged and fought briefly with an umbrella before it contorted and blew away. She watched it as it disappear into the night and then ran to the garage.

"In here," Teffinger shouted.

She approached, hesitantly, then opened the passenger side door and slipped in.

She was the department's hottie, Sophia Cruz, twenty-seven years old, too sexy for her own good, in spite of her daily garb of pants suits and bunched up hair. There wasn't a guy in the department who wouldn't crawl across a field of broken glass just to smell her neck.

Her hair was down.

Her glasses were off.

A short white dress rode up, showcasing serious legs.

"Whew," she said. "I'm half drowned."

"You want some dry clothes? Or a towel?"

She chuckled.

"No. Wine though, if you have some."

"Wine coming up."

He flicked the headlights off.

Everything turned to pitch.

He got her a glass of white wine over ice cubes and said, "Thanks for coming. Here's the deal. We're going to re-open the Jack Flamingo case."

Jack Flamingo.

She was processing the name.

"Yeah, I remember now, the light bulb guy. He got drunk and fell off a chair. Killed by a light bulb. That's not how I'm going, I can tell you that."

"Well, that's how it started. But a lot's happened in the last couple of days."

With that, he filled her in on the theory that Flamingo was murdered because he was getting close to finding out who killed September Stone, someone other than Jori-Ray Rose. He gave her all the information he had to back that theory up.

"The Jori-Ray case isn't getting re-opened, not officially on the record," Teffinger said. "But between you and the storm, we're going there. Here's where I'm at. I think John Stone hired a hitman named Axel Chard to kill Flamingo and make it look like an accident. I don't know why yet but I'm going to figure it out. Here's a picture of Chard."

He pulled up a photo of the man on his cell phone.

"I'll send it to you," he said. "Stone wants Jori-Ray dead. If she dies, this whole thing goes away. My suspicion is that he's going to hire Axel Chard to get the job done. What I want you to do is tail Stone and see if he meets up with his favorite problem solver. It may be as early as tomorrow morning. That's why we're meeting tonight."

"I've never done a tail," Sophia said.

"You'll do fine," Teffinger said.

"Should I plant a tracker?"

"No. This has to be by the book. Here's what's important. This doesn't go anywhere beyond you and me. Tell no one, including people in our own department. I don't want it working its way back to Stone. He'll retaliate against Double-F and I'm not going to let that happen. So you need to be discreet, okay?"

She took a sip of wine.

"Sure."

"Thanks."

"Jack Flamingo was my first case," she said. "I guess I screwed it up."

"You didn't screw it up," Teffinger said. "You got played, the same way any of us would have, including me. You'll be getting the bust when this is over. In the end, we might not have enough to tie John Stone back to either Flamingo or the Jori-Ray case. But if he's after Jori-Ray, we might be able to bring him down for what he's doing right now."

"Killing her?"

"Hopefully only attempting to kill her," Teffinger said. "Or conspiracy. If I could bring him down on either of those, I'd be happy. I wouldn't mind getting Axel Chard off the streets too, if there's a way. He's a suspect in the death of that actress, Lupa. Do you know her?"

"Yes."

"I've seen every movie she's ever been in."

"I'll bet you have. Why would Stone kill his own daughter? That's what I don't get—"

"Me either, to tell you the truth."

"I mean, it doesn't make sense, does it?"

"No. Not at all."

She mulled it over.

Then she said, "I bought a copy, I should confess that."

"A copy of what?"

"GQ," she said. "When they put you on the cover."

"Oh."

"Yeah, oh."

DAY EIGHT

May 24
Monday

33

Monday morning before dawn, Teffinger woke to regret that he'd brought Sophia Cruz in on the case, not because she wasn't qualified—she was—but because the assignment was too dangerous.

John Stone was a calculating snake.

Axel Chard was the grim reaper that no one ever saw coming.

Teffinger almost pulled her off before finally deciding he was underestimating her. She had the right to prove herself, just like everyone else. She had the right to take the same risks that he did.

Okay.

Continue on course, but watch her back.

Maybe she'll turn something up even as early as this morning.

That would be so sweet.

It would be nice to know that his theory actually had teeth to it.

He threw on sweats and headed out for a jog.

The world smelled like wet grass.

Puddles lay on the asphalt, waiting to get licked up by the inevitable sun.

Storm-battered leaves littered the yards.

A few clouds lingered from last night's storm but a clear dawn was already sneaking in. He felt good. There was nothing better than the start of a fresh day. He picked up the pace to six-minute miles, letting his knees lift and his lungs suck deep. A dog behind a fence gave him a warning bark. Second-story bedroom and bathroom lights began to randomly flick on. Two houses up, a fox scampered across the road, pausing briefly to check him out before disappearing behind a bush.

When he got back home there was a message on his phone.

It was from Catherine Stone, September's mother.

She wanted to meet with him, but not at her house; somewhere off-site.

Teffinger smiled.

The crack was about to get bigger.

An hour later, he pulled up in front of an abandoned warehouse near the BNSF switchyard, down by the South Plate—not far from Tarzan's old lair, actually—and killed the engine.

The place was Catherine's choosing; how she even knew about it, Teffinger couldn't figure.

Obviously, she wanted to be away from prying eyes.

Her husband's, in particular?

Ten minutes later the woman pulled up in an old pickup truck, killed the engine and hopped out. She was dressed down, in jeans and a pink T-shirt. Up top was a Rockies baseball cap with a ponytail pulled through the back. Oversized sunglasses hid most of her face. She wore no lipstick or paint.

She was young, considering; only about forty or so, attractive on every level, and well maintained. She wasn't afraid to work her body and it showed.

Her face, usually ordained with a big white smile, was now serious.

She removed her sunglasses and looked into Teffinger's eyes.

"Two different colors," she said. "I'd forgotten about that."

"You look well."

She shrugged.

"It's one day at a time, even now," she said. "You'd think it would eventually all just wash away, but it doesn't. It never really leaves you."

Teffinger nodded.

"I understand."

"With Jori-Ray escaping, it's, well, bigger." She paused and added, "How did she do that? Escape? I've been wondering—"

Teffinger raked his hair back with his finger.

It immediately fell back down over his forehead.

What she wanted was confidential information.

But she also deserved it.

"She had an inmate stab her in the stomach, bad, to the point where she needed to be taken off-site to a hospital for medical attention," he said. "She had three guards assigned to her, eight hours each, meaning around the clock, plus she was handcuffed fulltime to the bed, except for bathroom breaks and whatnot."

"But she got away anyway?"

"She did."

"I don't see how."

Teffinger exhaled.

"She's a beautiful woman. That's how."

"I don't follow."

"The night guard was a man named Pete Puller. Jori-Ray let him have sex with her, not just once, but every night. Then she threatened to expose him unless he loosened the handcuff enough for her to slip out of. He took a well-orchestrated bathroom break and she disappeared."

"He didn't think he'd get caught?"

Teffinger shrugged.

"He probably knew he would, but I guess he really didn't have much of a choice at that point. He was in too deep, no pun intended. Anyway, she made it out the back door of the hospital and someone picked her up."

"Who?"

"Unknown."

"But she had an accomplice, for sure?"

"Yes."

She processed it.

Then she said, "John said you asked him if September had a gun. We never found anything like that."

"That's what he said."

"We have a shed out in the back yard," she said. "Occasionally I'd see September go in it but I never thought much about it. Last night I checked it, just for grins. Up in the rafters, we were storing some tires from an old Austin Healy that John bought a long time ago. Inside one of those tires, I found some stuff."

"What kind of stuff?"

"I'll show you."

The woman grabbed a tote bag from the floor of the pickup truck and handed it to Teffinger.

Inside was a gun, four boxes of ammo, an 8.5 x 11 inch clasp envelope, and several large pieces of paper rolled up together and secured with a rubber band.

"I didn't touch the gun," she said. "I put a screwdriver in the barrel, lifted it out and set it right down here into this bag. The ammo, I had to touch but tried to keep my fingers at the edges; same thing for the folder. I opened the folder and looked inside. The rolled up papers are targets; souvenirs, I suppose. I don't know if any of this has anything to do with September's murder but figured you should have it."

Teffinger opened the passenger door of his Tundra, got Catherine's permission, and dumped the contents of the bag onto the seat, being careful to not touch anything.

The gun was a 9mm SIG.

The registration number was filed off.

Three of the boxes of ammo were full.

The forth had only 10 rounds inside.

Inside the clasp folder were several photos, a piece of paper, plus four rubber-banded stacks of money, all in fifty and hundred dollar denominations.

"I kept the bills in the rubber bands but did give them a count," Catherine said. "I got $10,550, if you put all four stacks together."

"Okay."

"I assume it's from John's safe," she added. "All he kept in there were fifties and hundreds."

"You're probably right. I have reason to believe she was sneaking money out of it."

He studied the photos.

They were of September and some older guy, 20 or thereabouts, mostly outside in terrain that looked like the foothills, maybe out around the Titan Road area.

"Who's the guy?"

Catherine shrugged.

"I've never seen him before in my life. The photos look

like he and September are out shooting somewhere; maybe practicing. Maybe he got the gun for her and was training her on how to use it."

Teffinger didn't disagree.

The piece of paper was a receipt from Starmakers Recording Studio in the amount of $5,000, for a four-hour block of studio time, dated two months before September was killed.

"I'm assuming September bought that for her boyfriend, Paul Bench," Catherine said. "He had a band, if you'll recall."

Teffinger nodded.

"I remember. Did you tell your husband about this stuff?"

"No."

"Why not?"

"He's a U.S. Senator," she said. "The gun's clearly illegal. I want him to always be able to say he never saw it, never touched it, and never knew anything about it." She paused and added, "He's a good man, Mr. Teffinger. He's an alpha male, to be sure, and he can be hard to take at times, even insulting, but deep down he's a good man. Keep that in mind."

"I will."

"He doesn't like you," she added. "Quite the opposite, actually. But you're not alone. There are a lot of people he doesn't like. It doesn't mean he's a bad man. That's just how he processes the world and interacts with it. He's had a charitable trust for a long time, which I run. A lot of his money goes to help people who have no idea where it came from."

Teffinger pondered it.

Then he said, "Did you ever hear of someone named Axel Chard?"

"No. Who's he?"

"He may go by other names," Teffinger said. "He's a hit-man. He's a good-looking guy who likes to live large and have high-priced call-girls sitting in his lap. Does that ring a bell?"

"No."

Teffinger remembered he had the man's photo on his phone and pulled it up.

"This is him."

Catherine shook her head.

"No, I've never seen him before."

"Okay."

"I would remember."

"Okay."

"Given where we're meeting, you're probably not going to be too surprised at what I'm going to ask you, which is this: can we keep this meeting between the two of us?"

Teffinger nodded.

"Sure, absolutely. I'll have to do a chain of custody report and book everything into the file, so there will be a record and your name will be in it," he said. "But it's not open to the public and there's no reason anyone would ever see it outside of myself and possibly a few other internal people. I won't tell anyone if you won't."

"Thank you. I don't want the media to work themselves into a frenzy and start pulling old Band-Aids off."

"I understand."

She got back into the pickup truck and started the engine.

Before pulling away she powered down the window and said, "John didn't have anything to do with our daughter's murder. Jori-Ray Rose killed her. I'm meeting with you, but it's mostly so I can tell you this to your face: go catch that bitch."

34

Suburban non-gang fifteen-year-olds aren't interested in a gun, not unless they needed it for defense, or offense. In September's case, Teffinger suspected the former. Either way, the one person most likely to know was the person who got it for her, which almost certainly was the 20-year old in the photos. If anyone knew what was going on weird in September's life, it was him.

He was key, just like that.

As soon as Catherine left, Teffinger took pictures of all the photos with his phone, texted them to Sydney, and then called her and explained the situation, concluding with, "Find out who this guy is. This is your top priority. Drop everything else. Please and thank you."

"Who is this?"

"Funny."

"Let's talk about the obvious," she said.

"Which is—?"

"Which is, what's in it for me?"

"How about a paycheck at the end of the month, just like the rest of us."

"Yeah, but I get that without dropping everything. You want me to drop everything, right?"

"Sydney—"

"That's the difference here, the drop thing. Come on, Teff. Give me motivation. You can do it."

He could argue.

He'd only be wasting his time.

"Okay, lunch," he said.

"Say, okay, lunch, on me."

"That's what I meant."

"You got to say it, Teff. I know your tricks."

He said it.

"Okay, lunch, on me. Happy?"

"Not yet. When?"

"Soon."

"Soon's a subjective word. We both know if you have even an ounce of wiggle room—"

"By the end of the month, okay?"

"No. On Friday. This Friday. Four days from now."

He groaned.

"Okay, Friday. Oh, one more thing as long as you're doing stuff," he said. "I got a call from Mary-Ann White's mom. Her heart's breaking. See if you can think of a way to move that case forward."

"God, Teff, I've racked my brain a hundred times."

"Rack it 101, okay?"

"Do I get desert on Friday?"

"I'll count your brain racks. If it's 101 or more, then yes."

35

Sophia Cruz called sounding like she just stepped off of a rollercoaster. "We got action! Stone parked off Colfax on a side street and got out of his car wearing a fake mustache and beard and a crazy-big cowboy hat. He walked a block to a sleazy hotel called the Paradise and disappeared into one of the second-floor rooms."

The Paradise.

Teffinger knew it well.

He'd personally responded to more than a few murders there.

It was a two-story, paint-peeling piece of junk with outside stairs that led to an exposed walkway that fed the second story rooms. It had twenty or so units that you could rent by the hour, day, week or month. It didn't take a PhD in quantum physics to figure out what the clientele was like.

"Where are you?"

"Down the street."

"On foot or in your car?"

"Foot."

"How long has he been inside?"

"Just a few minutes. I called you right away."

"Okay. Stay there. I'm heading over. If someone besides Stone comes out, follow him and forget about Stone. If Stone leaves alone, just stay there and see if someone else comes out after him, then follow that person. We don't care about Stone at this point. We care about who he's meeting with. Got it?"

"Yes."

"Don't get spotted."

Ten minutes later Teffinger drove past, spotting Sophia in shorts and a T-shirt thirty yards down from the sleaze-bag, standing behind a white van with a flat tire. A car had pulled up to her and the driver, a bald man, was leaned over and talking to her through the passenger window, no doubt checking to see if she was a whore.

Get out of there, asshole!

You're going to fuck it all up!

Teffinger was half tempted to pull up next to the jerk and flash his badge, but before he could do it, the guy took off. Two minutes later he was at Sophia's side.

"He's in Room 23," she said. "Third from the left, blue door."

"Okay."

"He's with a woman."

A woman?

Teffinger's chest tightened.

He was supposed to be with Axel Chard.

"How do you know?"

"Someone dropped her off right after I called you," she said. "She walked up, knocked on the door and disappeared inside. She wasn't dressed like a hooker but had a body, that's for sure; about twenty-five or so, blond hair. Could be an escort."

Teffinger grunted.

"Old habits, and all that. Who dropped her off?"

"A black sedan with tinted windows, an Audi, maybe. It

was expensive."

Teffinger mulled the options.

If the woman was an escort, which seemed more likely than not, Teffinger might be able to squeeze her. She might have dirt to cough up.

"Okay, here's what we do. I'm going to park down the street. You stay here and let me know when the sedan comes back and which way it's heading. Fair enough?"

"Yes."

Teffinger squeezed her elbow.

"You did good," he said. "Oh, take a few pictures if you can do it discretely; Stone, the woman, and the license plate of the sedan. At a minimum, we should be able to put some pressure on him. We'll be able to force him to leave the chief alone."

Then he was gone.

Catherine's words echoed in his brain.

He's a good man, Mr. Teffinger. He's an alpha male, to be sure, and he can be hard to take at times, even insulting, but deep down he's a good man.

Reality was not her friend.

Not any more.

36

Sophia's call came in thirty minutes. "The sedan just showed up. It's waiting outside. I was wrong about it being an Audi. It's a Mercedes. I got a picture of it. Let me check it. Yeah, the license plate shows. So far, no one's come out of the room." She paused and said, "Okay action. The woman just came out."

"Alone?"

"Yeah. Stone's still inside. The woman shut the door behind her. She's heading for the car. Hold on, I'm going to get a picture of her." Silence, then, "Okay, I got it. She just got in. It's pulling out. It's heading your way. What do you want me to do?"

"Get a picture of Stone when he comes out. Then get back to your car and call me. I might have you help me tail the Mercedes. Don't let Stone spot you."

"I won't. Cars keep stopping. They think I'm a whore."

"Don't flash your badge. Just tell them to fuck off."

The sedan passed Teffinger's truck.

He let one car get behind it, then pulled out and followed it east on Colfax.

A minute into it, his phone rang.

"Okay, Stone just left. He's walking back to his car with the hat way down over his face. I got as good of a picture of him as I could. Now I'm waiting for him to clear out before I head to my car. Do you want me to join you then?"

"Does the picture show his face?"

"Sorta, but not that good."

Teffinger exhaled.

"Position yourself to where he's got to drive past you. Try to get another picture of his face, and the license plate, too. Don't get spotted though. If you can't do it without getting spotted, don't do it."

"Got it."

"I think I have the sedan under control," he said. "When you're done there, head back to the office."

"You sure?"

"Yeah."

The sedan led him east to I-25, then north to 58th, then into an industrial area, and into the parking lot of a non-discreet building with a pink door that said Femme Confidential.

He knew the place.

It had a small members-only strip-club in the front.

The real money, though, came from the back, which was equipped with a stable of super-expensive escorts and sound-proof rooms ranging from dungeons to decadent to themed, a lot like the love hotels in Tokyo. The blond got dropped off at the front door and disappeared inside while the sedan took off.

Now what?

He weighed the pros and cons of confronting the woman.

The pros: she'd probably confess to just now meeting with Stone, and she might have dirt on him in exchange for Teffinger not hauling her in on a prostitution charge. He was only interested in Stone, not her.

The cons: she may tell Stone about Teffinger, especially if

he was a bread-and-butter client.

Okay.

Decide.

He decided he had no options.

He had no options because he had no time.

He needed to confront her, right now.

Wherever things were headed, he needed to get there.

There were twenty or so vehicles in a parking lot that could hold ten times that. Teffinger parked at the far end, walked to the front door and entered a small reception area, to find no one there. Ten seconds later a door opened and a punked-up woman walked in, dressed in patches of leather and lots of skin.

"Well aren't you the cute one," she said. "I'm half tempted to give you a freebie."

Teffinger smiled.

"You're too kind. The blond that just walked in; what's her name again?"

"You mean Scorpion?"

"Yeah, that's her. Tell her Nick's here. I need to talk to her for a few minutes."

The woman smiled.

"You know the rules, right?"

He shrugged.

"Not exactly."

"Two hundred dollars to the house for the room," she said. "You get thirty minutes with the girl, she'll dance for you. If you want more, you need to negotiate that directly with her."

"What are my options?"

"With Scorpion? She does bondage, you or her, but no pain on her end, teasing, wrestling, tickling, role-play, humiliation, just about whatever. She's a tough negotiator though, so be warned."

Teffinger checked his wallet.

There were three twenties and a ten.

The woman said, "We take credit-cards. The statement will show Anderson Services LLC."

Teffinger raked his hair back with his fingers.

"Yeah, sure, let's do the credit-card thing."

His phone rang.

It was Sophia.

She sounded like a balloon with half the air escaped.

"Bad news," she said. "I couldn't get another picture of Stone; his license plate, either. I only got that first one I told you about. It's not good. It could be anybody."

He stepped to the side where it was private.

"Don't worry about it. We're on the right track."

"Yeah, but sorry, anyway." A pause, then, "Some good news, though, a little. I ran the plate for the black Mercedes. It's registered to a guy named Shawn Anderson. He lives up in the mountains, in Genesse. There's no record on him."

"Run him down, just for grins; social media and all the rest. It probably won't end up being important but let's find out who he is. I don't want to find out later that he was a rock I should have turned over."

37

The pretty little punked-up one led Teffinger down a dark hallway to the back of the building, through a pink door, and into a dim-lit bondage room. There, she turned and wiggled her butt at him, and said, "Scorpion will be joining you shortly. Have fun." She blew him a kiss as she left, closing the door behind her.

He checked things out.

There was a rack, an X-frame, chains and bars hanging down all over the place, whips, dildos, feathers, leather cuffs, blindfolds, hoods, gags, and more and more and more.

Whatever your nasty was, you could get it done here.

Scorpion walked in ten minutes later wearing a Sailor Moon outfit and leather cuffs on her wrists and ankles. She smiled, locked the door behind her, and made her way seductively to Teffinger, where she rubbed her stomach against his, put her lips to his ear and whispered, "Stretch me out on the rack."

"I only came here to talk," he said.

"Talk is two hundred."

"I'm a homicide detective," he said. "I came here to talk to you about your meeting at the Paradise."

She ran a finger down his nose.

"Two hundred," she said.

"I already did you a favor by not hauling you in," he said. "Plus I did you a favor by not telling the punked-one out front who I am. No one will know that you're talking to me. All I want is five minutes of information. You're not who I'm after."

"Two hundred," she said. "Yes or no?"

He didn't like the idea but said, "Okay."

She kissed him.

"Stretch me out on the rack."

"That's not necessary."

"Do it," she said.

He complied, attaching her cuffs at both ends.

"Good boy. Now turn the wheel."

He complied, watching her arms stretch tighter and tighter above her head.

"More," she said.

He did it until it seemed like she would break apart.

"There, stop there. Now, see that phone over on the wall? Pick it up and tell the woman who answers to put two hundred dollars on your credit card."

He did it.

"Good," she said. "See, that wasn't so hard. Now, do what you want to me. When twenty-five minutes are up, a red light will flash. That means you have five minutes left. If you go over the five, you're automatically charged for another half hour."

"You went to the Paradise this morning," he said.

"That's true."

"Tell me about it."

"There's nothing to tell," she said. "There was no sex."

Teffinger put disbelief on his face.

"I was born on a Friday but it wasn't last Friday," he said. "What happened in there? With you and the Senator?"

"Senator?"

"Don't play games," Teffinger said. "John Stone."

"I don't know a John Stone."

Teffinger shook his head.

"Okay," he said. "Walk me through it, step by step."

"Someone called in and said he wanted a girl for half an hour. He would pay a thousand dollars, cash, at the room, in advance before anything happened."

"Who made the call?"

"John Doe," she said. "It's always John Doe."

"Are the calls recorded?"

"No."

"Okay, go on."

"I usually don't take assignments like that but decided to take a chance this time," she said. "When I knocked on the door, a guy in a cowboy hat answered. He handed me a thousand dollars in cash and said to go sit in that chair. Then he disappeared into the bathroom and he was talking to some other guy in there."

"Huh?"

"Yeah," she said. "I was getting ready to bolt because I thought they were going to tag team me. But, for better or worse, I just kept sitting there and the minutes clicked off one after the other. When the thirty minutes were up, the guy came out of the bathroom and said, "You can leave now. That was it."

"So you had no sex?"

"That's right."

"What about the other guy in the bathroom? Did you ever get a look at him?"

"No."

"What were they talking about?"

"I have no idea. I couldn't make anything out."

Teffinger pulled up a photo of John Stone on his phone.

"Is this the guy in the cowboy hat?"

"No. The guy in the hat had a mustache and beard."

"What if they were fake? If they were off, would he be the guy I'm showing you?"

"I have no idea. Maybe yes, maybe no. You tell me."

Teffinger released the tension on the rack and un-cuffed the woman who said, "You have fifteen minutes left."

"You can keep them."

"Do you at least want a blow job?"

"Maybe next time."

Then he was gone.

Driving back to homicide, Teffinger knew who the guy in the bathroom was. It was Axel Chard, confirming the mission and getting his money.

Scorpion had just been a diversion in case someone was following Stone. He got to the room first, she showed up, she left, and then he left. Anyone following Stone at that point would leave too. After that happened, the guy in the bathroom—Chard—would simply wait until the coast was clear and then disappear.

Teffinger didn't have Stone on a sex charge.

He didn't have a clear photo of him at the hotel.

He also had no photo of the man's license plate.

Scorpion couldn't identify him.

He had nothing.

38

Teffinger's office was a third-floor cubicle by the window, staring out at the bail bondsmen houses across the street, painted in cartoon colors. He could have had a real office with a real door that closed, down the hall, like everyone who preceded him, but the walls were too close and the windows too small and the air too full of non-oxygen and there wasn't enough noise. Equally important, the cubicle was closer to the coffee machine. He was barely able to get a cup and make it to his chair when Sydney plopped down in one of the worn leather things in front of his desk and gave him a long hard stare.

"You look down."

He couldn't deny it.

"A fish just wiggled off a hook."

"Well, man-up and re-bait," she said. "I've been racking my brain like you asked about the Mary-Ann White case. We pounded the pavement for the surrounding two blocks looking for video cameras. We can go wider, say four blocks. If you want, I can get flyers printed up with the date and time we're looking for and we can stuff every mailbox. You never know, maybe we'll get a call." She twirled a pencil in her fingers and must have read his thoughts because she added, "It's not much, I know."

He put hope on his face.

It was dark out that night.

The chance of getting any useful tape was somewhere between slim and none, and Slim just left town. Still, it was something.

"Run with it. Do one other thing for me, too, if you would. Call Jena Lake down at Channel 8. See if she'll do an updated story. Let's get that little girl's face back in everyone's living room. What about a reward? Where is it right now?"

"Ten," she said.

He frowned.

"That won't buy a used car. See if you can get it up."

She batted her eyelids at him.

"I will if you will."

He smiled.

"I'm going to call it one of these days, that little bluff of yours."

"I'm waiting." She blew him a kiss and said, "Don't forget about Friday."

"Get it up to 250," he said.

"The reward?"

"Yes."

"250? And how exactly am I supposed to do that?"

He shrugged.

"Just take what you have and make it 25 times bigger."

"So, simple?"

"No. Math's always hard. That's why everyone hates it."

Five minutes later Teffinger was out the door, to home, grabbing his passport and a small briefcase, in the throes of a sudden crazy plan that might be worth something or might be dumber than dirt, only time would tell.

He had to get back to Haiti.

Two hours later he was strapped into the aisle seat of a

crazy-big machine, charging down a runway at DIA, and hoping against hope that the thing didn't do a pancake right after it lifted.

The G's pushed him back.

Everyone was quiet, serious, and staring straight ahead.

The roar of the engines was deafening.

He clutched the armrests.

Two kids were in the seats next to him, seven or eight years old. The closer one tapped him on the forearm and said, "It'll be okay."

He smiled as best he could.

"Right. I know."

"Don't be scared."

"I'm not."

Sweat beaded up on his forehead.

The aircraft lifted.

The heavy rotation of the wheels immediately stopped.

Everything got smooth.

The craft rose higher and higher and started to bank to the left. The tightness in his chest eased. Okay, all was well. In ten minutes the seatbelt sign would be off and he could order a beer—the first of a bunch.

Then, suddenly, a violent explosion pierced the air and the plane shook as if falling apart.

Flames were shooting out of the engine.

The plane immediately slowed and began to drop.

The kid screamed.

Teffinger summoned everything he had and shook the kid's arm.

"Listen to me. Hey, listen to me!"

The kid's eyes met his.

"It's going to be okay," Teffinger said. "We probably just

hit a bird, that's all. It happens all the time. The plane's designed to fly on one engine. We'll circle back to the airport and be back on the ground in no time."

"I want my mom!"

"Where is she?"

"She's not here! She's back in the airport!"

Teffinger put his arm around the kid's shoulders and squeezed. "I got you. Don't worry about anything. I won't let anything happen to you. Okay?"

The kid looked distant.

Then he focused on Teffinger's eyes and nodded.

"Okay."

"Good. Just sit tight. We're going back to your mom."

DAY NINE

May 25
Tuesday

39

Mid-afternoon Haiti time, Teffinger climbed into an airport cab driven by a twitchy old guy with a gold tooth, and headed into the guts of Port-au-Prince.

He was lucky to be alive.

Yesterday, the plane did make it back to the airport just as he told the kid it would; but the landing, with one engine and a heavy crosswind, was hard, ending in a bounce, a crash, sirens, fire, emergency vehicles, foam, and lots of frantic bodies sliding out of emergency shoots, including Teffinger, with the two kids in his arms.

Then came the investigation.

What happened?

Was he hurt?

Did he take any phone video?

And on and on and on, because it had to, because two people ended up dead, because lots of lungs inhaled smoke, because bodies got cuts and bangs and concussions, and because the inevitable calls to lawyers were no doubt already in motion.

By the time he was finally able to walk away, it was too late to do anything but go home and try it all again the next day, if he could summon the courage.

That was yesterday.

Today was today.

He checked into the same sleazebag motel as before — Villa Blue — not just because he already knew the lay of the land, but because it was the last place he'd run into his target, Axel Chard. Out of an abundance of caution, he registered under the alias Nash Remington, paying cash in advance for three nights.

The plan wasn't complicated.

Stone had hired Chard to go to Haiti and either bring Jori-Ray back or kill her; more likely, the latter. All Teffinger really needed was to lay eyes on the guy. That, in and of itself, would confirm his suspicion that Stone was as slippery as a greased pig. In a more perfect world, though, Teffinger would actually be able to foil the man in the act and — maybe, just maybe — catch his little ass. Then he'd find a way to squeeze him.

Late afternoon, Teffinger rented a 27-foot Grady White with twin outboard motors and pulled up Janjak's lair with binoculars from calm waters a mile offshore.

What he saw he could hardly believe.

Janjak was in a Boston Whaler, alone, cruising on plane directly at him with her dreadlocks dancing.

He could easily outrun her, and his first instinct was to do exactly that.

He didn't, though.

Instead he just waited.

It didn't take long, five minutes at best.

The woman circled around him closely at high speed three times and then abruptly came off plane and drifted to his side.

She wore her usual; a white wrap-around skirt, and nothing else. In the front of her boat, minding its own business, was a large yellow snake with a twitchy tongue. Teffinger had no idea if it was poisonous or not but suspected it was.

Janjak killed the engine, then locked eyes with him as she loosened her skirt and let it fall to the floorboard.

He was about to ask her how she knew he was here.

Before he could, the woman blew him a kiss and dived over the side.

The easy movement of her perfect dark body in the crystal green water was the sexiest thing Teffinger had ever seen. He suddenly remembered why he'd fallen in love with her, way back when, and wondered if this was the magical continuation of something that would never end.

Maybe he was destined to be here.

Maybe he'd never leave.

Maybe, screw Denver and everything else.

The woman floated on her back with her face pointed at the sun and her eyes closed.

She looked so vulnerable, so at peace, so perfect in her own skin.

He took off his shirt, then—after a brief hesitation—everything else, and dived in.

Janjak swam to him and put her arms around his neck.

Her legs rubbed against his as she treaded.

Nothing had ever felt so perfect.

Nothing.

"A man's coming to kill Jori-Ray," he said.

"You?"

"No. His name is Axel Chard. He's a hitman. If my gut's right, John Stone hired him."

"That's the girl's father, right? September's?"

"Yes."

"So what's the problem? Is it eating him alive that Jori-Ray's out walking around free in the world?"

"Maybe," Teffinger said.

Janjak kissed him on the mouth.

It was pure electricity.

"But there might be more to it," he added. "I think he might be implicated in his daughter's death. He might have even been the one who killed her. If that's true, then killing Jori-Ray would be the best way to close the investigation."

Janjak pushed off and swam away.

She circled around the boats, then climbed up into hers and looked down at Teffinger.

"Jori-Ray's at my place. Meet me there."

She fired up the outboard.

Then she blew him a kiss and threw the snake in the water so close that it almost hit him.

"Bring him back with you," she said.

40

It took some time, but Teffinger got the snake scooped out of the water with a paddle, dropped it into the anchor locker head first and slammed the hatch before it could twist around and bite his eyes out. His phone rang just as he was about to fire up the outboards and Sydney's voice came through.

"Where are you?"

Haiti.

That was the answer.

It was also one he couldn't say.

"Right behind you," he said.

"Right behind me, huh? Should I back it up?"

He grinned.

"Your call."

"God, Teff. You better stay on my good side. You could get fired for all this stuff—"

He grunted.

"So I've been told. What's going on?"

"Okay, the Mary-Ann White case. We got those flyers out and believe it or not we already got a hit. A woman by the name of Desoto Brown has Ring camera footage from the night in question. She lives three blocks away. A car stopped right outside of her house that night, just around three in the morning. The driver was doing something with his phone. It lit up his face, to an extent, for about ten seconds. It's pretty vague so far but forensics is trying to enhance it."

"Damn! You got to love life sometimes."

"Yeah. Exciting, huh?"

"Send a copy of what you got so far to my email, please and thank you."

"Will do. Oh, almost forgot. We set up a Go Fund Me page for the reward and it's already over a hundred grand. And Jena Lake's doing an updated report tonight on the news. Maybe the log jam's finally breaking loose."

"Call the mother, Katrina, and give her an update. Show her the video. See if she recognizes the guy."

In his peripheral vision, Teffinger detected motion.

The snake was in the front of the boat, slithering its way towards him.

He threw his shirt on top of it.

A moment passed, then another, and the thing didn't come out. The cloth was still wet with saltwater. Maybe it was holding the thing down.

"I got to go," he said.

"Is something wrong?"

"No."

"You sound weird."

"I hate snakes."

"What's that mean?"

"It means I don't like them. Hate means not like."

"Tell me again why I put up with you—"

"It's a mystery, isn't it?"

He kept an eye on the shirt as he fired up the outboards and headed for Janjak's.

His gut churned.

He could be face to face with Axel Chard at any time. It would be unlikely that both of them would walk away alive.

Chard wasn't that kind of guy.

Teffinger was.

That was his weakness.

41

Hidden out of sight from prying eyes in the villa, Janjak and Jori-Ray sat on a sofa across from Teffinger, holding hands, as Teffinger filled them in on what he'd learned over the past few days, including his suspicion that John Stone may have killed his own daughter and had now hired Axel Chard to kill Jori-Ray. Stone may have previously hired Chard to kill a private investigator by the name of Jack Flamingo, who was working for Alabama, and made it look like an accident. Chard was also implicated in the murder of a movie star named Lupa, out in L.A. last year.

Janjak pondered it.

"When will he come?"

Teffinger shrugged.

"Lupa was at night. So was Jack Flamingo."

"So, tonight?"

He nodded.

"I think his instructions are ASAP," he said. "Stone wants me off his back in the worst way, before I actually find something."

Janjak tilted her head.

"I have a woman who owes me," she said. "She's white. With a wig, she could look like Jori-Ray from a distance. We can use her as a body double if we want."

Jori-Ray didn't hesitate.

"No. Absolutely not."

"But—"

"No, that's final. This is my mess. If anyone's going to die, it's me. End of discussion."

Janjak pondered it.

"So be it, then."

"I want to see Kimona," Teffinger said.

"No," Janjak said.

"Is she here?"

"No."

"Where is she?"

"She's not here. She's safe but you can't see her. If that's what you came here for, you can go back to Denver."

The pressure in Teffinger's chest rose.

He felt like a tire inflating to overload.

"Look," he said. "I'm gaining on John Stone, but I'm not going to have him by the time of the offering."

Janjak hardened her face.

"The date's set in stone. It has been for a hundred years. Don't think it's going to change because it isn't."

She gave Teffinger an evil eye, then gave Jori-Ray a kiss on the lips and left.

Teffinger looked deep into Jori-Ray's eyes and said, "Do you know where she is? Kimona?"

"It doesn't matter. I can't tell you."

"But you know, right?"

She stared into the distance.

"Look," Teffinger said. "I'm putting my life on the line to save your ass. A little reciprocation would be in line, don't you think?"

She nodded.

"I'll do whatever you want," she said "But I can't go against Janjak. You know that. Just talking about this puts us both in danger."

Teffinger stood up and put a scowl on his face.

"Then you do the offering," he said. "Tell Janjak that you'll do it and to let Kimona go."

She frowned.

"I've already tried that."

"Bullshit."

She shook her head.

"Honest, Teffinger, I've brought it up a whole lot of times. She won't budge." She hesitated and added, "I think she's in love with me. She knows I wasn't going to survive it the first time, the offering. If Kimona hadn't interceded, I would have died. I know that. She knows that. If I do the new offering, she'll lose me." She took a deep breath. "I'm sorry. If you can convince her to let me do it instead of Kimona, I will. Try if you want. I'll even join you. But telling you where Kimona is right now, that's not something I can do. I wish I could but I can't. I hope you understand."

Teffinger processed it.

"Do you love her? Janjak?"

"I don't know; she's been more than kind to me, you know that. I have feelings for her, I'll admit that, but to be honest, I'm not sure whether they're my own feelings or whether she's making me have them."

"Have you slept with her?"

She hesitated.

Then she said, "Yes."

42

Teffinger snuck around the grounds all day, silently searching for Kimona, only to convince himself that Janjak was telling the truth.

The woman wasn't there.

Janjak's men spent the day quietly checking hotels, to find no sign of Axel Chard. Somehow they even got their hands on the airline manifests into Port-au-Prince International Airport for today and yesterday and found no sign of him on connecting trips from Denver. No one at customs recalled seeing anyone like Axel Chard.

Maybe the man flew into the Dominican Republic.

Maybe, from there, he was going to rent a car.

With a guy like him, you never knew.

No one suspicious came anywhere near the grounds in a boat, or in a car, or on foot. If they had, they would have been spotted. Janjak had eyes everywhere. A frog couldn't hop in with getting noticed.

The man was out there, though.

He was waiting for dark.

Teffinger could feel him.

He had Jori-Ray wander around freely all day, walking on the beach, sunbathing, staying in sight, and otherwise being the good little bait that she was. It was important that Chard knew he was in the right place. Let him think that no one had a clue he was coming.

Get your guard down.

Believe it's a piece of cake.

The day passed and twilight came.

Jori-Ray and Janjak sat on wooden chairs in front of the main structure, ostensibly hanging out there because that's where they'd be sleeping tonight.

After dark, they retreated inside to the upper floor where the bedrooms were.

They got ready for bed.

Then they turned out the lights.

Two minutes later, Teffinger snuck Jori-Ray out into the dark and, with a rifle in hand and a knife in his belt, escorted the woman to a raggedy shed fifty yards to the south.

She headed inside, dressed in shorts and tennis shoes, in case she ended up needing to run, and laid down nervously on a mattress, where she'd stay hidden until morning.

Teffinger gave her a kiss on the cheek and said, "It's going to be fine."

She nodded.

"Be careful."

"Don't worry."

Two armed men were on guard, waiting in the darkness, one on each side of the shed. Janjak had already given them clear orders.

They were not to leave Jori-Ray's side for any reason.

If someone approached without announcing himself, they were to shoot to kill. Everyone else already knew they were not to come anywhere close to that area without first raising their hands and clearly showing who they were.

Janjak's men—twelve in total—hid in the shadows, strategically placed.

Teffinger took a position in the palms fifty yards south of

the shed.

Then he waited.

They all waited.

Minute after minute ticked off, then bigger chunks of time.

Clouds came in and blocked what little moonlight there was.

Then it started to drizzle.

Everything turned to pitch black. He could have been in a coffin fifty yards under the ground and it wouldn't have been any darker.

He sat there for a long time, rocking back and forth, waiting for something, anything, to happen as the rain soaked into every pore of his body and the storm got more and more evil.

He called Janjak.

"Everything okay in there?"

"Yes," she said. "Quiet as cotton. I'm starting to think he's not coming. I'm getting no visions."

"He's coming," Teffinger said. "Count on it."

He punched off, stood up and took a leak, fighting against a whipping wind to stay vertical.

Then he silently headed towards the shed just to make sure everything was all right.

When he got close enough he shouted, "It's me, Teffinger. Did you get that?"

No response came.

He stepped closer.

"Hey, it's me. Don't shoot. I'm just checking on things."

No response came, again.

His chest tightened.

Then he broke into a trot.

43

Lightning flashed.

What Teffinger saw he could hardly believe. One of the guards was sprawled on the ground, motionless. His face was a bloody mess, as if his eyes had been gouged out. The other was in the throes of death battle, overpowered by a man who had him from behind, with an arm around his neck. Feet kicked his out, and as he tumbled towards the ground, the man behind him twisted his neck violently. He hit with a thud that sounded like death itself and didn't move.

The killer wasted no time.

He was already busting through the shed door, splintering the wood into oblivion with the brute force of his shoulder, not even trying the handle, and disappearing inside.

Jori-Ray screamed.

Teffinger's brain flashed.

The man hadn't seen him yet.

His instinct was to shoot.

Shot now!

End it!

No!

No!

Don't hit Jori-Ray!

He got to the door. Inside, everything was blacker than pitch; he could see nothing, not a single thing, but he knew the sounds; they were punches, landing without mercy, smashing the life out of Jori-Ray.

Teffinger shot into the roof.

For a short nanosecond, everything lit up. The man had Jori-Ray on the ground, straddling her chest, and pummeling her face with his fists.

He turned.

His face contorted.

He wasn't alone.

Someone was in there with him.

Someone with a rifle.

Teffinger hesitated, not knowing whether to jump the man or shoot him. Then he fired again, into the air one more time, to get a final read on his mark, before he shot him dead. When the air exploded with light, everything had already changed. The man was behind Jori-Ray now with an arm squeezed around her chest and a knife to her throat.

"I'll kill her!"

Teffinger froze.

He couldn't shoot.

He couldn't get to the man without the knife carving into her throat.

"Let her go!" he shouted.

Suddenly his face exploded into pain.

He knew it was a punch but it felt more like a baseball bat swung by a crazed gorilla. The room swirled with the force of a hurricane and he fought to keep his balance. Then came another equally brutal punch, from out of the invisible blackness. His knees buckled. He dropped to the floor in debilitating pain and struggled to keep from passing out. A kick came to his ribs, knocking the wind out of his lungs, and then feet were stepping over him and disappearing into the night.

"Nick! Help me!"

Get to your feet!

Now!

Do it!

Don't pass out!

Don't give up!

He forced his body off the ground, picked up the rifle and made his way out the door, into the darkness.

"Nick!"

The shout seemed a long ways off.

He followed it as best he could, ever deeper into the wind and rain of the storm, hardly able to see a thing.

He was heading towards the water.

That much he knew.

The guy must have a boat waiting for him.

He fired into the air three times to get the attention of Janjak's men.

Bam!

Bam!

Bam!

Then he shouted.

"Get him! "

"He's going to the water!"

"He's got Jori-Ray!"

Suddenly outside floodlights kicked on at the villa, not strong, but enough for Teffinger to make out what was happening. The man was pushing a small inflatable dingy into the water. He jumped in and threw a punch towards the floorboard, no doubt at Jori-Ray, who wasn't in view but had to be there because she wasn't anywhere else. Janjak's men were charging at him, firing, apparently not realizing Jori-Ray was there and they might hit her.

"Don't fire!"

The guy frantically jerked the rope of an outboard, kicking it to life, and headed out into the whitecaps at a full speed. Before Teffinger or anyone else could get to the water's edge, the guy had completely disappeared into the darkness.

44

With he adrenalin suddenly gone and reality back in full ugly force, the pain in Teffinger's face and ribs took over, collapsing him to the sand at the water's edge, where the storm beat down on his already broken psyche.

He'd failed.

Not only that, he never even really got a good look at the man. He couldn't swear it was Axel Chard.

Suddenly from out of nowhere someone slapped his face.

He looked up to see Janjak.

"You!" she shouted. "This is your fault!"

He didn't deny it.

She was right.

Keeping Jori-Ray in the shed was stupid. He should have put her in a car and had one of the men drive her to somewhere safe in the city.

"Get up!" Janjak shouted.

He struggled to his feet.

He didn't care if she had a machete in her hand. He deserved whatever was to come. She lead him down the beach to the Grady White where she had her men pull it free off the sand where the waves had wedged it.

"Get in!"

He used all his strength to get himself and his water-soaked clothes up and over the gunnels.

"Go get her!" Janjak shouted. "I'll rot your soul in hell for a thousand years!"

He fired up one outboard, then the other, and headed into the black thundering whitecaps, holding on for dear life as they broke over the bow and washed out the back.

The sky was black.

The water was black.

Turning around, Janjak's place was black except for a couple of solitary lights, which were already starting to dim with the distance. In another few minutes they'd be gone entirely.

He fumbled at the toggle switches at the helm until the gauges lit up.

Good.

There.

The boat had a compass.

Which way would Chard have gone?

He couldn't get far.

It was doubtful he was heading out to sea to meet another vessel. The logistics of the meet would be too much in the dark. More likely he was headed up or down the coast, probably not that far, just distant enough to get to where he had a car or blue-water boat waiting to pick him up. Teffinger didn't know the topography well enough. Either direction, he didn't know if a road came close to the water, or if there was a lagoon that might give refuge to a pickup boat. It was a toss-up, a fifty-fifty gamble.

He headed due west, which should parallel the coast, at least in general terms. If Chard was going to get picked up, someone might be flashing a light to guide him in.

Watch for that.

He brought the speed up.

The boat crashed violently into the black invisible waves, throwing wall after wall of stinging spray into Teffinger's face.

No lights showed.

Maybe Chard had already hooked up.

Come on!

Where are you!

Something on the floorboard bounced up and hit him in the shin. He reached down to get it away and realized it was the rifle. Janjak must have tossed it in after him. He pointed it into the air and pulled the trigger to see if it still worked.

It did.

It hardly made a noise over the howling of the engines and the pounding of the hull against the water, but it worked. He kept it gripped in his left hand and clenched the steering wheel in his right.

Come on, Chard!

Show yourself!

He charged on for what seemed like a long time, keeping as close to a westerly course as he could, but not really having a clue if he was near the coastline or ten miles out to sea. All the time, he saw nothing, not a single light or sign of life.

Then he turned and doubled back, heading due east.

When he got to where he thought Janjak's place should be, there was no sign that he was in the right place. Her lights didn't appear. He kept his course until he was definitely past where he'd started, and held it for a long time.

No sign of anything appeared.

He had no idea where he was.

He was just a forsaken soul lost at sea.

He pounded his hand on the helm.

Then he turned off the outboards, laid down on the floor-board and closed his eyes. The waves tossed the boat like a toy but weren't strong enough to tip it over, not unless two rolled in together with one climbing the other, which was unlikely.

Go ahead and sleep for a few minutes.

It's okay.

There's nothing left to do.

Nothing.

DAY TEN

May 26
Wednesday

45

Teffinger woke up to realize he must have fallen asleep for some time, possibly hours. The waves were calmer now, much calmer in fact. The storm had passed. No more rain was falling. The howling winds had trickled down to a light breeze. While it was still some point in the middle of the night, the darkness of the sky wasn't quite as complete. His brain felt as if demons were inside trying to break out with ball peen hammers.

He muscled to his feet.

He could be anywhere at this point.

He could be twenty miles out to sea, maybe more.

He checked the gas gauge and was shocked to see that he was under a quarter tank. How far would that get him? Whatever the answer was, he couldn't afford to go an inch in the wrong direction. No one knew he was out here, only Janjak, and as far as her calling out for a search party, that wasn't going to happen. She'd be too busy rotting his soul in hell for a thousand years.

Hunger gnawed at his stomach.

He made his way to the bow, sat down and leaned back against the railing in the dark. Kimona had been trying to get through the chaos and into his brain for some time now, and he let her. He let her remind him of her smile, of her soft touch and easy kiss, and of the way the world felt so incredibly perfect when she was around. A song he hadn't heard in over a decade suddenly played in his brain.

Mississippi in the middle of a dry spell
Jimmy Rodgers on the Victoria up high
Mama's dancin' with baby on her shoulder
The sun is settin' like molasses in the sky.

He flicked it off.

The boat rocked peacefully, with a repeating rhythm. It didn't care that Jori-Ray was dead by now.

Chard—assuming it was Chard—hadn't come to haul her back to prison.

No, no way.

That was evident in the way he was pounding the woman's face. In another minute or two she would have been dead. The only reason he took her was for insurance. He stopped needing that hours ago. He probably slit her throat in the dingy and dumped her over the side.

Something weird happened.

He heard an engine, up above in the sky, getting closer and closer; a plane, flying low with the navigation lights on. It wasn't much more than a dark silhouette in a dark sky, but it was a small prop deal, and had pontoons. It was definitely some kind of seaplane, heading due west.

Was it going to pick up Chard?

Did it have to wait until the storm was over?

Teffinger fired up the outboards and followed it at full speed with his lights out. If he burned up all his gas chasing a wild goose, then that would just be the way it would have to be. Someone would probably spot him before he starved to death.

It slowly gained distance, with the navigation lights getting dimmer and dimmer with each passing minute, until they finally disappeared completely.

Teffinger maintained the course and speed.

The tank was under an eighth now.

Then something incredible happened.

A cove of some sort appeared on his left. The plane was in there, bobbing on the water, with a spotlight illuminating a small dingy that was motoring out to it.

A man passed a body to the pilot; Jori-Ray's body, no doubt.

Then he climbed in and pushed the dingy away.

The plane turned its nose out to sea.

Then it skirted across the water, faster and faster, now coming directly at Teffinger who was sitting there invisible in the blackness with the rifle in his hands.

The plane lifted, finally breaking free.

Just as it was about to pass mere feet over Teffinger's head, he fired at it.

46

The plane's engine sputtered and choked, broke into flames and then stopped completely. The plane immediately dropped and buried the propeller in the waves, flipping it over and bringing it to a rest upside down.

Teffinger got to it as fast as he could, shifted into neutral and dived in. The doors and cabin were completely under water. He tried to get a door open but couldn't. He had to surface for air.

Then he dived back under, to the other door.

That was a good move.

It opened.

Everything was pitch black.

He felt around until he found Jori-Ray in an air pocket and shook her.

"Can you hear me?"

She groaned.

"Hold your breath! Do you hear me?"

"Teffinger?"

"Hold your breath!"

He pulled her out the door and up to the surface where he kept her head above water as she coughed and choked and flailed. Then he got her to the Grady White and used every molecule of strength he had left to push her up and over the gunnels. She dropped inside, alive.

He hung onto the side of the boat, deciding.

Then, against his better judgment, he swam back to the plane, and pulled out the next body that made its way into his hands. There was no movement in it but he brought it over to the boat anyway.

Jori-Ray was on her knees now.

"Help me!" Teffinger shouted.

Together, they got the body in.

Just as they did, a massive rush of air came from the plane and it disappeared beneath the surface, with the spotlight still shining as it slowly dropped down deeper and deeper. Teffinger swam to it but it was already a good twenty feet under the surface by the time he got there.

When he got back to the Grady White, Jori-Ray was over the other person, giving him mouth to mouth.

Suddenly the man gasped and choked, fighting for air.

47

Teffinger wasted no time untying the rope from the anchor and using it to hogtie the man, who was already regaining strength and resisting. He pulled the man to front of the boat, flicked on the bow lights, and confirmed what he already suspected.

The man was clearly Axel Chard.

"Untie me," he said.

"Shut the fuck up!"

The man struggled, testing the ropes.

Teffinger gave him a warning kick.

"Move again and I'll throw your ass over the side."

The man got quiet.

"John Stone hired you. Right?" Teffinger said.

"Screw you."

Teffinger swallowed. He had the upper hand, but Chard was a snake. He needed to make absolutely sure the man didn't get a chance to make a move. If he pretends like he's choking or something, don't untie him. No matter what, don't untie him.

Gas was low.

The world was still black.

They sat in the cove bobbing and waiting, for an hour, then two, and then three, until the first rays of dawn finally began to creep into the sky. Then they headed east, which may or may not be the right direction, and getting lucky, finally making their way all the way back to Janjak's place, where they beached the boat in the sand as Janjak and a dozen armed men trotted out to intercept them.

Janjak looked at Jori-Ray's battered face and bruised body.

Then she threw her eyes on Chard.

Her face was hard with hate.

She climbed into the boat, dragged the man to the back and dumped him over the side. The water was only three feet deep there, but it was plenty deep enough to drown him. He laid on the bottom in crystal clear view, struggling violently against the ropes. Janjak dropped down into the water next to him, put her face under the water and stared directly into the man's eyes, watching him die. She stayed there a long time. Then she pulled her head out, took a deep breath and shouted to her men, "Pull him up!"

Three men pulled Chard off the bottom and dangled him just above the surface as he choked and fought for air.

Janjak got her face close to his.

"Who hired you?"

"Fuck you!"

"John Stone?"

"You'll never know."

Janjak shook her head in disbelief and said, "Wrong answer."

She motioned to her men and they dropped him back into the water. When he was almost dead, they pulled him up again.

He gasped wildly for air. Janjak waited until his lungs stopped convulsing and said, "Last chance. Who hired you?"

He looked at her, not defiantly, but almost as if grappling

with the reality of how this had to end.

"Kill me," he said. "Do it."

She motioned to one of her men, who handed her a machete. She passed it to Teffinger and said, "Cut my back. Don't cross over anything that's already there."

He knew why.

She was going to take the man's soul.

The end was coming for him.

"Stay still," he said.

He wrapped an arm around her chest so she couldn't flinch, then cut a shallow slit in the small of her back, about two inches long. Blood dripped down onto her white wraparound skirt, so very red.

As Teffinger went to hand the machete back to her, she refused to take it.

"You do it," she said.

"What, kill him?"

"Yes."

Teffinger stared at the man lying hogtied in the sand at his feet. One good slash into the man's neck or head would do the trick. He pictured it; the horror on the man's face, the swing, the flying blood, the slumping of the man's body, the gurgling of sounds from his throat.

He hesitated.

Janjak stared at him with defiance.

"You're the one who captured him," she said. "You're the one who brought him back here. So it's your privilege. And it's your responsibility."

Teffinger felt the cold weight of the machete in his hand. The murder was justified, no question. There was no telling how many lives the man had taken over his callous pathetic existence, including, most likely, Jack Flamingo and Lupa, not to mention two of Janjak's men, his attack on Jori-Ray, and on and on. Still, as justified as it was, Teffinger couldn't do it.

"I can't," he said.

"Do it!"

He dropped the weapon.

"I can't kill a defenseless man."

The veins in Janjak's neck pulsed.

She walked away. As she did, she turned and said, "I hope you're prepared for what's coming."

48

Exhausted, Teffinger got his fill of food and water, then wandered down the beach and slept in the shade of a palm tree, not waking up until the early afternoon. The insufferable storm of last night was long over, replaced now with calm green waters and full-on sunshine. Seagulls flew low over the water, back and forth and around and around, in search of unsuspecting aquatic life that had unwittingly come too close to the surface.

He headed back to Janjak's, gassed up the Grady White and motored west down the coast to the cove where he'd shot the plane down.

By the light of day, the aircraft was clearly visible, resting on the bottom, upside down, no more than fifteen or twenty feet under the surface. He dived in to have a look at the pilot. To his surprise, it wasn't a man; it was a woman, a black woman, floating upside down in the cockpit, not restrained by a seatbelt.

Her face was brutally smashed in and her head was hanging to the side, the victim of broken neck. A tattoo of a heart decorated her left arm.

The window was violently cracked.

She almost certainly died on impact.

In a way that was good. It meant that Teffinger never really had a chance to rescue her. He couldn't second-guess that he'd moved too slowly and that he might have been able to help her if he'd worked faster.

He grabbed a wallet sticking out of the back pocket of her shorts and swam as quickly as he could to the surface, barely breaking the air before his lungs gave out.

He treaded water for a minute, getting his strength, then made his way back to the boat.

According to her wallet, the woman was Lovely Dieudonne-Cyr from Port-de-Paix, Haiti.

There was a picture of her on the beach with a child about five or six. He knew it was her because of the tattoo. Unlike the face under the water, this face was pretty and carefree, with white teeth and compelling eyes.

Who was the kid?

Her son?

The very thought put a hole in Teffinger's chest.

He tried to rationalize his way out of it. He'd been forced into crisis mode through no choice of his own. Shooting the plane had been his only option, his only one. Somehow, the woman had gotten mixed up with Axel Chard. That was her doing, not Teffinger's. She had to have known that Chard was on a mission of murder. She participated anyway. That made her dirty. She might be pretty but she'd made herself an accomplice. Because of her, Jori-Ray might be dead right now if things had gone just a little differently.

The rationale was there.

It was logical to the ends of the universe.

But it did no good.

Soon, someone would be telling a little boy that his mommy would never be coming back.

That was the bitter, unchangeable reality that now existed in this world.

Shit.

Why couldn't she have been some ugly fat guy?

He dived back in, slipped the wallet back into the woman's pocket, and memorized the registration number of the plane, which was HH-UBP.

Then he headed back to Janjak's.

49

When he got back to Janjak's, her men intercepted him as he approached the main structure, shouting at him in words he didn't understand but which clearly meant stay back. They weren't only at the front, but all around. Jori-Ray walked out the front door with a basket in hand and made her way straight for him, grabbing his hand and pulling him towards the beach.

"Come on."

"What's going on in there?" he asked.

"You'll find out."

She led Teffinger down the beach for some distance, farther and farther away, until they were the only ones left in the universe. She brought him to the shade of a palm tree and eased down onto the sand, extending her hand in an invitation for him to join her. Then she pulled her shirt off, laid down on her back topless, and stretched her arms up over her head.

She smiled.

Teffinger knew what she was doing.

This was gratitude for what he did last night.

"This isn't necessary," he said.

"Don't deny me. Please—"

He turned his eyes to the surf, no more than twenty steps away, lapping gently on the sand.

The woman ran a finger over her bruises.

"Am I too ugly?"

"You know that's not it."

She put disappointment on her face, then sat up, opened the basket and pulled out a bottle of wine, half-sandwiches, pastries, fruit and chocolate.

Seeing it, Teffinger was suddenly starved.

They drank.

They ate.

They let the sunlight and the surf and the promises of unknown futures fill their world.

"You know I'm innocent, right?" Jori-Ray said.

Teffinger nodded.

"Chard got hired by Stone, that's a given, but he's not going to roll over on the man like I hoped he would. Honor among thieves, I guess. Where is he, anyway? Chard?"

"He's with Janjak."

"Where, inside?"

"Yes."

"What's she doing to him?"

"Not to him, with him. They're in the bedroom. She's dancing for him."

The words landed with the force of a rock to Teffinger's throat.

"Why?"

"To get him to talk," she said. "She's doing it for me. She's trying to get you the proof against Stone."

She laid back down on the sand, raised her arms above her head, and closed her eyes. "If you're not going to make love to me, can you at least give me a massage? I haven't had one in over five years—"

50

Teffinger opened his eyes to realize he'd been unconscious. The last thing he remembered was being on the beach with Jori-Ray. Now, he was in bow of the Grady White, speeding out to sea in calm waters. Janjak was next to him, holding his hand, and visibly happy that he was waking up. One of her men was at the wheel. A second was standing next to him at the cockpit, with one hand on the rail and the other on a rifle.

He sat up.

It was early evening.

Hours had passed.

"Where we going?"

"To do something."

"Like what?"

"You'll see."

The woman handed him a bottle of water.

He hadn't been thirsty until he saw it, then suddenly he was, and drained most of it in one long swallow.

"Thanks."

She kissed him on the lips.

"You're welcome."

They headed farther and farther out to sea, now joined by three dolphins, jumping in and out of the waves at the bow of the boat.

Janjak clapped her hands, excited.

"They're good luck!"

Mile after mile clicked off, the coastline disappeared, the dolphins dropped off and then, up ahead in the far distance, three small islands appeared. Teffinger recognized them immediately. They were the ghost islands; the very ones he'd been abandoned on before. His first thought was that Janjak was going to abandon him there again.

But why?

The woman patted his knee and said, "Relax. This isn't about you."

"Then, what?"

"You'll know soon enough."

The islands loomed larger and larger until the boat was right there, swinging around the edge of the closest one and beaching into the sand.

They headed inland, towards the palms, with Janjak and Teffinger in the lead and the two men following ten steps behind. Both had their rifles.

Up ahead, a man was sitting in the sand underneath a palm tree.

He wore no shirt.

He stood up as everyone approached and it was then that Teffinger recognized him.

Axel Chard.

He didn't come towards them to meet them half way.

He just stood there, waiting.

"I couldn't get him to talk," Janjak told Teffinger as they walked. "He had a hundred chances. Now it's time for him to die. Like I said before, it's your privilege and it's your responsibility."

Teffinger suddenly knew what this was about.

Janjak wanted him to do the deed.

"No," he said.

Janjak smiled.

"If that's your decision, fine."

As they got closer, what Teffinger saw he could hardly believe. Chard was attached to the palm tree with a fifty-foot chain shackled to his ankle. A second chain of equal length lay limp in the sand.

Teffinger knew who it was for.

It was for him.

His chest pounded.

"Back up," Janjak took Chard.

The man picked up an independent six-foot length of chain—his weapon—and swung it over his head as he complied.

"Don't run," Janjak said to Teffinger. "If you do, we'll shoot you in the leg."

She handed him her machete.

Then her men shackled him to the other chain.

He didn't resist.

It wouldn't do any good.

It would show weakness in front of Chard.

Janjak walked to the palm tree and looked first at Chard, then at Teffinger.

"No one moves for one minute," she said. "I'll be back in an hour."

Then she walked away with her two men in tow.

Teffinger watched.

She never looked back.

He cast his eyes on Chard.

The man was bigger than him.

He was stronger.

He killed people for a living.

He swung the chain over his head with a demon speed.

It made a horrible swishing noise.

A blow to the head would kill him.

A blow to his back would crush his spine.

He now realized why Jori-Ray had been with him this afternoon. She wasn't showing her gratitude for saving her life. She was a last meal. It was the same for Chard, being with Janjak. It was just like in the gladiator days; two men, getting one last sweet bite of life, before one of them would die.

Suddenly the man screamed a piercing war cry and charged.

An image suddenly sprang into Teffinger's psyche.

He was in the shed, last night.

Chard was on top of Jori-Ray, pummeling her face with his fists.

Teffinger's mind snapped.

Then he threw the machete as hard as he could at Chard's chest.

The man dodged wildly with the reflexes of a cat.

The machete flew past him.

He smiled at Teffinger.

"Oops—"

51

Chard slowly inched his way towards Teffinger, all the while swinging the chain above his head like a buzz saw, making absolutely certain that Teffinger had no opportunity to attack. Teffinger backed up inch after inch until his ankle snagged and he didn't have one more inch to get.

He couldn't go left.

He couldn't go right.

He couldn't go back.

Chard was in no hurry.

He kept the chain at full speed, reading Teffinger's eyes and waiting for that pitch-perfect moment to land a solid fatal blow to Teffinger's head or chest.

Then he lunged.

Teffinger thought he would try to break the impact of the steel with his hand or arm, but the speed and force was too horrific. His bones would shatter. He twisted his torso backwards at the last second as the chain came at him, avoiding it, but barely, in fact feeling it swish through his hair

His own movement brought him down, flat on his back.

He tried to get up but couldn't.

His foot was too far out in front of him.

Chard went for a deathblow.

Teffinger rolled wildly.

The chain hit the sand to his side.

Then he grabbed it.

Chard jerked at it, actually bringing Teffinger to his feet, and the two men struggled at close quarters for a long time, each with a hand on the chain and each trying to wrap it around the other man's neck.

They ended up back to back.

The chain was around both of their throats.

Each of them had an end.

Each of them pulled.

Teffinger's air cut off.

He couldn't breathe in.

He couldn't breathe out.

He pulled even harder at the chain, feeling it dig even deeper into his throat but knowing that it was cutting just as much into Chard's.

He tried to trip Chard's feet out from under him as Chard did the same to him.

Neither went down.

He couldn't breathe.

He had no air, but neither did Chard.

Come on!

Die!

Die!

Die!

Second after second passed, each one exploding fire in his chest.

His mind fogged.

His body lost its strength.

The chain came out of his grip.

His legs buckled and he dropped to the ground.

He felt Chard land on top of him.

Then everything turned black.

52

Sweet, sweet oxygen flowed through Teffinger's body and slowly brought him back to the world he'd been seconds away from leaving. He clawed his way out from under Chard's body, briefly confirmed that the man was unquestionably dead, and crawled over to where the shade was, where he sat in the sand with his back against the palm and his fists clenched in rage.

Janjak.

The little bitch.

Playing with his life.

Forcing him to kill.

She'd pay.

Somehow, some way, she'd pay.

Take that to the grave.

He focused on Chard's lifeless body.

It was a sight he'd seen before, in one form or another, a life extinguished, at his hands. If he were honest with himself, Chard probably wouldn't be the last. This would probably be a good opportunity to stop and reflect on who he really was, deep down.

He let it pass.

Every situation had been justified.

Chard had it coming.

Screw him.

The man's death, though, did put a wrinkle in the John

Stone deal. Chard hadn't turned on the man and now quite obviously never would. Teffinger was back to square one, long on suspicion but short on proof.

That meant that Jori-Ray would remain September's killer.

At this point, Teffinger would never bring her in. Someone would, though, eventually. Either that or Stone would eventually have his way with her.

Janjak eventually showed up, alone, without her men, smiling at the fact that it was Teffinger who was waiting there alive to greet her.

He stood up.

Kill her.

That's what he should do, right now, this moment.

Teach her a lesson about playing God with his life.

She ignored the rage in his eyes, wrapped her arms around his body and laid her head on his chest. "It had to be this way," she said. "It was your privilege. It was your responsibility."

"I could have died."

She kissed him.

"You didn't."

"And what if I did? What if he was the one here waiting for you instead of me?"

She shrugged.

"I would have let him go."

"After killing me?"

"I took his soul," she said. "Having his body free wouldn't do him any good. He'd be hoping to find death around every corner. He'd be nothing more than a shadow; a shadow that I could twist at my whim. You'd be avenged, trust me."

She freed him from the cuff on his ankle, and then the two of them carried and dragged Chard's limp body to the adjacent island, where the ancient pile of bones was, and threw him on top, to rot in the sun and get eaten by the birds and bugs. Teffinger wiped the sweat off his brow and said, "The plane that was helping Chard—the one I shot down—the pilot was a female. Her name is Lovely Dieudonne-Cyr, from Port-de-Paix."

Janjak scoffed.

"The world's better off."

"You know her?"

"Personally, no; but she's no secret," Janjak said. "She's the daughter of Emmanuel Dieudonne-Cyr, nickname Fou Reken. He's spent his pathetic existence building the Dieudonne-Cyr cartel, which is a hundred men strong the last time I checked, maybe more. Drug smuggling, human trafficking and slavery, that's their thing. He's crazy, he's violent and he's everywhere." She paused and then added, "He'll eventually find the plane. He'll figure out that it was shot down instead of just crashing. When that happens, he'll be hunting for the person who pulled the trigger. We need to get you out of Haiti."

He focused on her.

"What about Kimona?"

Janjak hardened her face.

"Nothing has changed with her," she said. "If you want her, get the charges against Jori-Ray dropped. You have five days left, until Midnight on May 31st. That date can't change and it won't. Don't think you can show up at the last minute and get more time. There is no more time. There are forces at work that you don't know about and never will. Five days.

That's it."

Teffinger locked eyes with the woman.

"If you hurt her, I'll kill you. Know that."

She ran her fingers through his hair.

Then she kissed him.

"No you won't."

DAY ELEVEN

May 27
Thursday

53

Teffinger arrived back in Denver late Thursday afternoon to find a white SUV in his driveway, one that he didn't recognize. The front door to his house was open. Inside, he found Jori-Ray's lawyer, Alabama, sitting on the couch and going through the three cold-case evidence files that Teffinger had pulled out of storage. A can of Diet Pepsi sat on the coffee table. She tossed her blue hair to the side, briefly cast those beautiful eyes of hers upon him as he walked in, and said, "Hey."

She was charismatic; he'd give her that.

But breaking in?

Acting like it was no big deal?

That was a kick in the gut.

"I had to bust a window in the back," she said. "You should leave a key under the mat like everyone else."

"Why?"

"That should be obvious," she said. "I'm going through the evidence files. I'm trying to find out if there's something in there that can help us."

Teffinger shook his head in disbelief.

"You break into a private house. Then you go through confidential police records. That's illegal on about a hundred levels."

"Yeah, I know," she said. "But we're running out of time. You told me they were here, so it's partially your fault." She patted his arm. "Here's the way I look at it. If I had asked for your permission, you've have said okay or not okay. If you said not okay, then I'd never get to see them. And if you said okay, then you'd be putting yourself way over the line, and if I found any exculpatory evidence that you didn't turn over to the defense at the time of trial but didn't, I'd have to file a motion. So, I decided to keep you out of it."

He ran though the implications.

"So all this is for me—"

She smiled.

"Exactly."

"You could get disbarred."

"Yeah."

He pulled two beers from the fridge, handed one to her, and downed half of his in one long gulp.

Good stuff.

Ice cold.

"So, what'd you find so far, anything?"

She frowned.

"Unfortunately, as in way, way, unfortunately, no. Looking at everything in here, Jori-Ray did it. There's no other conclusion." She took a sip of beer, set it down on the coffee table, and headed towards the front door. There, she turned and said, "Your neck's a mess, by the way. People are going to be asking questions. You better have a story ready. One that doesn't involve you killing someone."

"So you know what happened?"

The woman nodded.

"Janjak told me. Don't worry, I won't be telling anybody."

She blew him a kiss.

Then she was gone.

When she left, Teffinger called Sydney and said, "Did you have any luck tracking down that gun-guy in September's photos?"

"Teff?"

"Yeah."

"You're back?"

"I am."

"So what happened in Haiti?"

"A lot of stuff I can't talk about right now. I'll get drunk at some point and tell you, I promise, but until then just indulge me, please and thank you. The gun guy—anything?"

"A little," Sydney said. "His name's Brady Pointer; small record of drug possession; currently a safety officer with OSHA. I paid him a little surprise visit. He wouldn't come right out and admit that he got the gun for September, for obvious reasons, but he did admit that he taught her how to use it. He claims she never came right out told him why she wanted it but said she was clearly scared of someone."

"Who?"

"He didn't know. At least that's what he said."

"Do you believe him?"

"I might, actually," Sydney said. "I don't think they had a connection, other than the gun, and the drugs."

"The drugs?"

"He was her supplier."

"Did he admit that?"

"Not straight out. He was real careful with his words. Anyway, I got the impression that the two of them didn't have a physical or emotional connection, so she might not have confided in him about whatever it was that was going on." She paused and added, "Oh, I almost forgot. She did tell him one thing that's a bit curious. She was thinking about running away."

"Why?"

"She didn't give any details. It was just a random comment. She said she might head off to San Francisco and wanted to know if he knew any drug dealers there. He didn't, and that was the end of the conversation. It never came up again."

Teffinger processed it.

Then he said, "Who did she know in San Francisco?"

"I have no idea."

"See if you can find out."

Teffinger examined his neck in the mirror.

Baby steps—that's all he was getting; tiny, little, insignificant baby steps. He didn't have time for them. What he needed was a way to trick John Stone into admitting what he did.

Get it on tape.

That was the kill shot.

Stone would never confess directly to Teffinger, that was a given. He might, however, confess to someone else.

Set up a pretend blackmailer, maybe.

Set up someone who saw Stone plant the gun out in the open space.

Demand money.

Get the conversation going, all on tape. Get it going so it was based on the assumption that Stone was the killer and got spotted. Get Stone to fall into it and maybe even say something like, "You couldn't have seen me. It was too dark out."

Teffinger shook his head.

It was illegal.

No judge would ever admit it as evidence.

It was also dangerous as hell.

Get back to reality.

He pulled another beer from the fridge and downed it as he booked flights to Haiti on Monday. In case all else failed, he would be there at midnight, ready to do whatever the hell it took to get Kimona out of there alive.

That included killing Janjak, if necessary.

54

Teffinger made it to the office late afternoon, told everyone he accidentally got his neck tangled in a boat rope—no big deal, no permanent harm—and ended up in a conference room with Sophia Cruz, brainstorming a way to get John Stone to confess, and all the while trying to keep his caveman genes from kicking in and letting his eyes drop down to where they wanted to go.

"Maybe his wife could get him to confess to her," she said.

Teffinger shook his head.

"Spousal privilege."

"Not if she cooperates with us."

"Huh?"

"If I remember it right," she said, "the way it works is, if he tells her something, and we subpoena her as a witness, we can't force her to talk. That's the spousal privilege. But it's her privilege to assert, not his. So, for example, she can testify against him if she wants to, whether he wants her to stay quiet or not. What that means is, if we can get her to cooperate with us, and he confesses to her, she can testify to that confession in a court of law. It will come in as a valid, one hundred percent chunk of evidence."

Teffinger stood up and paced.

He tried to make it fit.

It was way better than some illegal blackmail ruse, which

could never be used as evidence, and, in fact, would probably just get him and the department sued.

In the end, though, he shook his head.

"Catherine. She stood by him even when the whole Jori-Ray affair exploded in her face. She won't go fishing for us."

"Yeah, but she brought you the gun and the pictures. Right?"

"Yeah."

"Behind his back, right?"

He nodded.

"So she's already fishing. Maybe she's willing to at least ask him some questions and let us know what he says. Who knows what the guy will end up telling her. If he actually does confess, do you think she'll swallow it and stand quietly by his side?"

Teffinger shook his head.

"Doubtful."

"So, let's do this: Ask her if she'll ask John about the stuff she gave you, the gun and photos. See what happens."

He chewed on it.

It could actually lead to something.

He nodded.

What the hell—

"Okay. Do it."

"Me? I was talking about you."

"Take her out to coffee or something. Do it away from the house, where she's not in the guy's shadow. Keep the focus on September, unraveling the secrets and getting to the facts, and all that. Don't let her know we're using her as bait."

"Are we?"

He nodded.

"That's why we can't afford to have this go sideways. Are you up for it?"

"We'll see, I guess."

He patted her arm.

"You are. Don't tell her about us following John to the hotel. Don't tell her about Axel Chard. We might pull that out at some point in the future if we need to drive a wedge between them and nudge her over to our persuasion, but for right now just keep it close to the vest. Do you need coffee money?"

She smiled.

"No."

"Good, because I don't have any."

55

The worst thing in the world is inaction; not knowing which direction to look; flapping around like a fish out of water. That was Teffinger right now, a pathetic bouncing fish, a man without a compass, disoriented to the nth degree, having no good ideas on how to bring John Stone down. He sat at his desk racking his brains. He had no concrete proof that Stone and Axel Chard were connected, meaning he had no concrete proof that Stone had engaged in a conspiracy to murder Jori-Ray Rose.

Would Stone try again?

Could Teffinger plant a fake hitman to make contact with him?

He chewed on it.

In theory, yeah, it was good.

The logistics, though; that was the problem.

Who could he get?

How could the contact be made so that Stone believed it was legit?

Maybe he could claim he was a professional acquaintance of Axel Chard's. Teffinger could get more details about Chard from the profiler, Dr. Leigh Sandt. Those could then be fed to Stone; the kind of things that would only be known to someone who actually knew Chard.

He smiled.

He felt like a fish that had flopped his way back into the

tank.

He called the FBI profiler, Dr. Leigh Sandt, and said, "I have it on good sources that Axel Chard is dead."

"What sources, exactly?"

He exhaled.

"Sources I can't reveal, unfortunately," he said.

"Seriously? You don't trust me?"

"I do, a hundred percent," he said. "You know that. This has nothing to do with you. He died in Haiti. We believe that he had been hired by the Senator, John Stone, to kill Jori-Ray Rose."

Silence.

Then she said, "You killed him. The source is you."

Silence.

"I was in Haiti at the time," Teffinger finally said. "I'd like to just leave it at that. Anyway, I've come up with a plan and you might be able to help."

It took a number of phone calls by a number of people, and over two hours of coordination, but in the end, Teffinger had a man, an agent out of Boston by the name of Roger West, who was the FBI's point man on Axel Chard, and knew as much about the man as anyone.

He'd come to Denver.

He'd present himself to John Stone; maybe walk up to Stone while he was heading to his car, something like that. He'd be wearing a wire. Teffinger and three or four others would be on other side of that wire, recording.

He'd say he was an acquaintance of Axel Chard. He'd give details. He'd convince Stone he was legit. He'd make it clear that he was in the same line of work as Chard.

He's say Chard got killed in Haiti before he could finish the assignment.

Jori-Ray Rose was still alive.

Then he'd get quiet.

He wouldn't go any further than that; not an inch.

If he offered his services as a hitman at that point, it would be entrapment. He needed to just stay silent as death and let Stone bring the subject up.

If Stone solicited him, then, wham!

The trap snapped shut.

Teffinger and company would arrest him immediately.

Sweeter than sugar.

The twitchy old clock on the wall said 5:02. West was scheduled to arrive at DIA at 9:48. He'd rent a car, check into a hotel downtown, just like a hitman would, and call Teffinger at eight in the morning.

They'd meet and hammer out the details.

With any luck, Stone would be in cuffs by noon tomorrow.

He headed over to Sophia Cruz' cubicle, plopped down in one the of worn wooden chairs in front of her desk and said, "Change of plans. Hold off on Catherine Stone for the time being. Have you called her yet?"

"No."

"Good. We're going to go in a different direction."

"And what direction is that?"

"Be sure you're in the office by 7:30 tomorrow morning. I'll brief you then."

"Sure." She paused and added, "It's Thursday."

"True. And?"

"And, there's a country bar down on I-25 called the Eagle Rose."

Teffinger knew the place.

It was big as a city.

It was loud as a bomb.

It was drunker than a skunk.

It was filled from the floor to the ceiling with stomping boots, cowboy hats, fights and swirling skirts. He'd spent many a drunken night of his youth down there chasing those skirts.

"Thursday's two-for-one," Sophia said. "Skinny George and the Telecaster Boys are playing. It's going to be insane. I'll be getting down there about eight, in case you were wondering. Maybe I'll see you there."

56

At seven o'clock, Teffinger took a shower and washed his hair, which he usually didn't do at night, and wondered if he was actually going to head down to the Eagle Rose in spite of negating the idea all day as batshit crazy. There were overwhelming reasons why even thinking about it was dumber than dirt.

Sophia Cruz worked under him.

He didn't want to lead her on.

And he needed to be at his best in the morning.

But the pressure of his near-death ordeal with Axel Chard had been building up in his psyche all day like an ever-deepening shadow. There was also the impending doom that might come his way from the Dieudonne-Cyr cartel. And, not least, there was whatever dark fate awaited him Monday at Janjak's lair when he went there to save Kimona.

He was an overinflated balloon about to pop.

He needed alcohol.

He needed escape.

He needed to be someone else for a few fucking hours.

Go or not?

At 8:13 p.m., he hopped into the Tundra and pointed the front end towards the Eagle Rose under a deepening twilight sky.

Just go.

Have a beer or two or three.

Get out of your skin.

Pick all the heavy stuff back up in the morning.

Easy peasy.

He drove east on 6th in the slow lane with She Loves You on the radio and no trucks tailgating his posterior.

All was good.

Then, just like that, it wasn't. As he cut through the mouse-trap onto I-25, a chill ran up his spine.

He sensed danger.

It was suddenly there, in every pore of his body, like some nefarious specter.

Something was going to happen.

Something bad.

It was almost as if he was being warned to turn around.

He ignored it and kept driving.

After spending an eternity to find a place to park, he paid a lot more at the door than he wanted, and made his way inside. It was exactly as he remembered it, totally unchanged, right down to the bras hanging from the ceiling and knife carvings in the pillars. The smoke and beer and drunken women brought him back to his getting-laid days. The band was loud, the bodies were wall-to-wall, and the air was filled with possibilities. There had to be at least a thousand people in there. Every guy was looking to get lucky and every girl was using it to her advantage.

Nothing had changed.

He elbowed his way to the bar, paid for a Bud light and got two shoved his way. He downed one in three quick swallows, set the empty on the bar and headed out into the crowd, towards the stage and dance floor, with the other in hand.

The alcohol kicked in.

A grin came to his face.

The hard corners in his brain softened.

Right now, this was the whole universe. There was nothing else. There were no crazy Janjaks or helicopters under water or chains around his throat.

The dance floor spun in a circle, like a skating rink, with stomping and beers spilling and faces that only got that look when they were sloshed.

A woman spun by Teffinger, almost passed, and then ran up to him and slipped her cowboy hat onto his head. He must have had a look because she laughed.

"Looks good on you!"

Then she was already disappearing, shaking her hair free.

She was nice—long hair, short dress, animated, moving around the floor with another little beauty.

She passed him again, blowing him a kiss this time.

He tipped his beer towards her.

The next time around, she grabbed his hand and pulled him to a table way back by the wall, filled with women, half-empty pitchers of beer and red solo cups. She motioned him into a chair and plopped down on his lap with her arm around his shoulders.

Someone said, "What you got there, girlfriend?"

"Something yummy."

She wiggled on his lap, grabbed a cup off the table and took a long hard swallow, then passed it to him.

She smelled like a rose and felt like heaven.

"You're cute, but that's not why you're here," she said. "Me and Sophia Cruz are old friends. I asked her to bring you here so I could talk to you."

"Oh?"

"Yeah."

"Is she coming? Sophia—"

"Yes."

She pointed across the room.

There she was, wearing a short white dress and a blouse tied above her navel.

"She'll come over after we're done talking," the woman said. "I've come up with a plan."

"To do what?"

"Save lives," she said. "Put away a killer. It'll work but you'll have to get a little dirty."

"Who's the killer?"

The woman topped off her solo cup, then Teffinger's, and said, "It'll all be in the files, everything you'd ever want to know. It has to do in part with Mary-Ann White. But there's a lot more to it than just her."

Mary-Ann White.

She was the six-year-old who disappeared from her bed.

Teffinger narrowed his eyes.

"You know something about that?"

The woman nodded.

"Some; maybe not all. There's a problem though. It's privileged. That's why I said before that you'll have to get a little dirty."

"I don't follow."

"Let me break it down," she said. "By the way, before I start, this conversation never happened. You have to promise me right here right now that you'll never repeat a word of it to anyone."

Teffinger frowned.

"I don't know if I can do that. I don't know what you're going to tell me."

She wiggled on his lap.

"Promise. Or I get up and walk away."

Teffinger took a long swallow of beer.

"It looks like I don't have a choice," he said.

She kissed him on the mouth.

"That seals it," she said. "My name's Hannah Taylor. I work for a lawyer by the name of Grace Springfield. Have you ever heard of her?"

He nodded.

He had.

Everyone had.

She was one of the best criminal defense attorneys in the state, maybe even the country. She worked solo, with no other lawyers in the firm and just a small staff, but more often than not had the front-page trial. A reporter once asked her how she was able to do that. "You keep it simple. Juries like it simple. So do I."

"She represents a certain person," Hannah said. "He calls her a lot and basically just confesses to her what he's done. He always asks for some legal opinion at the end, just to keep it all within the attorney-client privilege, but it's really just a mechanism for him to share. The one problem with doing bad things is that you really aren't able to talk to anyone about them. This is his way around that. Grace bills him $1,000 an hour, which helps her take on clients that otherwise wouldn't be able to afford her. Anyway, she keeps notes of her conversations."

"Who's the guy?"

"Slow down. You'll get there, maybe."

"What do you mean, maybe? What's your game?"

"Grace is out of town until Monday. I made a copy of the files," Hannah said. "Grace doesn't know I did it. They're in the bottom drawer of my desk. Do you know where the office is?"

He nodded.

It was an old standalone house converted into an office, down near the hospitals.

"Yes."

"There's a security camera in the back. I've unplugged it," Hannah said. "There are two security cameras inside the building that I've also unplugged. The key to the back door is in a small magnetic container that's hidden underneath the electrical panel at the side of the structure."

Teffinger pondered the scene.

Breaking into a lawyer's office and taking confidential files was almost too extreme to even think about.

"Why don't you just give them to me?" he said.

"Can't. They're privileged."

"So, I steal them?"

The woman shrugged.

"They're not the originals," she said. "If you took them no one would ever know. I appreciate you could never use them as evidence or anything like that. But you'd know a whole lot of stuff that you don't know now."

"This is pretty extreme," he said. "Something like this could cost me more than just my job. I could end up in jail."

"That's true. That's why we absolutely have to keep it a hundred percent secret. You have to never tell anyone and neither will I. We both take it to the grave. If this ever got to light of day, the guy would kill Grace for betraying his trust. He'd take her someplace private and do it real painfully."

"So how do you justify this, then? Putting her in danger like this?"

"She's already in danger," Hannah said. "He's going to kill her in the end anyway. At this point, she knows it, but doesn't have a way out. She's running scared. She's so par-alyzed with fear that she can barely function, to be honest. She'd never betray a client so I'm doing it for her. What I'm trying to do is save her, do you understand? If you can take this guy down, we all win. That includes Mary-Ann White. You may have enough in the files to find her and bring her home."

"So, she's alive?"

The woman shrugged.

"I can't guarantee that for sure but I hope so."

57

Just like that, the woman's weight was suddenly off Teffinger's lap and she was disappearing into the crowd. He watched her for as long as he could to see if she turned around and gave him a final look, which she did, then got up, headed to the bar for a fresh one, and set out to find Sophia Cruz, who instead found him and jerked him to a stop from behind with a hand to his belt.

Her face came close to his.

Close enough to kiss, actually.

"So, what did little princess Hannah want?"

"Secret stuff."

"Secret stuff?"

"Yeah. Impossible stuff, actually."

"You're not going to tell me?"

He took a long swig and said, "I'll tell you this; it was a waste of time." He looked at her, deep, and said, "You look nice." It was the truth, too. "Did I say that out loud?"

She chuckled.

"It's called beer goggles."

His knees wobbled and the room spun.

He said, "Can you do me a favor?"

"Sure."

He wiggled the bottle in front of his face and said, "I need to get home but the last thing I should be touching right now is a steering wheel."

She came in close.

"Then touch something else."

Five minutes later, they were in Sophia's car—something too low for Teffinger's taste—merging into thin traffic on I-25 and heading south. Sophia's dress hiked up as she worked the clutch and her legs were paradise by the dashboard lights. Teffinger tried to keep his eyes off them but the beer wouldn't let him.

When we get there, open the door and get out.

Do it fast.

Say, Thanks. I'll see you in the morning.

Give her a big smile.

Then head straight for the front door.

Do it fast.

Don't look back.

Don't invite her in.

Don't screw her.

"Tell me a secret," she said.

"How's that?"

"A secret. Tell me something that no one in the world knows. Then I'll tell you one."

"Sure," he said. "Why not? You know Jena Lake, the TV reporter?"

She did.

"Well," he said, "back in my high school days in Fort Collins, she was the younger sister of Matt Lake, my best friend. She was sort of a tomboy and hung around all the time. I always had kind of a crush on her but she was three years younger so nothing ever happened, other than we'd wrestle her down and tickle her now and then. Anyway, another one of my friends, a guy named Travis, lived on this farm that had a mountain lion in a cage, one they'd raised since it was a little cub. It was real friendly and Travis and Jena and I used to go into the cage with it and hang out, just to see how long we could stay in there before freaking out."

"Cool," she said.

"That's not the story, though," he said. "One day Travis dares me to spend the whole night in the cage. No one had ever done that before. Jena's with me and I said I would if she would. Being the tomboy that she was, she said she would if I would. So we go there one evening just before dark. Travis opens the lock and Jena and I get in the cage. Travis locks us in and leaves. After a couple of hours, the mountain lion starts to get freaked out with us being in there so long. That freaks Jena out and she's hiding behind me, wanting more than anything in the world to be out of there. Somehow we survive all the way to morning. It was the longest night of Jena's life, mine too for that matter."

She thought about it.

"So what's the secret?"

Teffinger smiled.

"The secret is that I had the key to the lock in my pocket the whole time. Travis slipped it to me before he left."

"You never told her, afterwards?"

He shook his head. "She still doesn't know, to this day."

"So you put her life at risk just so you could get a little squeezing—"

"Yeah, right. But I also gave her a story she could tell for the rest of her life."

Suddenly they were at Teffinger's house.

"Your front door's open," Sophia said.

His heart pounded.

She was right.

He hadn't left it like that.
He'd double-checked it before he left.
"Wait here," he said.
Then he approached.

58

Inside, it was as if a pack of demons had gone to work on the place for an hour. Everything was trashed. Furniture was overturned.

Drawers were pulled out and dumped.

The TV was in a million pieces.

The walls were smashed.

The worst, though, was in the bedroom, where a cat had been sliced open at the gut and tossed on the pillow like so much garbage.

Suddenly Sophia was at his side, staring at the carnage.

"That's Mikey," Teffinger said, pointing. "He belongs to the kid two doors down, Jason. It came here a lot for milk. It must have come around looking for some and got this instead." He shook his head. "It's weird. When I was driving down to the bar, I had this crazy feeling that something bad was going to happen tonight. It was tangible. I almost turned around and came home."

"Well, good thing you didn't." She was right, maybe. "So who did this?"

"I don't know," he said.

"There's a lot of rage here, Teffinger. It has to be someone in your life."

He racked his brain.

Rage.

The cartel?

John Stone?

Janjak?

A friend of Axel Chard?

Someone from his past; Michael Northway, or Tarzan, even?

"I don't know."

"Were they looking for something?"

"I don't have anything. Wait, let me check—"

Back in the living room, the cold case files had been dumped out and lay scattered and kicked on the carpet but appeared to be complete; same for the box of Jack Flamingo's notes. "Those all relate to Jori-Ray Rose, meaning John Stone," he said. "It doesn't look like anything's missing though."

"You think he did this, Stone? Rattle you up, back you off—"

"It's certainly possible."

"He's got the money to hire people."

"Tell me about it."

Suddenly Teffinger had a terrible thought and headed for the garage. His worst fears were true. The '67 Corvette was destroyed. Someone had taken a hammer to it, all over—the windshield, headlights, taillights, sides, dash, you name it.

Sophia put an arm around his waist.

"I'm sorry, Nick."

He grunted.

"I'm going to have to tell Jason about his cat. That hurts a lot more than the car if you want to know the truth. I'm going to lock up and get a hotel for the night. I'll file a police report tomorrow. We got Stone coming up and I want to be ready for him."

"Why don't you just stay at my place?"

He checked his watch.

It was insanely late.

He needed to be up at six.

HR would have a fit if it ever found out, but it might save time, and the department would never reimburse him for a hotel, not unless he could show it was related to Stone, and probably not even then.

"Where do you live?"

"Near Belmar Park. Ten minutes."

"Can I use your car in the morning?"

"Absolutely. I'll even make you coffee."

He smiled.

"Coffee. You have me at coffee."

DAY TWELVE

May 28
Friday

59

Friday morning, Teffinger awoke when the first rays of dawn crept into the room and pulled at him until he could resist no longer. He was in a bed that wasn't his, next to a sleeping woman who, when he brushed her hair back, turned out to be Sophia.

Then he remembered.

He remembered intending to sleep on her couch only to find it impossibly small. He remembered her invitation to share the bed. He remembered laying there, with all the beer in his brain making him think about flipping her over and taking her like the devil himself. He remembered battling those demons until everything got numb and the darkness finally swallowed him.

He swung his feet over the edge of the bed and stood up.

The motion pulled the covers.

Sophia's back came into view.

She had no top on.

Teffinger turned his eyes away and headed for the shower. When he got out, Sophia was in the kitchen flipping pancakes and drinking coffee, dressed in a long T-shirt that barely made it past her butt.

She poured him a cup of coffee, smiled and said, "We didn't have sex. In case you were wondering."

"Trust me, that's the kind of thing I remember."

She ran a finger down his nose and added, "We never got

to finish the conversation last night. You told me your secret but I never told you mine. Do you want to know what it is?"

He had no interest but nodded anyway.

"Sure."

She grabbed the bottom of her T-shit, flipped it up, and flashed him.

"I'm not wearing a bra. That's my secret."

His first thought was to nip it in the bud, to tell her in no uncertain terms it could never happen, that it was wrong for a million reasons, plus ten more that he couldn't even think of yet, and the sooner she got it out of her head, the better off they would both be.

But those weren't the words that came out of his mouth.

Instead the words were, "That's a pretty impressive secret."

"Well, thank you. Pancakes?"

As she filled a plate, he took a sip of coffee, walked to the window and looked out.

The sky didn't have a single cloud.

A bright Colorado day was headed their way.

"We're going to get John Stone today," he said. "It's going to be sweet."

60

The Hideout in lower downtown—LoDo—was an art deco café that had chocolate coffee and catered to clandestine meetings, with few windows, dim lights and a no-see, no-tell policy. Teffinger sat in a red vinyl booth at the far back, near a framed wall poster of Marilyn Monroe, with his hand on a hot mug and his eyes on the door, fifteen minutes early.

Hardly anyone was there.

A punked-up girl behind the counter, no more than twenty or so, paid him no mind.

Teffinger was on his second free refill, at exactly eight o'clock, when the door opened and a man walked in.

He was about forty, in great physical condition, with a heavily tattooed left arm. He wore tight jeans and a blue cotton T-shirt that showed lots of muscle.

His face was manly.

He wasn't the kind to back down or take bullshit.

Teffinger waved him over and extended his hand.

"Nick Teffinger."

"Roger West."

"I have to admit, I'm relieved," Teffinger said. "I was afraid you'd turn out to be some kind of pencil pusher or something. You look like a hitman."

"We'll see."

The punked-up one came over.

"You need anything?"

"Coffee, black, like my heart, please and thank you," Teffinger said. Then to West, "So, give me your vision."

For the next half hour, they went over the details, exactly what to say and what not to say, to be sure it all didn't amount to entrapment. The tricky part was going to be making contact. They had no idea what Stone's schedule was today.

"Hopefully, he's going to go to his office and then out to lunch," Teffinger said. "We'll have people in place to track him, whether he walks or drives, and we'll be documenting it as well as we can with photos and video. Once he lands wherever it is that he's going, you can swoop in and make your pitch. We'll need to get the van within a block or so before you do it to be sure the sound comes through nice and clear. Without the recording, all we'll have is your word against his and that won't be enough, as I'm sure you already know." Teffinger took a sip of coffee and added, "Nervous?"

West chuckled at the thought.

"No."

"Good. What name are you going to use?"

"Poet."

Teffinger chewed on it.

"That's not an FBI codeword or anything, is it?"

"No. There's actually a guy out there that goes by that name," West said. "No one knows much about him or if he's even real. But, to get to your question, no; it's not the name of an FBI file or suspect nickname or anything like that. Even if he gets into our files somehow, it won't pop up."

Teffinger nodded.

"I'm feeling good about this." He stood up. "Let's go put a notch in your belt."

"Why not?"

Halfway to the door Teffinger's phone rang.

Sophia's voice came through.

The words were stressed.

"Bad news," she said.

61

Bad news.

Those were the words that came out of Sophia's mouth and into Teffinger's ear. Those were the words that slammed into his gut like a punch.

"What's going on?"

"Stone just hit a woman on a bike," she said.

"What do you mean?"

"He was on his way to his office. About a block before he got there, he made a right hand turn and ran into a woman on a bike, one of those e-scooters or whatever you call them. She's on the ground, lying there. There's a big crowd around her. I don't know if she's hurt or dead or what, but I saw the impact and it was hard. She literally flew up into the air. A squad car's coming."

Teffinger could hear the sirens in the background.

"What's Stone doing?"

"He's waiting," she said. "He's by the side of his car talking into his phone. A couple of guys are walking up to him. Hold on— Oh, shit. One of the guys just shoved him. Oh, man, Stone shoved him back and the other guy decked him in the face! He's down now. He's on the ground. It looks like he's hurt."

"Where you at exactly?"

"Colfax and Grant."

"I'm heading over."

He hung up and told West, "We got a complication. I'll call you as soon as I can. Stay low and wait. Thank you."

Then he was out the door and gone.

Colfax & Grant was a ten-minute walk at normal pace, in a normal crowd. Teffinger got there in three, to a chaotic scene—five cop cars, an ambulance, dozens and dozens and dozens of lookie-loos, and a news crew running up. He watched, second after surreal second, as a body got lifted off the ground and loaded into the ambulance. It belonged to a black female, youngish, like a high-school student.

Her face didn't move or show signs of life but it wasn't covered, meaning she wasn't dead. The ambulance honked and slowly jagged through the crowd, trying not to kill anyone, until it broke free and sped off.

Four or five cops were trying to move the crowd away from the scene.

Stone was in the back of one of the cop cars, sitting there with his head bowed slightly forwards.

Two men were in the back of another one, right next to it.

Teffinger's phone rang.

It was Sophia.

"You seeing this?"

"Yeah. I'm across the street by the Subway."

"Yeah, okay, I see you," she said. "Stone was on his cell phone when he swung around the corner. I'm a witness. What should I do? I don't want to blow our cover—"

62

Teffinger got all the behind-the-scenes updates as the morning hours clicked off. Stone was taken to the station for a statement but called an attorney, a high profile muck-maker by the name of William (Wild Bill) Night out of Jones & Night, LLC, before he said anything. Wild Bill, after consulting in private with his client, immediately started shouting in the district attorney's ear.

The woman wasn't in the crosswalk at the time of the accident; close to it, agreed, but not actually in it.

Although she had the green light, as did Stone—don't forget that—she wasn't in the street when Stone began his turn. She entered the street at a high rate of speed while he was already in his turn. The crosswalk was for pedestrians. She shouldn't have even been around it on an e-bike, much less at the speed she was going.

Stone did in fact have his cell phone up by his face. It wasn't on, however. He wasn't on a phone call or texting or checking messages or anything like that. The fact that he might have been about to press his stocks app and see what the market was doing was irrelevant. He had been watching where he was going. The simple truth is that he didn't have time to react. No one would have.

The fight with the guys was self-defense.

They struck him first.

In fact, he might even press charges. He hadn't made up his mind yet.

Stone was a U.S. Senator. Did the D.A. really want a high-profile case that would be their's to lose? Talk about a career ender—

By noon, the investigation was still ongoing, and Stone was released without charges pending a final decision regarding fault.

None of that was of any particular importance to Teffinger.

The only thing of importance to him was that the press had gone into a feeding frenzy and pushed Stone into bunker mode. The man was holed up in his house right now with three news crews waiting at the end of his street at the gate.

The public was already flashing pitchforks.

The victim was Breanna Wilson, a straight-A student at East High; a girl with four younger sisters and a mother who was trying to make things work on the salary of a nurse. She had no father. He'd left a long time ago.

Witnesses said she was in the crosswalk at the time of the accident. The car swung around the corner, far too fast for her to react. She was on an e-scooter, true, but wasn't moving any faster than a normal pedestrian. And, even if she wasn't in the crosswalk exactly, did that really excuse anything? Drivers needed to be diligent heading into a zone like that. If someone was a few feet past, it was the same as if they were in.

Stone was on his cell phone, distracted to hell and back and clearly not giving a rat's ass about anyone other than himself.

Most importantly, Stone was a white U.S. Senator.

The fact that he hadn't yet been charged with anything reeked of prejudice.

Double standards.

They needed to end.

Now!

Teffinger's chest pounded.

He'd lost his chance to trap Stone, definitely for rest of today, and probably for the weekend too.

After that, he'd have to head to Haiti and try to get things done the ugly way.

He kicked a can.

It rattled down the street and fell into a gutter.

Yeah.

I feel it.

Suddenly his phone rang.

It was Roger West.

"I've been watching the news," he said. "I've got a plan."

The words felt good but Teffinger couldn't imagine how they could be real.

"Which is what?"

"I sneak through the open space behind Stone's house and knock on his back door."

Teffinger considered it.

"When, after dark?"

"No. Now."

63

It was impossible to know how old Fugin was; he could be twenty, he could be fifty. He'd only been in the forensics department for a couple of months and Teffinger hadn't even crossed his path in a stairway yet much less talked to him. Right now, mid-afternoon in a white van with no markings on the sides, he was cueing up Poet and working controls on a digital recorder as Teffinger and Sophia silently watched. The more the man worked, the more comfortable Teffinger got with him.

The connection wasn't as clear as crystal but it was still pretty damn good.

The man played back three sample recordings.

Each was as it should be.

He handed Teffinger a mic and said, "Good to go."

Teffinger gave a documentary introduction—the date, time, location, weather, persons involved, target—and then patched into Poet and said, "We're live. Whenever you're ready."

"You can hear me?"

"Just fine. Confirm the safe word."

"Alligator."

"Okay."

"I'm going to take the earplug out now," Poet said.

"Confirmed. You got your platter with you?"

Poet chuckled.

"Roger that. Will be serving up one dish of John Stone in ten minutes."

"Good luck."

"Get the oven ready."

Muted sounds of walking and breathing came through.

Then, after a time, "A hundred yards out."

"Fifty yards out."

"Entering the back yard at the pool area. No dogs or problems in sight."

Knuckles rapped on glass.

No one answered.

Knuckles rapped again.

A door opened.

A male voice said, "Who the fuck are you?"

It belonged to John Stone.

"I'm an acquaintance of Axel Chard," Poet said. "There's no need for a gun. I just want to talk and it will only take a second."

Sophia looked at Teffinger.

He's got a gun!

He nodded at her.

I heard.

"Axel's dead. I don't know if you knew that or not."

Silence.

Something moved and a door shut.

It could have been Stone stepping outside for privacy.

Then Stone said, "I don't know anyone by that name."

"I know you don't know me from shit," Poet said. "Jori-Ray's still alive. Me and Axel have worked on a number of cases together. We're in the same business."

Poet let the words hang.

Teffinger's heart raced.

Come on, Stone, you little fucker!

Bite!

The silence lasted forever.

Then Stone said, "Tell me about a case."

"Jori-Ray, actually," Poet said. "I'm the one who got Axel in touch with the Dieudonne-Cyr cartel in Haiti. I've done business with Emmanuel Dieudonne-Cyr for over a decade. Do you know what his nickname is?"

"No."

"Fou Reken. That means Crazy Shark. His daughter Lovely was killed in the mission. She was giving air support and someone shot her plane down."

"Who?"

Silence.

"Someone who's going to die a horrible death."

Stone cleared his throat.

"Like I said, I don't know anyone named Axel. If I were you, I'd put an ad on Craigslist, under services, skilled trade. See if someone wants to hire you. You never know."

"Yeah, I'll try that," West said.

Then he was gone.

64

Teffinger busted out the door of the van, paced frantically back and forth for a second, and then kicked the side panel.

Pain shot up his leg.

"Sneaky little shit— "

"He's a lot smarter than I thought," Sophia said. "So now what? Craigslist?"

Teffinger nodded.

"It's all we have. He better bite. I'm getting sick to death of being the nice guy."

An hour later, they posted an ad on Craigslist:

Experienced handyman for hire.

No job too big or too small.

Reasonable prices.

Free quotes.

References available.

Axel Chard.

Time passed, then more, without a reply.

Teffinger felt like a mouse riding on a cat.

Come on, Stone!

Do it!

As the seconds clicked off, the windows got too small and the walls closed in. He headed outside for air, initially intending to simply take a walk and let the sunshine clear his head, but deciding instead to numb the time. He took an Uber to the Eagle Rose to pick up the Tundra, then headed home and called the Lakewood PD to make a police report.

A young kid showed up; Officer Sheldon Cooper, to be precise.

He couldn't have been on the force more than a day.

"Sheldon Cooper," Teffinger said. "You're not the only one with that name."

"Yeah. I know—Big Bang Theory. I'm the one who doesn't get to hang out with Penny."

"Bummer for you."

"Exactly." The kid looked around. "Was anything taken?"

"I don't think so."

"I've never seen anything like this."

Teffinger nodded.

"It's something, huh? You a dog man or a cat man?'

"Dog."

"Good. That'll make your day easier. The place is yours, do as you wish," Teffinger said. "Photograph it to hell and back. I got to head over to a neighbor's house for a few minutes. I'll be right back."

With that, Teffinger took a walk up the street.

Jason was headed down the driveway on his bike, wearing a Rockies hat on backwards.

"Hey, buddy. How's my best-bud doing today?"

"Good."

"Is your mommy home?"

"Yeah. She's in the house."

"I'm going to talk to her for a minute."

"Do you want me to get her?"

"No. I'll just knock."

His phone rang.

Sophia's voice came through.

"Teff—"

"Told on." To Jason, "You be careful on that bike, okay?"

He waved.

"I will."

Then to Sophia, "What's up?"

"We got a reply. He's what is says:

May be interested in your services
Project site is 9938 South Santa Fe Drive
Project start time is 10 p.m. tonight
Apply in person if interested."

She continued, "The reply came from an email account called Haiti Unfinished 002. So it's definitely Stone. No question. The address is in that dilapidated industrial area up on the north edge of the city where the tracks are. 9938 is an old cinderblock building. It caught fire last year and got boarded up. It's just sitting there now like something out of a horror film. It's the kind of place Stone could hand over a suitcase full of money and finalize a deal with no nasty little security cameras around."

Teffinger wanted to smile, and would have, if he wasn't about to have to walk through a door and break a heart or two or three.

"I'll be back at the office in twenty minutes," he said.

Then he turned and stared at the door.

His feet didn't move.

He swallowed and forced them forward.

65

At nine o'clock, in deep twilight that would soon be night, no one was around. The whole forsaken area was deserted. The buildings were quiet and dark and locked up tight against vandals and riffraff until the morning. Stationary railroad cars sat dead and unmoving on the spur tracks at the north edge. Teffinger, Fugin and Sophia arrived in the white van an hour early and squeezed into an alley between two creepy looking buildings a block away.

He studied the area through the outside mirror.

He didn't like it.

What he could see was hardly anything.

It would be too dangerous to get the van any closer but, still, he didn't like it.

"Just stay here and do your thing," he said. "I'm going to go get a vantage point."

"Want me to come with you?" Sophia said.

He almost said, "No. You're not dressed for it," which was true. She should have worn pants. But she was in a T-shirt and mid-thigh black skirt, meaning her arms and legs would pick up the light, especially during movement.

Instead he said, "Sure, if you want."

"I want."

To Fugin, "Looks like you're in charge. Don't forget to do the intro. Call me if you have any problems. Do you have my number?"

"No."

Teffinger gave it to him.

With that, he checked the mirrors one more time, then quietly slipped out and headed further down the alley, between the buildings, to the back where the spur ran, with Sophia two steps behind.

They headed a block up the tracks, came back to the street, and crossed after making sure no one was around. Then they made their way along the backs of the buildings on the other side until they were behind the building that was directly across the street from the target address.

The twilight was deeper now, almost night in fact.

Teffinger rolled an empty 55-gallon drum underneath a small window about ten feet up. Then he climbed on the drum, reached up and pushed against the glass.

It actually slid open, unlocked.

"Think you can get through that?" he said.

Sophia looked dubious.

"Maybe—"

They both climbed up on the drum. Teffinger cupped his hands and boosted Sophia up to where she could get her head through.

"I think I can fit," she said.

"Okay, here we go."

He boosted her up as high as he could, to where she could get her upper body through, until she was half in and half out. Then she disappeared inside.

Something metal made a horrible sound when she dropped.

"Are you okay?"

"Yeah, sorta—"

Ten seconds later she swung the man door open and Teffinger entered.

"Come on."

The building was a large hulking space that looked like it hadn't seen activity in over a decade. Old forgotten machines and shelves sat abandoned, covered in dust and spider webs.

On the street side, there were no windows.

They made their way up four flights of open metal stairs to the roof access, where they pushed a metal door open, and stepped out into the night.

The vantage was perfect.

They were looking directly down on the target building.

Teffinger checked his watch.

9:33 p.m.

A full moon shined.

Everything was quiet.

Stone hadn't shown up yet.

Neither had Poet.

A skinny dog with a bowed head walked slowly and silently down the middle of the street.

Then Teffinger saw something he didn't expect.

Blood was flowing down Sophia's leg.

She hadn't even noticed yet.

"Houston, we have a problem," he said.

She looked to where he was looking, and then pulled her skit up to get a better view.

The wound was deeper than Teffinger thought.

There wasn't a dangerous gush of blood coming out, but blood was coming nevertheless, and it was steady.

He took off his shirt, ripped a sleeve off and tied it around her thigh.

Then he applied pressure, keeping his hands locked tight in place.

"Thanks," she said.

He nodded.

"It's the least I can do . . . and that's what I always do."

Suddenly headlights approached from up the street.

They slowed in front of the target building, crept slowly past, and then continued down the street.

It had to be Stone.

Poet wasn't supposed to show up until 9:58.

"He's making a sweep," Teffinger said. "We're almost there."

66

Keeping her voice low, Sophia said, "Nick, I'm worried about that break-in at your house. I really think someone's out to kill you."

He exhaled.

"Doubtful—"

"I know you're trying to minimize it and put on the macho-man face, but that was extreme. Gutting a cat, I mean, that's way beyond normal. That's a seriously sick mind at work. I don't think you should stay there at night anymore until you get it figured out. Stay at my place."

"Suppose you're right," he said. "That would only put you at risk."

"I don't care."

"Maybe I do."

"We can keep each other's back covered," she said. "It would be hard for anyone to even figure out where you were." She paused and then added, "I'm serious about this, Nick. Don't just flip it aside."

He chewed on it.

Deep down, he agreed with her a thousand percent. He'd been trying to push it into a corner of his gray matter but it kept crawling out and sucking at his breath. Something serious was going on and he'd better get ready to face it before it swooped up from behind and wrapped a rope around his neck.

Ignoring it wasn't going to save the day.

"We'll see," he said.

"No, not we'll see. We'll do."

"We'll see."

"At least for tonight," she said. "Agree to at least that much."

He chewed on it.

They'd leave in the van.

From there, he could slip into Sophia's car.

No one would know he was with her.

She'd be as safe as she could get.

His place was still a mess.

He would never run from his own turf but he really didn't want to be there, either. He'd needed a new pillow, minimum, and didn't have the time or inclination to go get one.

Stone wouldn't be a problem. If everything went tonight as planned, they still wouldn't arrest him until tomorrow. Teffinger didn't want to squeeze him about September's murder until he was good and rested and had plenty of daylight ahead of him.

"Okay, tonight."

"Good."

"Thanks, by the way. I don't think anyone really cares about me all that much."

She patted his hand.

"You'd be surprised."

Suddenly his cell phone rang.

It was Fugin.

"Teffinger, fuck! Headlights are pulling right up behind me. The door just opened. Someone's getting out!"

"Stop talking! Just stay quiet. Power off!"

The line died.

A minute passed.

Teffinger said nothing.

His chest pounded.

Then he saw headlights racing up the street from the vicinity of the van.

It was the same car as before.

It swept past at a high rate of speed and disappeared around a corner.

Teffinger's phone rang.

"I think we're busted," Fugin said. "Whoever it was came up to the window and looked inside with a flashlight. The keys were in the ignition. Here's the worst part though. I had my clipboard on the passenger seat."

"So?"

"My notes were on department stationary. Even if he couldn't read the writing, he could still tell it was cop notes."

"Fuck!"

"I'm sorry, Nick—"

67

Stone was gone and he'd never come back. Not only had he figured out that he was being lured into a trap, he undoubtedly knew who was behind it: Teffinger. His guard going forward would be sky high. As good as Teffinger felt at 9:30 having Stone in the cusp of his grasp, the descent into sudden and unexpected failure a short half an hour later was the likes of something he'd seen few times in his life.

His soul was empty and his heart was dark.

His one, perfect option was gone.

Just like that, poof!

Gone!

Gone!

Gone!

He did have a couple of things incriminating Stone, one being the reply to the Craigslist ad, which they might be able to pin on him if they could get a search warrant for his computer. But even that was next to nothing.

May be interested in your services

May.

It wasn't a solicitation for murder.

It wasn't an offer.

It wasn't a contract.

It wasn't anything illegal.

In fact, the "services" Stone was responding to were for a

"handyman."

He also had the fact that Stone had shown up tonight, which he might be able to prove if Stone's car had GPS tracking and they could get a search warrant for it.

Stone had never actually met with Poet, though.

Again, there was no solicitation for murder.

There was no contract; not by words, not by actions, and certainly not by transfer of money.

In fact, the only words directly out of Stone's mouth on the subject were the ones he initially spoke to Poet at his house when he denied that he knew anyone named Axel Chard.

Halfway back to headquarters, Sophia said, "Teff, you're awfully quiet."

"Just thinking." To Fugin, "It wasn't your fault."

The man looked straight ahead through the windshield, keeping the van on the road and saying nothing.

"Seriously, don't beat yourself up. Tomorrow's another day."

The man looked over.

He must have seen something in Teffinger's eyes because his face relaxed.

"I'm sorry man—"

"Let it go. Seriously. Okay?"

"We'll see."

"Do it. And promise me one thing," Teffinger added. "Next time I have an operation like this, I want you to be the guy."

"You sure?"

Teffinger nodded.

"Yeah."

After dropping off the van at headquarters, Teffinger told Sophia he'd meet her at her place, and stayed behind to call the D.A., Clay Pitcher, Esq., who was a decent lawyer but scared to death of messy cases.

He liked sure wins.

He had nightmares about hung juries.

Teffinger knew he'd be waking the man up.

He'd just have to apologize and owe him one.

Clay answered on the forth ring with sleep in his voice.

"Teffinger?"

"Yeah. Listen—"

With that, he explained that he wanted a search warrant for Stone's computers. He wanted it first thing in the morning. He wanted Clay to come in early and work it up.

"Look, we cue it up as potential evidence that Stone was attempting to hire a hitman," Teffinger said. "Between you me and the walls though, what I really want to do is see if there's anything in there that relates to September."

Clay grunted.

"That case is done and over and dead and buried."

"Not to me it isn't. Stone's implicated somehow."

"How?"

"I don't know yet."

Clay exhaled.

"Nick, look, nothing personal. But this Stone thing; you're not following the evidence, you're ignoring it. Jori-Ray Rose killed September. I tried the case, in case you forgot."

"Clay, stretch for me this once, please."

"There's nothing there."

"Come on, man—"

"Nick, there isn't enough there for a warrant. I wish there was but there isn't. Not to mention, September was more than five years so. Whatever computer Stone was using back then probably isn't the one he has now."

"So you won't even try?"

"It's a broke-dick dog, Nick. I can't drag a broke-dick dog into court. Not even for you. I'm sorry."

The line died.

Teffinger paced.

Clay's pushback was exactly as he anticipated but, still, hearing it in words from the man, out loud, it was a swift kick to the dick.

Nothing was working.

He shifted gears to the little girl, Mary-Ann White.

If he couldn't catch Stone, maybe he could at least help her.

He took the stairs down to the parking garage, fired up the Tundra and headed for the law office of Grace Springfield, Esq.

68

Grace Springfield's office turned out to be an old converted two-story house next to the Five Points area, a block from Saint Joseph Hospital. To the left was a string of old but well-loved houses. To the right was large pay parking lot, which might have security cameras.

Teffinger drove past.

The office was dark.

A six-foot high cedar fence encircled the structure at both sides and along the back.

The parking lot had only a few straggling cars left in it.

Teffinger parked a block over, circled back on foot and muscled his way over the fence at the rear. If the pretty-little Hannah Taylor's cowgirl lips had been telling the truth, she had the security cameras unplugged. The key to the back door would be in a magnetic box under the electrical panel.

It's not too late.

You can still turn back.

The parking lot sprayed enough light into the area for him to find the electrical box. Underneath was the key, exactly where it was supposed to be.

He held it in his hand.

His head spun.

This was wrong.

He had only one chance to stop it and that was right now.

The second he put the key in the door and entered, everything would be forever different.

He put the key in the lock, gave himself one final chance to come to his senses, and then entered.

The interior was dark, very dark, but not pitch; some light came through the front windows. He stood there quietly, letting his eyes adjust, until he was able to make out shapes and spaces.

The first floor largely consisted of a heavy wooden conference room with book-lined walls, an office which no-doubt belonged to Grace, a restroom and a kitchen.

Teffinger took the wooden stairs up to the second floor.

There he found a storage room filled with boxes, a copy room, a small bathroom and an office.

He entered the office without turning on the lights.

In the bottom drawer of the desk, he found a thick expandable folder filled with files.

He grabbed it, wiped his prints off the few things he'd touched, put the key back where it belonged, and got the hell out of there.

He encountered no one.

Back in the Tundra, he powered up the radio as he pulled away.

One of his favorite songs in the world came on.

He turned the volume up and sang along.

> Well it's been building up inside of me
> For oh I don't know how long.
> I don't know why
> But I keep thinking
> Something's bound to go wrong . . .

When the song was over, he called Jori-Ray's lawyer, Alabama, and said, "Do you have a way to contact Janjak?"

"Maybe. Why?"

"My house was trashed last night. Can you call her and ask her if the Dieudonne-Cyr cartel knows about me?"

"Sure, if you want."

"I want."

He was almost to Sophia's place when a dark thought crept into his brain.

What if Hannah Taylor was working for Stone?

What if the security cameras were actually on the whole time?

What if this was nothing more than a big trap to take him down?

Pulling into Sophia's driveway, Teffinger's phone rang.

It was the person he really wanted to hear from, Alabama.

"Janjak said one of her men disappeared yesterday morning. He went to town for groceries and never came back. The cartel might have snatched him. She doesn't know that for sure, but can't think of any other explanation."

Teffinger's chest tightened.

He pictured the man strapped down in a cinderblock cell, screaming about a white man from Denver as they cut his knuckles off one by one and burned holes in his chest with a blowtorch . . .

69

Sophia was asleep in bed, face down, with the sheets covering the lower half of her body, breathing deeply with a slow musical rhythm. Teffinger studied the way her hair fell against the pillow as he wondered what he was feeling about her, deep down, where he didn't often look. Something was happening, he couldn't deny it and wasn't in charge of it. He was a leaf floating on the surface of a stream.

He softly closed the door.

At the kitchen table, he opened the files he'd just taken from the lawyer's office.

The top one was labeled

Locke, Pierce / Janie Cooper

Teffinger immediately recognized the name, Janie Cooper.

She was all over the headlines—when was it?—three or four years ago, it must have been, she got abducted out of her beach bungalow bed down in Cancun while her parents slept in the next room. Day after day went by, conspiracy theories raged, the safety of Americans vacationing in Mexico became the newest debate, and the FBI eventually flew down. Her father—Austin Cooper—was a U.S. District Court Judge in Washington, D.C. Her mother was a Vietnamese woman named Hue who met Austin while studying in the United States. After ten days, the girl was spotted on a street corner, hungry and dirty but very much alive and well. Whatever had happened during those ten days was never made public and the case slipped into oblivion.

The file consisted of three pages of typed notes and dozens upon dozens of news articles regarding the case. The notes were apparently taken by the lawyer, Grace Springfield, documenting several phone conversations she had with her client, Pierce Locke. Locke had prided himself on being able to find out that the Vietnam woman, Hue, was the heir of the Windflower Hotels chain, and had more money than God. Locke abducted the daughter and demanded ransom. The parents denied having any substantial savings, which, according to Locke's own words, "Really, really pissed me off. I almost killed the fucking little brat right then and there to teach them a fucking lesson about lying to the wrong fucking person." On the tenth day, which was their last, they paid what he demanded—five million dollars—and he dropped the girl off on a street corner. All parties involved, including the FBI, agreed to keep the incident confidential, so that Hue's wealth would remain secret and nobody would try to do a copycat on her.

Locke kept his word.

Apparently, he only bragged to his lawyer, who was obligated to keep it confidential.

Teffinger flipped three more files and a pattern quickly emerged. Locke kidnapped kids for ransom. But he wasn't just a kidnapper. When the parents didn't pay, the kid never came back. He didn't kill them, though.

He sold them.

A ten-year-old girl named Aimee Marie Miller was sold to an undisclosed person or persons outside the United States.

So was another named Michelle Carter, who was the daughter of a hedge fund giant named Joe Carter.

The lawyer's notes indicated, "I keep trying to get him to tell me who he's selling to. It's the one thing he won't disclose, even to me."

Teffinger opened a file labeled:

Locke, Pierce / Amber Madison Hall

There, right in the opening paragraph, was something that made Teffinger's chest pound.

The conversation took place three years ago. Locke was calling the lawyer from Haiti.

Haiti.

"Nick, what are you doing?" The words came from Sophia, walking into the kitchen with sleep on her face. "It's past midnight."

He checked.

She was right.

He had no idea.

Friday had snuck into Saturday. The thought hit him with the force of a piano dropping out of the sky. He had Saturday and Sunday left, that was all. Then he'd be off to Haiti on Monday to do what he could to save Kimona.

"I'm coming," he said.

Hannah Taylor had said there would be information in the files regarding Mary-Ann White. He flipped through and found one labeled:

Locke, Pierce / Mary-Ann White

Yeah, baby!

DAY THIRTEEN

May 29
Saturday

70

Mary-Ann White!

Teffinger rifled through the file with the intensity of a starving wolf ripping into a carcass.

Michael Ravenfield.

He was at the heart of it all.

He won over $18,000,000 in the Virginia lottery three years ago. Pierce Locke targeted him and set out on a relentless quest to see if the man had any weak spots.

It turned out that he did.

He had a brief affair seven years ago with a woman named Katrina White.

Together they produced a daughter, Mary-Ann White.

After Katrina got pregnant, but before the kid was born, Ravenfield beat feet back to Virginia. Daddy was the last name he ever wanted to be called. Call him deadbeat, call him gone, that was fine, but don't call him the D-word.

Still, Locke figured that the man had enough money to pony up at least $2,000,000 to save his own flesh and blood. So he snatched the girl from her bed on April 1st.

Then he contacted Ravenfield.

The man turned out to be the most selfish, callous fuckface on the crust of the planet. Over the ten-day period that followed, he never offered up a single red cent.

On the tenth day, Locke sold the kid—and, as far as Ravenfield went, he'd have to live the rest of his days believing that the kid was dead because he was too fucking greedy to fork over even the cost of a new iPhone.

Normally, that would be the end of it.

But Ravenfield was a special case.

He'd been as frustrating as hell.

"Screw you, asswipe!"

That's what he'd said to Locke.

A lot more than once, too; every single time.

The more Locke pondered the guy, the more he decided that the world didn't need him. On July 7th, Locke paid a little visit to Ravenfield at his beach house. Locke strapped him into his own leather recliner by the window, looking out onto the ocean and the sailboats on the horizon. Then Locke took a kitchen knife to Ravenfield's flesh until the man tried to buy his way out, which was a neat little turn of events. It turned out that Ravenfield had two million dollars in cash in a vault in the basement behind a trap wall. Locke got it in hand and said, "See how easy that was. That's all you had to do back when I asked. But you're more of a screw you, asswipe, guy, aren't you?"

"That's all I have! Take it and go! I won't ever tell anyone. I swear! You got your money. That's what you wanted, right?"

Locke nodded.

A vial of cocaine sat on a fancy contemporary end table next to the chair. Locke twisted the cap off, held the glass up to the Ravenfield's nose and said, "Go ahead."

The man took a snort.

Lock said, "The ocean is so damn beautiful, isn't it?"

Ravenfield smiled.

"Yeah."

"Take a look at it."

Locke waited as Ravelfield took a look.

Then he slit the man's throat.

The account was true.

There were lots of local news articles in the file. Michael Ravenfield, one of the state's biggest lottery winners, was found murdered in his beach house Thursday morning.

An unknown amount of cash may have been taken.

The police have no suspects at this time.

He ran the name of the client, Pierce Locke, through Google and social media. Although they were a few hits, they all belonged to people who were either the wrong age or otherwise not viable suspects.

Teffinger wasn't surprised.

The name was clearly an alias.

His crimes had obviously been investigated to death, not only by local jurisdictions, but by the FBI as well. Somebody, somewhere, had to have something on him.

He checked the time.

It was almost one in the morning, meaning three, Quantico time.

Dr. Leigh Sandt was a woman who was slow to boil. But even she might get dragged past her limit if he called her at this hour of the universe.

Wait?

Or call?

He paced for a few seconds, decided he didn't have time to wait, and braced himself.

She answered on the third ring and sounded as if she'd just been pulled from the depths of non-existence.

"Hey, Leigh, it's me. I'm really sorry to wake you—"

"Teffinger?"

"Yeah. Listen, I'm—"

"It's three in the morning."

"Yeah, I know, but I've got something serious going on and I need your help."

"Is someone there killing you?"

"No, it's nothing like that. I need some information on a guy."

Silence.

"Un-fucking-believable, even for you."

The line died.

He bowed his head on the table and closed his eyes. At some point later, the soft touch of a hand lightly shook his shoulder.

"Nick, come to bed. You're exhausted."

71

As soon as Teffinger woke Saturday morning, he could tell by the brightness of the room that he'd slept well past when he wanted. His watch confirmed it—9:42. He remembered Sophia waking him at the kitchen table last night, then grabbing his hand and leading him to bed. He remembered her helping him get his clothes off and covering him with a sheet. She might have given him a kiss goodnight on the cheek. He wasn't certain about that. Maybe it was just wishful thinking.

The files!

He'd left them on the kitchen table!

He bolted out of bed and found Sophia in the kitchen, drinking coffee and going through the files with a serious look on her face.

"Jesus, Nick," she said.

Shit!

The woman's eyes fell to his midsection. He looked down, relieved that he still had his boxers on, and said, "Good morning."

She nodded.

"You hungry?"

"Always."

He took a quick shower, where he tried to get the day organized in his head, and came out with towel-dried hair to bacon and eggs and coffee and Sophia.

"This is important," he said. "You can never, ever tell any-body about these files."

"This is what Hannah Taylor wanted to see you about, isn't it?"

"Yes. They're confidential and privileged. I'm not sup-posed to have them. If anyone ever finds out, I could lose my job. Worse, if this guy Locke ever finds out, there's a good chance he'll go after the lawyer."

"Grace Springfield."

"Right, her," he said. "She doesn't know I have them, by the way. Only Hannah does." He took a sip of coffee and added, "Do you have her phone number by any chance?"

Two minutes later he called the woman.

As the phone rang, he bounced back to the Eagle Rose, and could feel the weight of her body on his lap.

"Hannah, quick question," he said. "Pierce Locke is an alias, I'm assuming."

"So, you got the files—"

"Apparently."

"I honestly didn't think you'd have the guts. Yeah, as best we can figure, it's an alias."

"Do you know his real name?"

"Unfortunately, no. Grace has tried to figure it out a hun-dred times," she said. "Every time the guy calls, his number is blocked. He never really says much about himself other than the crimes themselves. A few times, he indicated where he was calling from; one was Haiti, I remember, and another time it was San Francisco."

San Francisco.

There's where September Stone wanted to run away to.

"Whenever he did that," Hannah continued, "Grace would

put it in the notes. Plus we know what cities he was when the crimes were committed. Other than that, though, the guy's a ghost."

"What about recordings?" Teffinger said. "Did Grace ever record the conversations?"

"I think she did record some of them—the ones that came to the office phone. She has a recorder on that line," Hannah said. "But a lot of them went to her cell phone. He would just call out of blue. She'd never knew when to expect them."

"So, the ones she recorded, where are they?"

"I think they're in the safe in her office but I'm not sure. I've never actually physically seen them. And, to preempt your next question, no, I don't have access to the safe."

"Okay."

"Sorry—"

"No worries," Teffinger said. "Do you think she might have stored them digitally? In her computer, maybe?"

"I've never noticed them there. I'll check and get back to you if you want. I guess we've gone this far—"

"That would be great," Teffinger said. "What about money? How did the guy pay his bills? There has to be something we can track."

"Cash would just show up."

"How?"

"Someone would throw it over the fence, usually at night. He'd call the next morning and say, There's an envelope outside by the electrical panel, or something like that."

"Did you ever get any video of that?"

"We don't have cameras on the sides. Only the front and back, and inside, of course."

Teffinger grunted.

"Come on, Hannah, give me something."

She exhaled.

"Like I said before, I think he's going to kill Grace. That's why I got you involved. And that's why he's being so careful, in my opinion."

"All right."

A second passed, then another and another.

Teffinger was about to punch off.

Then Hanna said, "There's only one small possible thing I can think of. Grace almost always stops to get a coffee on her way to work, at a place called Lava Java, which is over by 17th and Downing. There's a guy in there sometimes that gives her the creeps."

"In what way?"

"I don't know," she said. "Grace said it's like he's watching her or something. Once, she spilled coffee on the guy's table on purpose, and said Sorry, and made a bunch of apologies as she cleaned it up. She wanted him to say something back so she could hear his voice, but he never said a single word. The next time he showed up there, she pretended to be texting while she was waiting in line. There's a mirror behind the counter. She took a picture of the guy using the mirror."

Teffinger's heart raced.

"Does she still have the picture?"

"Yeah. She downloaded it to her computer. I can send you a copy if you want."

"I want," Teffinger. "I definitely want."

"I have remote access to the computer from home," she said. "You should get it in a couple of minutes. I'll check for those audio files too."

"Beautiful."

72

Teffinger made his way over to the front picture window and pulled the curtain back. There wasn't a cloud in the sky. Weather wise, it would be perfect today. Way down the street, it looked like two people were seated in a parked car. They didn't show any significant motion. It was almost as if they were waiting for something.

His phone pinged.

It was a text, from Hannah, with a photo and the words, "Creepy guy attached. Sorry, no audio files."

Sophia came over.

The creep was a strong, manly guy in his mid-thirties, with a prominent nose and a small black tattoo on the left side of his neck.

"This is him," Teffinger said. "Meet Pierce Locke."

"You think?"

He nodded.

"He's exactly what I pictured."

"So now what?"

"We run him through every database in the world. He knows who he sold Mary-Ann White to. What he doesn't know yet is that he's going to tell me."

He headed back to the picture window.

The car was still there.

The figures were still inside, not moving.

"Do you have binoculars?"

"Yes."

Thirty seconds later, he pulled the figures in. They were both black men with dreadlocks.

"We might have company," he said.

"Who?"

"The people who killed my neighbor's cat."

"How would they know you're here?"

He shrugged.

"I don't know. They could have followed me from headquarters last night. Or maybe they have a tracker on my truck. I'm going to take a little drive and see if they follow."

"I'm coming with you."

He thought about arguing.

He already knew he'd lose.

More importantly, he didn't want her to be alone right now. They might well snatch her to get to him.

"Fine," he said. "Bring your gun."

Before they left, Teffinger called forensics to see if anyone was there, and actually got an answer, from Fugin no less.

"I'm going to send you a picture of a man," Teffinger said. "I need to know who he is and I need to know it as soon as possible. Spare no effort. This is a scorched earth assignment. Clock your time to the Mary-Ann White case."

"Understood. Did you hear that noise?"

"No. What noise?"

"Me, dropping everything else."

"Funny. And thanks. I owe you one."

Teffinger checked outside one final time.

The car was still there.

They walked out to the Tundra, backed out of the driveway, and headed down the street in the opposite direction, putting the right-hand blinker on when they came to the first cross-street. Just as they turned the corner, the other car pulled out.

"It's them," Teffinger said.

73

Teffinger headed west, towards the old BNSF switchyard at the edge of the city, in fact, the same place he'd met with John Stone's wife, Catherine, not so long ago. It was remote and there was less risk of a bystander getting shot if bullets started flying.

"These guys—if they're who I think they are—are part of a Haiti organization called the Dieudonne-Cyr cartel, which is a hundred men strong. Drug smuggling, human trafficking and slavery, that's their thing. When I was down in Haiti, I got on their radar screen. They're out to kill me but they'd rather take me back alive if they can. The bottom line is that they're extremely violent and they're my fight, not yours. They won't be afraid to make a move on a Saturday morning in broad daylight."

"I'm not going anywhere, Nick. Don't even insult me by asking."

He looked over.

That stubborn look of hers was all over the place.

He said, "It's my belief that the guy who kidnapped Mary-Ann White actually sold her to that organization. We know she was sold to somebody, and we know that the guy who took her—Pierce Locke, for now—has ties to Haiti. Here's where my thoughts get crazy. Are you ready?"

"Let's find out."

"I'd like to catch the two guys alive and use them as leverage to get Mary-Ann back."

He let the words hang.

Sophia said, "That actually is a little crazy, Nick."

"Well, I warned you."

"So, how to we catch 'em?"

"We're heading to the old BNSF switchyard," he said. "They'll end up shooting at some point. We defend ourselves."

Sophia's face laced with shock.

"You're actually serious. A gunfight at the O.K. Corral—"

"We can do it now, while we know where they are, or do it later, when we have no idea that they're sneaking up on us. Like I said, I'll drop you off somewhere. That's not a problem. In fact, it's my preference."

"No. No dropping off." She looked in the side mirror and said, "Shit, Nick! There's three of them. One must have been lying down in the backseat, sleeping or whatever."

Teffinger checked.

She was right.

There were three.

The rail yard was approaching fast. "I can still swing out of here," Teffinger said. "It's not too late."

He looked over.

Sophia had her weapon in hand, checking it over with quick, deliberate movements.

"Just keep going," she said.

Two minutes later they pulled up in front of a boarded-up, three-story brick building that butted against the tracks.

No one was around.

The yard was silent.

The switchers were nowhere to be seen or heard.

"This was Tarzan's lair," Teffinger said.

"Never heard of him."

"I'll tell you the story sometime. Follow me."

They disappeared down the side of the building. From behind a rusted drum, Teffinger took a look back. The car was stopped a hundred yards away, just sitting there in the middle of a vast acreage of dirt and gravel.

Two men got out.

They had guns in hand.

One ran to the north and the other ran to the south.

After a few seconds, the driver started heading straight in, coming slowly.

At the back of the building were several parallel sidetracks with strings of rail cars, mostly boxcars, but some flatbeds, tankers and specialty cars as well.

Teffinger and Sophia made their way into the tracks and hid in the shadows of a boxcar.

Then they waited.

"Remember, they have to shoot first."

"Got it."

"Then we have as much self-defense justification as we need."

"To tell you the truth, I feel like we already have it."

"No gray areas," he said. "Let them shoot first unless it's absolutely life or death."

Suddenly a shot rang out.

They dropped to the ground.

"Nick, you're bleeding!"

He followed her eyes to his left arm.

There was blood.

He'd been hit.

"Come on!"

74

Teffinger and Sophia rolled under the boxcar to the other side and ran as shots came from behind them and bullets ricocheted off metal. Suddenly Sophia swung around and fired. Teffinger turned to see one of the men drop to the ground. As soon as he turned back, a figure was in front of him, swinging out from behind a rail car thirty yards away.

He fired, aiming at the man's chest.

The bullet went high.

The man's face splattered.

He took in the sight for a second, then kept running in that direction, unsure where the last man was. When Teffinger turned, Sophia was on the ground, fallen or tripped.

He stopped.

"Come on!"

She got to her feet.

Then, just like that, a man came from out of nowhere, punched her in the face and got her in his grip from behind. The barrel of his weapon mashed into the side of Sophia's head. Blood ran down her forehead and a frantic fear screwed into her eyes.

He shouted to Teffinger, "Drop your gun!"

Teffinger froze.

They were fifteen yards apart.

"Do it! Right now!" the man shouted. "Drop it or she

dies!"

"Don't do it!" Sophia shouted. "Shoot the dog!"

The words were like a fog in Teffinger's brain. He heard them, he understood them, but he couldn't process the act of firing. He couldn't think it through fast enough. He couldn't gauge how accurate he was from this distance, or even how far apart they were. His heart beat like a thousand maniac drums. All he knew for sure is that both he and Sophia might be dead in a few seconds. He could barely breathe.

"Let her go," he shouted. "Then you can walk away. We'll call it quits."

"Drop the gun! Last chance, man!"

Teffinger raised his gun, almost to where it was now pointing at the man's face. The guy was like lightning, suddenly pulling his weapon from Sophia's head and swinging it towards Teffinger's body.

That's when Teffinger held his breath and squeezed the trigger.

The bullet struck the man at the top of his skull.

It splattered with a horrific cracking sound.

He wobbled.

The gun fell out of his hand.

Then he dropped to the ground.

75

Teffinger told Sophia, "That hell that everyone always talks about? Get ready for it to break loose."

Per department protocol, he called 911 to report the shooting. From there, dispatch would immediately inform everyone on the call-out list:

Deputy Chief of Police Operations

Major Crimes Commander

Assistant District Attorney

Homicide Unit Personnel

Director of the Crime Lab

Crime Lab Technicians

Denver District Attorney

Chief of Police

Etcetera.

The guy Sophia shot was laying in the dirt face down. With his weapon pointed at the man's back, Teffinger nudged the guy with his foot and got no response. Then he rolled the man over. Blood covered his chest. Teffinger put a finger on the man's neck to see if there was a pulse. To his shock, the guy opened his eyes and looked right at him.

"He's alive!"

He applied pressure to the wound and gave the man CPR until the ambulance arrived.

Cars and bodies rushed into the scene from all over.

Teffinger and Sophia were immediately separated and sequestered into separate vehicles some distance apart. Teffinger's weapon was taken and bagged.

The Chief, Tanner, poked his head in.

"You want to lawyer-up before we interview you?"

"No."

"Didn't think so."

Teffinger swallowed.

An officer-involved shooting was a serious matter, especially when it resulted in death. It could affect the entire relationship between the police and the community. It could lead to lawsuits. It could have all kinds of consequences. Every news channel would be all over it.

Investigations of these incidents were always exhaustive.

He'd be immediately interviewed until they had every detail and he'd repeated himself six times over.

The interview would be videotaped.

They'd want to know why he believed the suspects were from a Haitian cartel and, more importantly, why they were targeting him. He'd need to have an answer ready for that. It would also come out that he'd slept over at Sophia's for the last two nights.

Blood samples would be taken for a toxicology report.

All of that would take time, a lot of time, and there was nothing he could do about it. At the end of all of it, they would probably temporarily relieve him of field duty or put him on administrative leave.

Hours clicked off, filled with faces and questions and pauses and bathroom breaks and coffee cups and everything else under the sun. Substantively, Teffinger wasn't worried. It had all been self-defense. In fact, he had actually been shot in the arm before he ever fired a single bullet; a superficial flesh wound, granted, but potentially fatal just an inch or two over. The suspects had never gone into retreat. They weren't running away. None of them had been shot in the back. The threat had been constant from moment one.

The chief, however, wasn't happy.

"You knew all this gunplay was coming," he said. "You basically set it up. Not to mention, you never called for back-up."

"I didn't have time."

The chief creased every wrinkle in his forehead.

"You almost got Sophia killed. Hell, you almost killed her yourself."

"Well, I didn't . . ."

"Yeah. We have a name for that. It's called luck." The man leaned back in his chair, studied Teffinger, and said, "Are they going to be sending more men after you? This Haiti cartel—"

Teffinger shrugged.

"That would be my guess. I don't think I made too many friends today."

The chief frowned.

"Ordinarily I'd put you on administrative leave," he said. "But I don't want you running around without your gun. Go get a replacement weapon."

Teffinger nodded.

"Thanks. I owe you."

The chief leaned forward.

"Sophia's a good person," he said.

"I agree."

"Don't break her heart."

76

Teffinger finally broke free of the time suck around 2:00 and headed to Sophia's to find her sitting on the front steps with a bottle of water in hand and a Bluetooth speaker at her side, spitting out some kind of rapper crap, stressed to the breaking point.

He dropped down next to her and put a hand on her knee.

"That guy you shot," he said. "That probably saved both our lives. Don't ever doubt yourself about that. You could be dead right now or in a wheelchair for the rest of your life. Same for me. So, let me say it right now so it's real clear: thanks for that. Thanks to the end of time."

She looked into his eyes.

"He died, Nick," she said.

"Seriously?"

"They just called me."

"Well, fuck him."

"I'll be on their radar now, the cartel's, just like you. Won't I?"

Teffinger went to say, No, I don't think so.

Instead he said, "This is all my fault. I'm sorry."

"No. you offered to drop me off. It was my choice. I wouldn't go back and change it. Know that."

Teffinger's eyes fell to a large Channel 8 news van coming down the street. He grabbed Sophia's hand, pulled her up and said, "Incoming."

They headed inside.

On the kitchen table was the folder of Grace Springfield's files. Teffinger picked it up and flipped through the tabs to see if there was anyone famous that he hadn't gotten to yet. What he saw he could hardly believe. The very last file was labeled:

Locke, Pierce / September Stone.

September Stone.

September Stone.

September Stone.

He dived in.

Locke targeted September for kidnapping and broke into her room to snatch her. This was back when she was fourteen. Things went wrong. She woke up before he could inject her. They struggled and it was all he could do to keep his hand over her mouth. It became clear that he'd never get her out of there without her screaming. Her parents were home at the time, sleeping.

He didn't want to kill her.

He told her to just go back to sleep and never tell anybody anything. If she did, he'd kill her mom and dad. Then he'd kill her.

He left.

A year went by and as far as he could tell, the girl had never told anyone about what happened.

It bothered him, though, that she'd seen his face.

She was a witness.

She was a loose end.

Sooner or later, as she got older and stronger, she'd spill it out. She'd read a news article about a girl being kidnapped. She'd decide that it might be him. She'd decide that she needed to step forward so that what happened to her never happened to anyone else.

He decided to take her again. If the ransom didn't go through, he'd sell her. If it did go through, he'd still sell her. Either way, she was never coming back.

The loose end would be forever tied up.

He snuck into the house.

He made his way to her room.

She was asleep.

He was about to inject her.

He was this close to having the whole thing go perfectly.

Then, suddenly, September woke up and headed for the kitchen. Someone else was in the house, a woman, who he later learned was someone named Jori-Ray Rose. A fight ensued between the two women in the kitchen. September got the upper hand and knocked the other woman to the floor.

Locke decided to abort, but September had already spotted him. She had a gun and got it trained on him. He tried to talk her down but she wasn't having it. The woman on the floor moaned and shifted. That drew September's attention, for just a second, but it was enough.

Locke charged.

He wrestled the gun away from her but she still kept struggling. All he wanted to do was leave but she kept on after him. It was like she wanted to kill him.

The weapon went off, splattering her face.

The girl made a horrible sound and dropped to the floor, already dead before she hit.

He ran out the back way into the open space. He'd had gloves on the whole time, but he wiped the weapon clean anyway, just in case his DNA was on it. Then he threw it into the brush and disappeared into the night.

Behind the attorney's notes were printouts of articles about the murder as well as the trial of Jori-Ray Rose, all the way up to the conviction.

It must have been hell for the lawyer to know that an innocent person was going down for the murder and not being able to tell anyone the truth.

Teffinger looked at Sophia.

"Have you read this?"

"Yes, of course. This morning. I thought you already saw it. So it wasn't Jori-Ray after all. Pretty crazy, huh?"

Suddenly Teffinger's phone rang and Fugin's voice came through. "Got a hit on your man."

It took Teffinger a second to figure out what he was talking about, namely the picture of the man from Lava Java, the creepy guy, who may or may not be Pierce Locke.

"Go on."

"He's a San Francisco guy named Lance Rockwood. We got a facial recognition match from Facebook. We pulled a California driver's license under that name, Lance Rockwood, and the photo is definitely him, so the name he uses on Facebook is definitely his real name."

"This is beautiful. You got an address?"

"It's on his license. I'm texting it to you now. Oh, I almost forgot. The guy's got no record. He's squeaky clean."

"You the man. Text me."

Ten seconds later the license showed up on Teffinger's phone.

He went to Zillow and typed in the address.

It turned out to be one of the famous Painted Ladies near

Alamo Square Park. Zillow had the value of the property at several million dollars.

"This is our guy," Teffinger said. "He's living large."

"So what do we do?"

"This file we have is good, but we can never show it to anyone. Even if we did, it's privileged. It can't be admitted into evidence. As I see it, we only have one option. We head to San Francisco."

"And do what?"

"We get evidence. We find out who he sold Mary-Ann White to. And we make sure his sorry ass never touches another human being again. Not in this lifetime, or the next."

Sophia studied him.

"Are you going to kill him?"

Teffinger stared straight ahead.

"That would be illegal."

77

On the flight from Denver to San Francisco, Teffinger drank beer, cast an occasional glance at Sophia's legs, and let his mind drift. The information he recently obtained regarding September getting a gun, it made sense now. She was afraid that the guy who came into her room, whoever he was, would eventually pop back out of the shadows.

She was scared.

She was getting ready to protect herself, not to mention her mom and dad, if it came to it.

It must have been hell for her, not telling anyone. That hell no doubt accounted for the shift in her personality that everyone was starting to notice.

What a weight to carry.

Sophia put her hand on Teffinger's forearm.

"You okay?"

He shrugged.

"I don't know. A lot of this is my fault. I had Jori-Ray in my sights and never dug past her. If I had, I don't know, I might have figured out some things."

"Don't blame yourself."

"I'm not," he said. "This isn't a pity party. But when I think back, if I could have just kept my eyes wide enough to spot our little friend lurking out there in the shadows, I might have been able to shut him down back at the gate. Maybe

Mary-Ann White would have never happened—"

Sophia squeezed his forearm.

"It's hindsight Nick. Don't let it fuck with you."

He grunted.

"I'll tell you one thing. Fool me once, shame on you. Fool me twice, shame on me. He's not going to wiggle away again. I guarantee you that." He paused and then added, "You know, the way this little fuckhead tells his story to the lawyer, he makes it like he's the victim—all I wanted to do was leave, and crap like that, as if it's September's fault that she's fighting him after he's the one who broke into her house. It really pisses me off. I'm going to take this guy down and I'm going to enjoy every single second of it." He looked at her and said, "Sorry for the rant. Was I saying all that stuff out loud?"

She smiled.

Then she said, "I saw you looking at my legs."

"Sorry about that."

"Don't be. That's what they're for."

A violent storm pounded San Francisco with maniac fists just as night fell over the sky. Teffinger watched it from his window seat as the plane slowly descended deeper and deeper into it. A relentless string of lightning flashes lit the sky below them, illuminating thick menacing clouds, and showing for the briefest of a blink the black lonely silhouette of another plane, far below them, looking dangerously small and frail.

He double-checked his seatbelt and gripped the armrests.

"It's okay," Sophia said.

He swallowed.

Sweat poured down his forehead.

The plane kept descending. They were still above the storm and everything was still calm.

Then came the first wobble.

"Here we go," he said.

Within seconds, the plane pitched and twisted and dropped and bottomed out and shook and made horrible sounds, fighting for its life.

Twenty minutes later they were on the ground, alive.

He said, "That wasn't so bad."

Sophia chuckled.

"You should have seen your face," she said. "I wish I'd gotten a picture."

They rented a Dodge Challenger and headed north on the 101 into San Francisco.

Teffinger checked his watch.

9:04 p.m.

He had whatever was left of tonight, and then tomorrow.

Then he'd have to head to Haiti.

The realization was like a python slowly tightening around his chest.

78

Teffinger and Sophia booked a room in the Hotel Emblem on Sutter Street in the pulse of the city where Nob Hill meets Union Square and the Theater District. The Obscenity Bar called Teffinger's name as he passed but he forced himself to not listen. Instead, they got situated, then headed out into the storm to Lance Rockwood's house, parking on the other side of the park where they had as clear a view as was possible given the storm.

All the houses had lights on inside except Rockwood's.

His was dark.

On the right hand side, the structure had a one-car garage with glass panels at the top. The door was down and dark. To the left of that was a staircase that led to the front door.

Teffinger said, "I'm going in."

"He might be there. Sleeping—"

"It's a chance I have to take. I want you to stay here and keep an eye on the place. If he shows up, call me immediately. Can you do that?"

"Yes."

"Okay, good."

"Be careful."

"Always."

For reasons he didn't quite understand, he gave her a quick kiss on the cheek. Then he opened the door and stepped out into the darkness of the night. The weather assaulted him immediately, driving cold rain like a maniac into his clothes and face and hair. He stayed on the sidewalks and made his way to the front of the house.

He saw no life inside.

There wasn't a single light on.

Not seeing a Ring camera or other form of video security, he walked up the stairs and knocked on the door.

No one answered.

He headed back down the stairs and kept walking. At the end of the street, he turned right, then made another right into an alley that ran behind the houses, and approached the house from the shadows in the back.

The adjacent houses were only five feet apart but no dogs barked.

He made his way to the back door, busted the glass with his elbow and entered, to find himself in a kitchen.

"Anyone home?"

No one answered.

"Hello?"

Silence.

He closed the door, wiped his fingerprints off the knob, and powered up his cell phone to flashlight mode.

The man was clearly living the good life—Sub-Zero fridge, Wolfe appliances, white cabinets, hardwood floors, marble countertops, a fancy espresso machine, a built-in wine cooler, all top line and all expensive.

He saw no interior cameras.

He made his way into the living room where he paused just long enough to get the lay of the land, and then headed into the next room, his target—the den.

There, he rifled through bills, papers, drawers and books. He found Visa bills for several different names, not only including the man's real name, Lance Rockwood, but also in several other names, which must have been aliases, including Ray Johnson, Andrew Kent, Christopher Mills, and Stephen Cooper. Other than that, nothing appeared out of the ordinary, except for the fact that there was no computer or tablet to be found.

Upstairs, in the master bedroom, the bed was made.

On it was a clasp-envelope labeled Andrew Kent.

It was the kind of thing that might be used to hold alias tools, like a fake passport, driver's license and credit cards.

Nothing was inside.

It was empty.

The master bathroom was clean and opulent.

In a small trash receptacle under the sink, Teffinger found an empty canister of Alvesco 160, indicating that Rockwood might have some degree of asthma. There was no new canister on the countertop or anywhere else that Teffinger could find, which was unusual, because it wasn't a rescue inhaler, it was for daily use. There wouldn't be any reason for someone to take it out of the house, unless, possibly, there were going somewhere for a period of time.

Nothing else unusual showed up in the bathroom.

In the master closet, he found a mix of high/low, designer clothes on the one hand, and street clothes on the other. He found no strange boxes, trap doors, or photo journals. He was almost out when he pulled back some shirts just for grins. In the rear of the closet, down at floor level, was a trap door.

Behind it was a safe, securely attached to the floor with some kind of metal banding.

Teffinger wiggled the handle just in case it had been left open, which it hadn't.

At the end of the hall upstairs was another room.

Teffinger went to open the door to find it locked. He hesitated for a second, weighing the pros and cons, and then kicked it open. Inside were piles and piles of boxes.

His heart raced.

This is where the evidence was.

He could feel it.

He opened one of the boxes on the top to find it filled with old comic books. Two more gave him the same. A box on the floor held old LPs from what appeared to be the 1960s: The Byrds, Rolling Stones, Beatles, Bob Dylan, Love, Mamas and Papas, The Flying Burrito Brothers, Terry Knight and the Pack, Beau Brummels, Who, Buffalo Springfield, Herman's Hermits, Phil Oches, Kinks, Paul Revere and the Raiders—

Teffinger didn't despair.

This was the decoy stuff.

Somewhere, buried behind it, were the souvenirs and notes and details and shrines; the stuff that would burn him, once it was found.

This is how Teffinger would have done it.

He could probably tear into it all and find the treasures, but it would leave a mess. It would be better to just leave everything as it was until he could get justification for a search warrant, and then come in and miraculously find it, untouched and pristine.

He headed downstairs.

On the kitchen table was a small notepad he hadn't noticed before. On it was a handwritten phone number with an area code that didn't belong to California.

Teffinger dialed the number.

"Starlite Hotel."

"Yes," Teffinger said. "Has Andrew Kent checked in yet?"

"Let me see—"

"Yes, as of two hours ago. Should I ring him for you?"

"No, that's fine. I just wanted to be sure he made it okay. I'll call him tomorrow when it's not so late. Thanks."

Three minutes later, Teffinger slipped in the Charger, wiped the storm off his face and told Sophia, "Rockwood just checked into a place called the Starlite Hotel. He's travelling under an alias name, Andrew Kent. Hold on a minute . . ." He pulled up Google on his phone and searched for the phone number. It belonged to the Starlite Hotel, in South Beach, Florida. "It's in South Beach."

"Are we going there?"

Teffinger nodded.

"He's there to kidnap someone."

"How do you know that?"

"My gut."

DAY FOURTEEN

May 30
Sunday

79

The Starlite, it turned out, was an artsy four-story art deco hotel on Ocean Drive smack dab in the middle of the buzz. Walk out the front door, weave through the yellow umbrellas and food tables on the sidewalk, cross the street, and you're on the beach. Bodies, young and old, pretty and otherwise, strutted up and down and sideways and round.

Teffinger and Sophia sat in the sand under the shade of a palm and kept an eye on the entrance, like snakes waiting for a rat.

They didn't know if Rockwood was in his room or not.

Probably not.

It was two in the afternoon.

He was out doing something to further his goals.

He wasn't watching cartoons.

Ten minutes later, a yellow taxi pulled to a stop in front of the Starlite and a man stepped out, dressed in jeans, tennis shoes, a baseball cap and a red T-shirt that highlighted a strong, lanky build. Teffinger wasn't sure if he could take the man in a fair fight.

"Is that him?"

"I think so."

He disappeared into the hotel but the taxi didn't drive away.

"He's just stopping for a minute," Teffinger said. "Come

on!"

They trotted to the rental, a white Camry which was parked a good fifty yards away in the wrong direction, and made it back to the hotel just as the taxi was pulling away with Rockwood in the back seat.

The timing couldn't have been better.

"Fate," Teffinger said. "It's smiling on us."

They followed, directly behind in a bumper-to-bumper parade of vehicles, not letting anyone slip in, even though the guy would probably recognize Teffinger if he turned around. Teffinger was the lead detective on both the September Stone case and the Mary-Ann White case. The guy had no doubt followed both investigations closely and seen Teffinger on the news a number of times.

Yeah, he knew who Teffinger was.

He'd closed his eyes in bed and fantasized about what would happen if Teffinger ever showed up to take him down.

He'd felt his fists pounding into Teffinger's face.

He'd seen the blood splatter.

The ride didn't last long. The taxi pulled into a parking lot a mile down the road. Rockwood got out and made his way to a white 4Runner as the taxi pulled away.

Teffinger followed, farther back now with two cars in-between, given that Rockwood had the benefit of a rearview mirror. Rockwood led them west out of South Beach onto the MacArthur Causeway, over the water.

He turned right on Fountain Street, drove across a bridge to Palm Island, and then headed across a second bridge to Hibuscus Island, which was an enclave of multi-million dollar waterfront mansions with impeccable views of both Miami and South Beach.

Teffinger didn't follow him in.

It would be too obvious.

Instead he hung back on Palm Island and waited.

Ten minutes later, Rockwood drove past them, heading back the way he'd come.

They let him get out of eyesight and then picked up the trail.

At the MacArthur Causeway, Rockwood turned right and made his way to a place called South Florida Boat Rentals. There he walked down a dock and into the marina office. Twenty minutes later, he made his way down another dock, fired up a 30-foot go-fast boat and headed out to sea.

80

From the boat rental, Teffinger and Sophia headed back to Hibiscus Island and walked the streets. It was basically a long oval island with ninety or a hundred mansions on the outside, with waterfront footage, and a smaller number on the interior.

One of these had to be Rockwood's target.

Teffinger called Sydney back at homicide.

"Hey," he said. "I need a favor."

"I think I figured out who September knew in San Francisco."

Teffinger remembered now.

September might have been planning to run away.

"Who?"

"Someone named Amber Hunt. They were school buddies. Amber moved to San Francisco."

"With her family?"

"No, on her own. She ran away."

"Well, how was she living?"

"On the streets, apparently."

"Later on that," he said. "Look, the guy who took Mary-Ann White, I'm pretty sure he's down in South Beach right in the middle of his next adventure. I think his target lives on a place called Hibiscus Island, which is off the MacArthur Causeway. Do you know the area?"

"No. Never heard of it."

"Well, no matter. Everyone here is rich, so the target could be anyone. What I need you to do is find out who on the island has kids."

"I suppose I could somehow figure that out—"

"Here's the problem," Teffinger said. "Rockwood has already rented a go-fast boat. I think that's how he's going to get in and out, by boat. I think he's going to strike this afternoon or tonight, probably the latter, but you never know. So time's short."

"Understood. You're going to owe me like crazy."

"Good. Because I'm going to pay like crazy."

"So you say. Hey, Teff, you still there?"

"Yeah."

"Sophia Cruz is with you, right?"

"Yeah."

"Are you falling in love with her?"

He paused.

Then he said, "I don't know. I'll figure it out later."

Almost every mansion with waterfront access had its own private dock. Rockwood could pull up after dark tonight, tie off, snatch his pray from her bed, throw her in the boat, and slip away like a ghost into the darkness of the sea.

Then, what?

Where would he take her?

He might have to keep her for up to ten days.

Where would that be?

"Can you drive a boat?" he asked.

Sophia shook her head

"I can't even swim."

"Okay, then. I think I have a plan, anyway," he said.

"Which is?"

"We're going to rent a boat and hang out on the water after dark. We'll follow Rockwood in. He'll tie up somewhere and head up to the house. When he does, we sneak up to his boat. You're going to disable it while I follow him to the house."

"Disable it, how?"

"It has a key start," he said. "If he leaves the key in the ignition, you pull it out and throw it in the water. If he takes the key with him, you jam a toothpick into the slot and break it off."

She considered it.

"That's great if he comes in by boat," she said. "But what if he comes in by land? He's got that 4Runnner. It's a perfect abduction vehicle. And it's white. There's a million of them."

Between houses, Teffinger cast his eyes out to sea.

"Look," he said, pointing.

Sophia followed his lead.

Way, way off in the distance was a low boat, bobbing. It was hard to tell but it looked like someone was standing up and surveying the island with binoculars.

"That's got to be him," Teffinger said. "I'd give twenty bucks for some binoculars right now."

Sophia smiled.

"They cost a hundred."

"Okay, then. Twenty-five."

81

After dark Sunday night, following hours of down time, Teffinger and Sophia bobbed in the warm waters north of Hibiscus Island in a 22-foot Grady White walkaround, with the bow and anchor lights on, to all intents and purposes just a couple of night fishermen should anyone be curious enough to cast an eye on them.

A stiff wind blew, churning up enough chop to get Sophia good and nervous.

This afternoon, Teffinger's plan sounded good on paper.

Out here in the real world, in the dark and with the water slamming against the hull, it wasn't so pretty.

There were lots of boats out.

It was almost impossible to tell one type of boat from another. They were all just bow lights and anchor lights. If one of them was a go-fast, they couldn't tell.

Worse, from this vantage point, they couldn't see the south side of the island or the waters beyond. Sydney had located over thirty waterfront properties that had kids. They were on both sides of the island and none of them stood out as a better target than any other.

Teffinger fired up the engines.

"We got to get closer," he said. "We'll hug the island and circle around it until Rockwood shows up."

Then he hammered the throttle.

The bow rose up and then slowly leveled off as the vessel

picked up speed and got on plane.

It was a lot harder to see things than he'd anticipated.

There were enough houses lit up to define the perimeter of the island, that wasn't the problem. The problem was that most of the docks were dark. It was hard to tell if a boat was tied up. If Rockwood got past them and got his boat tied up while they were on the other side of the island, they'd never be able to see it.

Teffinger circled around the island still on plane, keeping a couple hundred yards offshore, while Sophia tried to pull it in with binoculars, which was almost impossible given the pitching and twisting of the hull.

A full rotation showed nothing of interest.

He brought the vessel off plane and kept the course.

Then something happened when they came around the north side of the island.

Sophia pointed and said, "Look."

The bow lights of a boat tied to one of the docks had suddenly turned on. Now it was pulling out to sea.

Rockwood?

Have you been doing your dirty work all this time?

The engines were loud, with a through-hull exhaust. It could well be a go-fast, but just as easily it could be nothing more than a throaty sport boat. It sped up, working to get on plane, and then headed due north towards Biscayne Bay, with the bow lights no longer visible and the anchor light being the only marker of its location.

What to do?

Chase it?

Stay here?

Decide!

Now!

"Nick!"

"I know. Hold on!"

He turned the lights off, hammered the throttle and gave chase in the pitch black of the night. It led them up the Intracoastal waterway past Miami Beach, past North Beach, and then through Bal Harbour and finally right, out into the Atlantic Ocean. Then it opened up and headed due east, straight out to sea, now doing at least seventy.

They followed at full throttle.

The anchor light got dimmer and dimmer.

Then it disappeared altogether.

82

Teffinger and Sophia headed back to Hibiscus Island in the event the boat they chased wasn't actually Rockwood at all. They circled around like before and, on the south side, Sophia pointed to a dock and said, "See that boat there? I don't remember it being there before."

Teffinger killed the engines.

Rockwood?

Is that you?

The house was dark.

Over the next few minutes, no lights went on, and the boat didn't move. It didn't seem to be a kidnapping in progress, unless, perhaps, Rockwood was inside, waiting silently in the dark for his targets to return home from wherever they might be. Teffinger fired up the engines, killed the lights and slowly motored in until he was close enough to make out the boat.

It wasn't a go-fast.

Circling back around, the boat they chased earlier hadn't returned to the dock. Teffinger made his way in, tied off and told Sophia, "I'll be right back. Stay here and keep a lookout for Rockwood. If you see him, call me."

"Okay."

"Five minutes."

He cut through the back yard to the rear of the house and

found that the back door wasn't completely closed. It was ajar an inch or two.

His heart raced.

Did Rockwood leave it open to avoid the noise of closing it?

Teffinger silently pushed it open.

No sounds came his way.

The house was quiet.

Having no probable cause to enter, he made his way around the perimeter of the house to the front door, which was a large fancy architectural piece surrounded at the sides and top with glass panels. He silently looked inside and found a large foyer with modern paintings and abstract sculptures. Past that was a massive vaulted living space. In that space was a contemporary white leather sectional couch. On that couch was a girl, a young teenager, maybe thirteen or fourteen, dressed in shorts, a T-shirt and socks. Her shoes were off.

With her was a boy, older, maybe fifteen or sixteen or seventeen. He was nibbling on her neck and feeling her up with his right hand under her shirt.

Teffinger knocked on the door.

The two teens jumped.

The look on the girl's face was pure fear that someone had seen her. Teffinger understood it only too well. He'd been young once himself.

The girl made her way to the door and pressed an intercom.

"Who's there?"

"Police," Teffinger said.

The girl's face appeared in the glass. Teffinger showed her his badge and flashed his best smile.

The door opened.

"There have been reports of some suspicious activities in the neighborhood," he said. "I'm just checking to be sure if everything's alright."

Relief flooded over the girl's face.

"Yeah—"

"Everything's okay?"

"Yes. Perfect."

"Is there anyone else in the house besides you?"

"Well, my boyfriend, he's not supposed to be here, but he is. I'm just babysitting. I don't live here."

"Where are the owners?"

"At some event. They'll be back around eleven."

Teffinger nodded.

"Okay, fine." He smiled and added, "Can you do me one small favor, and then I'll be out of your hair. Who are you babysitting, again?"

"Revy."

"Revy," he said. "Can you just check on her real quick and made sure she's alright. Then I'll be out of here."

"She's upstairs sleeping."

"If you could just double-check, that would be great," Teffinger said.

"Are you serious?"

He nodded.

"Don't worry. I won't ever tell anyone that your boyfriend's over. I did the same thing when I was a kid. Just check real fast on Revy. Then I'll go."

She hesitated.

Then she said, "Wait here," and closed the door.

Thirty seconds she swung the door open.

Panic gripped her face.

"She's not there!"

"Call 911!" The girl stood there, frozen. "Do it!"

Suddenly Teffinger's phone rang. The number was unknown but he answered anyway.

"Detective Teffinger," a voice said. "My name is Lance Rockwood. I think it's time we should meet."

Lance Rockwood!

Teffinger pulled to the side.

"Sounds good."

"Are you available now by any chance?"

"Yes I am."

"That's good," Rockwood said. "Get in your boat and head north. Go the same way you did before . . . that was you chasing me, I assume?"

"Yes."

"I thought so. Head out into the ocean directly east for a mile or so and then kill the engines and wait. Bring the woman with you."

"Sure. No problem."

"And leave your guns behind. We're only going to talk. We're not going to try to kill each other. If you try to take me in, bad things will happen to good people, if you catch my drift. You'll be making a mistake that you'll never be able to recover from."

"I'm on my way."

83

Teffinger did exactly as instructed, bobbing at the appointed location with his lights on and the engines off and the wind blowing. A half hour passed. Rockwood, no doubt, was making sure there were no police boats or helicopters lurking around. Then the go-fast was suddenly there, materializing from out of darkness with its lights off.

A flashlight shined in Teffinger's eyes.

"Take your shirt off and show me your hands," Rockwood shouted.

Teffinger hesitated.

Then he complied.

"Turn around."

"No gun, no wires," he said. "It's just me. Like you said."

The flashlight pointed at Sophia.

"Your turn."

She pulled her T-shirt over her head.

"All of it."

She unclasped her bra, slid it off and tossed it on the floor of the boat. Then she raised her hands and turned around.

"Okay. Jump aboard. Both of you."

They did it, finding the go-fast bigger and more stable than the Grady. They took a seat on the transom pad, once again showed they had nothing in their hands, and Teffinger said, "Your show."

Rockwood briefly flashed a gun.

"I know, I know, I'm cheating," he said. "I'm not going to use it unless you make me."

"That's fine," Teffinger said. "We only came to talk."

Rockwood stayed up by the windshield, far enough away that he'd have plenty of time to pull a trigger if Teffinger or the woman got stupid enough to make a move.

"Let's talk about a deal," Rockwood said.

Teffinger nodded.

"Sure."

"Right now at this moment, Revy's a hundred percent safe and well."

"How old is she? I've never even seen her."

"Four."

"She's just a baby."

"All her needs are being attended to."

"So, what, you have someone helping you?"

"Always," he said. "But that's not important. What I want to know is, how'd you come onto me? I'm guessing it was Grace Springfield."

He paused.

The silence grew.

Teffinger knew that Rockwood knew that he was struggling to find a good way to deny it but was unable to find the perfect lie.

"That's okay," Rockwood said. "You don't have to affirm it out loud. That's very disappointing, though. A client's supposed to be able to count on the silence of his lawyer." He paused and added, "Thank you for giving me that. I want one more thing. Then I'm going to give you something that I'm sure you'll appreciate."

"Go on," Teffinger said.

"I want you to stay out of the Revy case. I don't want you to tell anyone about me. I don't want you to tell anyone I'm staying at the Starlite. I don't want you to tell anyone that I rented this little go-fast here. I don't want you to tell anyone you chased me. I don't want you to tell anyone about this little meeting we're having. I don't want you to tell anybody anything. I want you to get out of town. I don't want you talking to the Miami police."

Teffinger cocked his head.

"That's a pretty tall order."

"It's even taller, what you're getting in return."

"Which is what, exactly?"

"Two things," Rockwood said. "If you do what I'm asking, you get my promise that no harm will come to Revy. I'm going to try to negotiate for a ransom. But whether I get something or not, I'll return her after ten days. I won't sell her. I won't harm her. She'll be absolutely fine, and it will be because of you; because of the deal we're making right here, right now. You're saving her, that's what it comes down to."

"What else?"

"Mary-Ann White," Rockwood said. "I'll tell you where she is."

"Is she alive?"

"As far as I know."

"What I'm looking for is a ten-day head start," Rockwood said. "What I want to do is finish my negotiations over Revy. Once that's over, you can come after me, Miami can come after me, and all the rest. All's fair at that point. In exchange for those ten days, you get my promise that I won't hurt Revy, win lose or draw on the negotiations. I'll return her safe and unharmed. You also get the location of Mary-Ann

White." He exhaled and added, "That's the deal. Pretty simple, actually. Be warned, though. If you make this deal, you better not breach it. There will be dire consequences, personal and otherwise."

Teffinger chewed on it.

He'd get Revy back.

He'd get Mary-Ann White back.

He could still hunt Rockwood; he'd just have to wait ten days.

Sure, Rockwood would be able to wipe the San Francisco house clean in the meantime, but there was enough external evidence at this point—including this conversation—to put him away for life.

"Here's the problem, even assuming you're not lying," Teffinger said. "You're going to be negotiating for ten days. Miami's going to be trying to catch you."

"Agreed."

"They might succeed," he said. "They might kill you in the process. If you die, how do you return Revy?"

"My associate does it," Rockwood said.

Teffinger frowned.

"I need more than that," he said. "I need to know where Mary-Ann White is. I need to know where to find her in case you die."

Rockwood considered it.

"If I agree, do we have a deal?"

Teffinger worked it over one more time.

Leave town.

Don't help the Miami cops.

No action for ten days.

Revy comes back.

Mary-Ann White comes back.

He can then hunt Rockwood to the ends of the earth.

"Yes," he said.

"You're positive?"

"Yes."

"Okay, Rockwood said. "Here we go. I sold Mary-Ann White to a man named Emmanuel Dieudonne-Cyr, who operates a cartel in Haiti. He, in turn, sold her to a woman in El Salvador named Luciana Serrano. She's the queen of child pornography. If you can get into the dark web, you'll probably be able to find pictures of Mary-Ann if you look hard enough."

Teffinger's gut clenched.

It was all he could do to not beat Rockwood to death with his fists right then and there.

He tried to stay focused.

"What about Revy?"

"Like I said before, she'll be returned either by me or my associate," Rockwood said. "What you would do to locate her if you absolutely had to, you'd go to Nassau. There's a backroads bar there called the Rolling Coconut. Talk to a guy named Ajay. Give him the code word, Witch Dog. He'll take you to her. You can't do any of that, though, unless I'm dead. That's the deal."

Teffinger nodded.

"I'll see you around at some point."

"Back at you."

84

When Rockwood pulled away in the go-fast, instead of firing up the Grady White, Teffinger called Alabama out there in the dark choppy seas as Sophia slipped back into her clothes.

"Here's the deal," he said. "Jori-Ray is innocent. She didn't kill September. A guy from San Francisco by the name of Lance Rockwood did it."

"How do you know that?"

"It's complicated, but it's a hundred percent true. Rockwood was in the house to kidnap September when Jori-Ray showed up. He killed September after Jori-Ray got knocked out. I have a ton of evidence but unfortunately right now all of it's inadmissible. Jori-Ray's freedom is coming but it won't be here by tomorrow. I need a little more time."

"How much?"

"At least ten days," he said. "Between ten and thirty days is my best guess. What I need you to do is call Janjak and get an extension for me. I don't want her hurting Kimona."

Silence.

"She'll never go for it."

"Try," Teffinger said. "Call her right now. I don't care if you're waking her up."

"You're certain about this guy, Lance Rockwood?"

"Yes. He kidnaps kids and shakes the parents down for ransom. He was in the house to kidnap September and then shake the mom, Catherine, down. He's done it a whole lot of times, all over the country. All the cases are well documented. Now that we know who he is, we'll be able to go back and tie him to them."

"This isn't a trick to bide time or anything like that, is it?"

"Alabama, trust me. Jori-Ray's going to be free but I can't get it done by tomorrow."

The woman exhaled.

"Okay. I'll call her but this better be real or she'll take us both down."

"It's real. Thank you."

85

It was late by the time they got back to the hotel, but Teffinger was wound up tighter than a roll of barbed wire, plus there was no reason to get up early—he wasn't going to be talking to Miami P.D., and his plane for Haiti wasn't scheduled to leave until noon. So he bought a bottle of wine at an all-night liquor store and took Sophia down to the beach where they sat on hotel towels just feet from the lapping waters.

It was dark.

The moon was just a sliver.

The stars were hardly there.

Their bodies were close but not touching.

Teffinger took a swallow of wine, passed the bottle to Sophia, and said, "It's going to be tough not helping Miami. There's no legal obligation, though. It's not our case. It's not in our jurisdiction. Here's the really tough part, though. They're probably going to think that I'm the kidnapper, being at the property right when everything was happening, pretending to be a cop, and then mysteriously disappearing. If the girl's any good at all at facial recognition, there well may be a composite sketch of my face in the morning paper."

"What about physical evidence?"

Teffinger shook his head.

"I don't think I left any," he said. "The back door was

slightly open and I pushed it in, but I used my knuckles. When I knocked on the front door, again, it was with my knuckles. I didn't see any security cameras. If it's true that there weren't any, then there's no way they can physically tie me to the scene. All they have is what the girl saw and what we said to each other."

"You showed her your badge, right?"

"Yeah."

"Maybe she saw Denver."

"Let's hope not."

Sophia took a swallow of wine.

She said, "I know we're under no obligation to help Miami, but what I'm worried about is whether it's legal, you know, making a deal with a criminal, one that actually helps him get away with his crime— Are we aiding and abetting, or conspiring, or something?"

"Maybe, to a point," he said "But the bottom line is Mary-Ann White. If what Rockwood said about her is true, we would have never found that out on our own. Not in a hundred years."

Sophia nodded.

"I want you to head up her rescue," Teffinger added. "This will be your move up and you deserve it. I want you to go back to Denver tomorrow and start immediately. Call Leigh Sandt with the FBI. She knows people at the CIA. She'll know how to get it rolling. Don't let anyone wrestle it away from you though. Be there on the ground when it all goes down. I want it to be you who personally delivers the girl back to her mom."

"What about you?"

"I'm going to Haiti tomorrow."

"Even if Janjak gives you an extension?"

"Yes."

"Why?"

"I need to get Kimona out of there."

Sophia got quiet.

Then she pushed him backwards and straddled his chest.

She pulled her shirt off, then her bra, and said, "Forget Kimona."

Suddenly his phone rang.

Sophia wiggled.

"Don't!"

"It's probably Alabama."

He answered to find out he was right.

"Bad news, Nick. Tomorrow's the deadline and it's not going to change. Everything's going forward at midnight. Janjak told me to give you a warning."

"Which is what?"

"Don't come to Haiti. Don't try to stop it. If you do, she'll kill you."

Teffinger pictured it.

"That fucking bitch."

"There's more, Nick. Remember I told you about Janjak's guy that went out for groceries and never came back?"

He remembered.

"Yeah."

"His head showed up in a box."

"The cartel?"

"Yes. Things are ratcheting up like crazy. They sent ten men in a boat to burn Janjak to the ground. They almost made it. They weren't any more than a couple of hundred yards from the beach when Janjak spotted them. She poisoned their brains and made them all chop each other to death. When the boat crashed into shore, there wasn't a single one of them alive. Janjak personally cut off all of their heads with her own two hands and then had her men turn the boat around and point it out to sea. Some fishermen came across it more than five miles out. Everyone's talking about it as if it's the plague from hell. The whole island is like a terrified little kid cowering in the corner."

Teffinger processed it.

"It sounds like she's too busy to kill me."

Alabama grunted.

"Don't fuck with her, Nick. You'll regret it."

DAY FIFTEEN

May 31
Monday

86

Monday morning, the disappearance of four-year-old Revy Hutton dominated the front-page of the Miami Herald. The girl's father was Owen Hutton, a real estate tycoon who had developed a large portion of Brickell, Miami's famed financial district, also known as Wall Street South. The child disappeared from her bed while Owen Hunter, and his wife Jovanna, were at a fundraising event for Kids Advantage. A babysitter was home at the time. Police are pursuing every measure to locate the child. They would like to talk to a person of interest shown in the sketch below. If you know who this person is please contact them immediately.

A composite sketch accompanied the article.

It had some semblance to Teffinger but not enough to worry about. He'd be able to board his plane later without interference.

A photo of the parents, Owen and Jovanna Hutton, also accompanied the article. The man was about forty-five, with a seasoned boardroom face that looked like it could cut through anything. The woman was much younger, closer to thirty, with kind eyes and an easy smile.

Right now, those eyes were filled with terror and tears.

Teffinger knew that.

He could feel the weight.

It was consuming enough that he thought briefly about

heading to Nassau and getting the girl back.

He swallowed it down.

If he broke the deal, Rockwood would know, immediately; Ajay would inform him. He might well place a call to the woman who had Mary-Ann White. She'd be killed within the hour. All traces of her would be erased. Her body would never be found.

In the bathroom, the running shower shut off.

Two minutes later the door opened and Sophia stepped out with a towel wrapped around her body and a mischievous look on her face.

She had no makeup.

Her hair was wet.

Her beauty shook Teffinger to the core.

It was as if he'd never really looked at her before. This was something he was seeing for the first time.

"What's that look?" she said.

"Nothing."

"Good. I've been waiting for nothing."

She dropped the towel to the floor.

Then she walked slowly towards him.

87

On the flight to Haiti, Teffinger used the time to do a little research on the Dieudonne-Cyr cartel. The big news was from yesterday, when ten people believed to be associated with the cartel were found chopped to death and beheaded in a boat. A photo of the cartel's leader, Emmanuel Dieudonne-Cyr, aka Fou Reken, "Crazy Shark," accompanied the article, although he was not one of the victims.

He was older, maybe fifty, but taut with muscles.

Tattoos covered his arms and chest.

His face was rough.

His eyes were black holes.

A red teardrop tattoo dripped from the left one.

In the photo, the man was standing between two other men. He towered over them. Teffinger recognized the guy on the right as one of the three guys who had come to Denver. He was the one who had a gun to Sophia's head. He was the one Teffinger shot in the face. Given his height, Teffinger calculated Crazy Shark to be six-five, maybe more.

He swallowed.

The man knew who Teffinger was.

There was no shortage of photos of Teffinger on the web, including the one on cover of GQ. That was a lot of material to use to memorize Teffinger's face.

Hopefully the man was fully focused on Janjak.

Still, Teffinger needed to be careful.

The man might know about the ritual tonight.

He might suspect Teffinger to show up.

He might be on the lookout for him.

Shortly after 1:00, Teffinger's flight landed at Port-au-Prince International Airport. There he bought binoculars, a flashlight, a baseball cap, a Haiti T-shirt, and stuffed them inside a newly purchased backpack, together with a few essentials such as extra clothes, toothbrush, and the like. The rest of his stuff, including his suitcase, went into the trash container in the Men's room.

Then he rented a motorcycle with the biggest engine in stock, a six-year-old Harley-Davidson Roadster, from the same place as before. It was battered and worn and spit gray smoke but it fired right up. Teffinger checked it three times just to be sure.

"If you get in an accident, you're automatically at fault," the skinny guy with white teeth and sloped shoulders told him.

"Why?"

"Because you're a foreigner. The police will take you in. What you need to do is give them money, so be sure you have some with you. Oh, I almost forgot. We're out of helmets."

Teffinger grunted.

"No worries."

He pulled five twenties out of his wallet and handed them to the guy.

"You never saw me," he said.

The man shoved the bills in his jeans.

Then he put a serious look on his face and said, "Be careful. There's craziness going on."

Teffinger said, "I will," and almost took off. Instead he said, "Hey, you don't have a knife you'd like to sell me, do you."

The man raised his eyebrow.

Then he cast an eye to see if anyone was around.

No one was.

They were alone out in the yard.

He sized Teffinger up and said, "Are you sure that's all you want? I have other stuff, too."

88

Teffinger suspected that Janjak would have brought Kimona back to the grounds by now to be sure there were no complications going into tonight. He rented a Boston Whaler from the same marina as before, left the Harley in the parking lot, and motored down the coast. A mile offshore he killed the engines, stayed low in the boat and pulled in Janjak's lair with binoculars.

Men were swarming all around.

There had to be at least twenty-five of them; and those were just the obvious ones he could see.

A number of strategically placed sentinels silently guarded the perimeter with rifles.

The sight hit him like an uppercut.

How was he supposed to get through all that?

He laid down on his back on the floor of the boat next to the backpack and closed his eyes. The sun tried to burn through his eyelids but couldn't quite do it.

He could feel Kimona.

She wasn't far away.

She was at Janjak's.

There was no question about it.

Alabama's words twisted in his brain. "Don't fuck with her, Nick. You'll regret it."

He had to admit, he didn't understand Janjak's powers. They always seemed to be shifting. She'd poisoned the minds of the cartel men who were coming to burn her down. She'd somehow made them chop each other to death. But, if that was true, why hadn't she used those powers against Axel Chard when he came for Jori-Ray? For that matter, why hadn't she used them against him and Kimona when she was chasing them out there in the ocean?

Were those powers not available then?

Were they still in an infancy stage, charging up?

Or maybe they were something in the nature of a bee's sting; something she could use at her discretion, but only once in her lifetime, something to be jealously held in reserve until there was absolutely no other option.

He didn't understand it.

He never would.

Right now, at this minute, he didn't know what weapons or curses or voodoo tricks the woman had against him. Maybe she sensed his presence but maybe she didn't.

He pulled the place in again with the binoculars.

To his horror, three boats were heading directly at him.

Janjak was at the wheel of one of them.

Teffinger fired up the engines as fast as he could and then punched the throttles.

The vessel sprang up to plane almost immediately and took off like a fire-charged banshee.

Shots fired behind him.

Up ahead there was no traffic.

He got down on the floor, faced backwards and steered with one hand at the bottom on the wheel, heading directly out to sea while his body jarred and bucked wildly from the slamming of the hull against the waves.

89

Teffinger's boat hit something, hard—possibly a submersed log—slamming his body into the console and filling the cockpit with rushing water. The engines still raced at full throttle, forcing the bow under the water. He pulled them back into neutral and frantically focused on the damage, which was extensive. Most of the bow was gone. A massive jagged hole had been ripped open under the waterline. The boat wouldn't sink—the hull was filled with flotation foam—but it wasn't going anywhere, either.

The three boats were closing in fast.

He killed the engines and waited.

Alabama's words ricocheted in his head. "Don't fuck with her, Nick."

He kicked the gunnel.

Fuck!

He couldn't believe he was out of it, just like that. At a minimum, he pictured himself sneaking up after dark and reeking havoc. And now, here he was, immediately spotted and at Janjak's mercy. It was like training for a fight for six months and then getting knocked out in the first ten seconds.

Janjak circled around him.

As always, she wore no top.

All she had on was a white wraparound skirt.

One of her men stood by her side, pointing a rifle at Teffinger's chest. All Janjak had to do was say the word.

Teffinger said nothing.

He wasn't about to beg.

Screw that.

The only thing he had left at this point was going down like a man.

He studied Janjak's face but couldn't read it.

It was as if she was swinging back and forth, conflicted about whether to kill him or not.

Suddenly she told her man, "Come back in two hours."

Then she dived over the side of the boat and splashed into the water.

The man hesitated and waited for her to surface, not wanting to abandon her unless he'd absolutely heard the orders correctly.

"Go!" Janjak shouted. "Come back in two hours!"

Then the boats were gone.

In the water, Janjak wiggled out of her skirt and tossed it up into Teffinger's boat where it landed on the backpack.

"Come in," she said. "It's warm."

"So what is this?" he said. "A dying man's last meal?"

Janjak splashed water at him.

"You love me," she said.

The words were a sudden drug in his blood. He knew he could fight them but it would do no good. They were already fogging his brain.

He took off his clothes and dived in.

90

Under the golden Caribbean sun, Teffinger found himself playing in the sparkling aqua waters with Janjak, feeling her body brush against his, letting his hands run over her skin, and anticipating with increasing urgency what would inevitably soon follow.

The water was warm.

The sky was endless.

Land was just a sliver on the horizon far, far in the distance. They were the only two people left in the universe. He knew it wasn't real but he also knew that if he could make this moment last forever, he would.

Screw the rest of the world.

Screw Denver.

Screw work.

Screw everything.

He was addicted to the moment. It might eventually kill him but he didn't care. Whatever happened next, this was worth it. Janjak was a drug and she'd injected herself into his blood.

They made love in the bottom of the boat.

They made it slowly.

They made it tenderly.

They put their entire souls into it.

Then they laid on their backs and stared up at the sky, laughing, and amazed at what they'd just been able to do.

Teffinger closed his eyes.

The darkness felt like a desert oasis.

When he opened them again, Janjak was gone and he was still in the boat, alone.

91

Time passed, lots of it.

Teffinger bobbed alone out in the ocean with his eyes cast on the distant shore.

Janjak was still in his blood but not as strong as before. She was no longer the entire universe. Now there were other people, including Kimona, and including Sophia.

Sophia.

She'd come onto him a number of times. So far, he'd deflected her every time, although it had been anything but easy. He owed it to Kimona to stay strong enough to do that, though. He owned her more time. He owed her the right to get back to where they were before they'd been interrupted. He owed her the opportunity to dig deeper into his heart, if that's what she still wanted to do. He was pretty sure she was the one. Their time had been short, though. He could be wrong. If he was, he knew where his destiny lay.

Sophia.

She made sense on almost every level.

All that assumed, of course, that he would still be alive. Of that, he wasn't sure. He couldn't figure out what Janjak's intentions were.

She might have left him out here to die.

Or, she might just be keeping him out here in a watery prison, until the ritual tonight was over. Then she might come back for him.

He didn't know.

He could think about it for a million years and he still wouldn't know.

Suddenly a sound came from behind him.

It was a small dingy, approaching from behind, steered by a man with his hand on the handle of an outboard motor. Quite a ways beyond it was a yacht. It didn't look like it was moving and could possibly be at anchor.

"Are you okay, mate?"

He was about thirty, dressed in a Guns N Roses T-shirt and beige board shorts. He looked a little like a pirate, deeply tanned, with long black hair pulled back into a ponytail and a wide, toothy grin.

Teffinger waved.

"You don't have a spare bow with you by any chance, do you? Mine got eaten by a log or a whale or something."

The pirate surveyed the damage.

"Wow. That's not going to buff out—"

Teffinger smiled.

"No. I don't think so."

Then the pirate motioned Teffinger over.

"Well, come on, mate. Jump aboard."

92

The pirate turned out to be New York photographer by the of Porter Zane, in the midst of a cover shoot for Rolling Stone magazine featuring a pop singer named Likki Lix, who Teffinger had never heard of but liked a lot when he met her, partly because she knew every Beatles song and wasn't afraid to sing them to him, but mostly because she reminded him of a squeeze named Lulu Blanche who sat next to him in Calculus back in his freshman year at CSU.

"We have something in common," Likki said. "Or will, soon."

"And what might that be?"

"Both on the cover of a magazine," she said. "You were on GQ. Am I right?"

He shrugged.

"That was just a weird street shoot that I stumbled into," he said. "It was a one-off."

She turned to the photographer and said, "Porter."

"Yeah."

"Get some photos of me and Nick, will you?"

"What'd you have in mind?"

"I'm going to take my top off. He'll be behind me, wrapping his arms around and covering my tits with his hands."

Porter frowned.

"That's been done."

"I know but I've always wanted to do it."

"He's older, too."

"Yeah, I know. That's the point. People of different ages should be allowed to be together if they want. Come on, please? He's pretty enough, don't you think? Plus, people will be freaking out trying to figure out who he is."

The man looked at Teffinger.

"No pay," he said. "And you'll have to sign a release."

Teffinger shrugged.

"It's the least I can do. And that's what I always do."

One pose led to another, and the shoot ended up taking a whole lot longer than Teffinger thought. He didn't care though, because they filled him up with food and drink, plus he pretty much needed to stay off the grid until after at least twilight in any event. One of the yacht's engines was down and the crew was working on it, meaning they couldn't take him to shore.

Since he was such a good sport about the shoot, though, they gave him the dingy plus an extra can of gas, which should be enough to get him to where he needed to go. All he had to do was promise to call Porter later and figure out a way to return it, if possible.

To be honest, they weren't too worried about it either way.

They could write it off as an expense.

Shortly after dark, after a long bumpy hour, Teffinger arrived at beach a mile or so west of Janjak's lair. He dragged the dingy into the palms where it was good and hidden.

Then he set off on foot in Janjak's direction.

93

Teffinger made his way ever closer to Janjak's lair, not walking by the edge of the surf, but staying farther back in the shadows of the palms. He had no plan, other than to try to get eyeballs on the place and see if he could come up with a plan. A mere three hundred yards away, he spotted a figure walking in his direction down at the water's edge.

He slipped behind a palm and held his breath.

The figure was nothing more than a black silhouette but Teffinger already knew it was one of Janjak's men, no doubt with instructions to shoot on sight.

He silently slipped the knife out of his backpack.

The steel was warm in his hand.

As the silhouette got closer, it began to take the shape of a female. Long hair was now visible, together with rounded hips. Whoever it was, she almost got to where he was, then sat down on the sand and leaned back on her elbows. Teffinger made sure she was alone and then quietly approached from behind.

Before he knew it, he was there.

In a quick motion, he slipped to her side and sat down on the sand next to her.

She jumped.

A noise came from her mouth, not exactly a word, more in the nature of some kind of startled utterance. Teffinger recognized that voice.

"Jori-Ray!"

The woman stared at him.

"Nick? Is that you?"

"Yes!"

She hugged him.

He said, "Where's Kimona? Is she here?"

"She's still off-site."

"Is the ritual still going forward?"

"Yes. But there's more. Janjak's at war with the Dieudonne-Cyr cartel. She's going to chop off the crazy shark's head tonight."

"You mean Emmanuel Dieudonne-Cyr?"

"Yes. Fou Reken. He's personally coming for her sometime tonight."

"How do you know?"

"She told me."

"Well how does she know?"

"I don't know. Maybe she invited him. Maybe she cursed him. Who knows? She's going to kill him with her own bare hands."

Teffinger pictured it.

The Crazy Shark was six-five.

Janjak was five-three.

"There's no way," he said.

"She thinks otherwise. The only thing certain is that one of them will be dead by dawn."

Teffinger exhaled.

"How's Kimona? Have you talked to her or heard anything about her?"

"No. The last I heard, Janjak had her off-site somewhere in something like a comatose spell." She held Teffinger's hand. "If that's true, she'll be weak as a baby. She won't even be close to having strength enough to deal with it. Between you and me, I think Janjak knows that all too well. She doesn't want Kimona to survive. She's setting an example."

"Has Kimona even agreed to the ritual?"

"I don't know. If she hasn't, Janjak will simply kill her. Well, I shouldn't say simply. It will be something horrific. The ritual will still go on though. She'll just pull somebody else into it at the last second."

"You?"

She shrugged.

"You never know with Janjak. I'm more than a little worried about it, if you want to know the truth. Nick, you should get out of here. There's no way you can stop it. She has men running around all over the place. Two hours from now, this whole place is going to be batshit crazy." She stood up and added, "I have to get back."

He pulled on her hand before she got away.

"Hold on," he said. "I found out the truth about September."

She hesitated.

"What'd you find?"

"There was another person in the house that night, a guy from San Francisco named Lance Rockwood. He was there to abduct September and shake down the parents for ransom. Things went a little wrong, then you interrupted everything, then September and this guy ended up struggling while you were passed out, and the gun ended up going off, and she was dead. He took off to leave you holding the bag."

Her hands shook.

Then she pulled away.

"That's good to know and I appreciate you getting to the bottom of it but it's the last thing on my mind right now, to tell you the truth. I have to get back. Nick, get out of here. Save yourself while you still can."

She disappeared into the darkness.

94

An hour passed, and then things began to get real crazy, real fast. Bodies appeared from out of the darkness like ghosts, lots and lots and lots of bodies, both men and women, all topless, all with demonic markings and exaggerated motions.

It felt like an uprising of bloodthirsty souls from hell.

This was no ordinary ritual.

This was something big, something that only came around once in a long time. Teffinger understood now why Janjak couldn't postpone it.

She wasn't in control.

No one was, except maybe the devil himself.

Torches swung wildly.

And then the drums began to pound, at first, unorganized, and then slowly melting together in a syncopated rhythm until they sounded as if they were coming from one fiendish hand.

A circle of torches lit up.

Inside were two vertical poles.

Four men walked into the light, carrying a struggling naked woman above their heads.

It was Kimona!

They roped her wrists and ankles to the poles until she was stretched tight in a standing spread-eagle position. Then the bodies circled around her in a frenzied dance.

The drums beat louder and faster.

Kimona pulled wildly at her bonds.

Suddenly a woman stepped into the circle and everything froze.

It was Janjak.

She was naked.

All movement stopped.

The drums died.

Everything got eerily quiet.

No one said a word.

Janjak circled slowly around the tied woman. She had something in her hand but it wasn't clear what. A snake? A machete?

Then she snapped it into the air.

It was a whip.

Kimona pleaded with sobbing incoherent words.

Janjak continued to circle.

Then she slashed the whip across the woman's back.

Kimona screamed and twisted wildly against her bonds.

A line of blood dripped down her back.

A third person entered the circle. It was a man. Janjak handed him the whip. Then she got behind Kimona and spread her legs and arms out behind the woman as if protecting her.

The man circled.

Once.

Then again.

Then yet again.

Then he lashed her.

Janjak screamed and her body twitched.

Blood dripped down her back.

The man pulled his arm back and swung the whip at her

again, with all his might.

The sound was like insanity itself.

She dropped to the sand and curled up in a ball. Then, slowly, she pulled her body back up and retook her position behind Kimona.

The man lashed her again, even harder if that was possible.

She dropped down hard to the earth and didn't get up.

Then the whole world suddenly erupted.

The drums pounded with a horrific tempo and the bodies circled around in a wild possessed dance.

95

With each second another eternity, Teffinger waited in the shadows for his chance. Kimona hung limp, either unconscious or dead. Janjak was still splayed out on the sand where she'd fallen, unmoving.

Nothing stopped.

The drums continued to beat.

The bodies continued to gyrate.

The torches continued to flash.

It went on and on and on and on, deeper and deeper into the night, as if locked in time and destined to keep beating, like a live heart, until something rose up and stabbed it.

An hour passed.

Maybe more.

Then Janjak's body moved, slow and uncertain at first, almost as if pulling itself out of the depths of hell. She got to all fours, the then to her knees. She stayed there for a few moments, gathering her strength, and then struggled up to her feet.

To Teffinger's shock, the woman turned directly towards him.

There was no way she could see him.

He was way off the grid, back in the palms.

Still, his heart pounded.

The woman's right arm rose and pointed a finger directly

at him.

A dozen or more men immediately charged in his direction.

He ran.

He was fast.

He lost them twice.

Then a pain shot into his back.

He knew what it was—a blow dart.

He fell to the ground, twisted his arm back to the breaking point and tried to pull it out.

It was way back by his spine where he couldn't reach it no matter how much he struggled.

His brain fogged.

Then everything turned black.

96

Teffinger awoke to find himself in the middle of absolute chaos. He was on his back, staked out spread-eagle in the sand. Janjak was on top on him, straddling his chest as would a lover. A large circle of people surrounded them, but they were back quite a ways, a hundred feet or more in all directions. They swayed back and forth trance-like to the beating of the drums.

Janjak leaned down and whispered in his ear.

"You love me."

He tugged wildly at the ropes.

They dug tight and raw into his wrists.

They had him good.

He wasn't going anywhere.

Janjak rocked her body back and forth sensually on top of him. She licked his face and said, "You love me. Say it."

"No!"

"You love me."

"Fuck! You know I do."

"Say it."

He tried to resist.

He couldn't.

"I love you."

"You'll always love me," she said. "And I'll always love you."

She raised her arms up over her head. To Teffinger's horror, she had a machete in each of her hands. At any second she'd swing one of them down into his skull.

He twisted frantically.

Suddenly the woman stood up.

It was then that Teffinger noticed he wasn't alone. Another man was staked out right next to him. He was bigger. His arms and chest were filled with tattoos. The flaming of the torches brought his face in and out of focus. He looked familiar. Then Teffinger recognized him.

He was Emmanuel Dieudonne-Cyr.

He was the Crazy Shark.

He was the sick fuck who bought Mary-Ann White from Lance Rockwood. He was the one who resold the girl into child pornography.

Janjak dropped to her knees between the two men.

She raised the machetes up high over her head.

Then she slammed them down.

The rope on Teffinger's left wrist cut apart.

He immediately pulled his arm down.

Janjak tossed a machete on his chest.

He grabbed it and frantically started to cut himself loose. Then he realized that the other man was doing the same.

They got to their feet at the same time.

With weapons in hand, they squared off, circling each other, as the voices around them screamed and people started throwing torches at them.

Then the other man lunged forward with the speed of a viper and swung the blade at Teffinger's face. He pulled back but not fast enough. The tip of the blade sliced into his cheek.

Blood came.

Lots of it.

He wiped it with the back of his hand and was aghast at

how much there was.

A torch suddenly slammed into his back, almost knocking him down before it dropped to the sand.

He grabbed it and swung it with all his might as the other man charged again, catching him squarely on the side of his head. The man fell to the ground, damaged but clearly not dead. He began to muscle back up to his feet. His hair suddenly burst into flames. He swiped at it desperately but it did no good. The fire only got bigger and hotter and deadlier. He fell to the ground and flailed his head wildly in a last-ditch effort, all the while screaming with insanity. Then he stopped moving and just laid there, burning.

Teffinger watched him for a few seconds.

Fifty or more people were breaking from the ring now and heading for boats.

They were cartel men.

Janjak's men let them pass.

The war was over.

Teffinger cast his eyes around until he spotted Kimona, about fifty yards away, hanging limply from the poles like yesterday's laundry and no one paying any attention to her.

He headed in that direction.

Suddenly Janjak was in front of him, blocking his way.

"Take her," she said. "Take her now. Take her and get the hell out of here and don't ever come back."

He looked at her.

Then he said, "You love me."

She nodded.

"It's my curse."

He kissed her.

Then he headed for Kimona.

THREE MONTHS LATER

97

Teffinger and Kimona grabbed gas and chips in Glenwood Springs, then headed even farther west on I-70, ever closer to Moab, where they had a motel waiting and mountain bikes already reserved. The Colorado terrain lost its mountain edge, turning more arid and hilly. The traffic fell off considerably and the eighteen-wheelers began to outnumber the cars. A severe thunderhead was building up in the north, twenty miles away, maybe farther, looking like it would spit lightning any second. The sky overhead, by contrast, was bright blue and dotted with solid, white, cotton-ball clouds, seriously stunning.

Teffinger felt good.

Kimona was at his side.

The Tundra wasn't breaking down.

A string of cases was behind him.

No one had tried to kill him recently.

And vice versa.

They were at a point in the road where they could only get three stations on the radio, all country. Kimona had never really listened to country before. "Three chords and the truth," Teffinger said. "That's what it is."

"And pickup trucks."

He smiled.

"True. You got to have them in there somewhere."

"And cheating hearts."

"Even truer."

The Colorado River appeared on their right, running wide and brown and powerful, escorting them into Grand Junction. The interstate and the river funneled into a canyon and rubbed against each other like lovers. The road tightened and twisted and the speed limit dropped. When they were just a few miles from the first exit into town, Teffinger pulled over next to the river and killed the engine.

"Come on," he said.

They stretched their legs and skipped rocks into the rapids.

It had been three months since they'd left Haiti.

A lot had happened.

Lance Rockwood succeeded in his ransom attempt with Revy, miraculously netting five million dollars and, true to his word, dropping the girl off alive and well back in Miami. He'd also used the ten days head start to wipe his entire world, including his San Francisco house, free of any and all evidence of crimes. He dropped off the face of the earth and Teffinger never could get a handle on where he went. Then the man got greedy. He snuck into Grace Springfield's house one dark rainy night last month to kill her.

She got him first.

End of Lance Rockwood.

Mary-Ann White was right where Lance Rockwood said she'd be. Sophia Cruz coordinated the rescue effort, which not only saved Mary-Ann, but more than fifty other exploited kids. She was reunited with her mother, Katrina, and the two of them moved to Park City, Utah, in search of a quieter life and a new beginning.

Jori-Ray Rose didn't kill September Stone, but getting her freed was a serious project. Lance Rockwood had destroyed all his files and documents, assuming he had them, which Teffinger didn't doubt for a second. The guy was a souvenir collector. Teffinger was responsible for that since he gave the man a ten-day head start. He really hadn't thought that through at the time and, at the end of the day, all he really had left were the files he'd taken from Grace Springfield's office. Those files were privileged and confidential and, legally speaking, that confidentiality didn't end with the death of the client, Lance Rockwood, alias Pierce Locke. So, in the end, Teffinger had no concrete admissible evidence of what Lance Rockwood had done.

So he went to work behind the scenes.

At considerable risk, he told his former enemy John Stone about the stolen files and his resulting dilemma in that he couldn't use them in court.

Stone made it clear that he didn't want Jori-Ray in prison.

He wanted the guilty party in prison.

Now that the guilty party was Lance Rockwood, everything was different.

Stone made a number of discreet telephone calls and ended up in several private meetings with the district attorney and others.

In the end, the district attorney, in conjunction with Jori-Ray's lawyer, Alabama Avery, filed a joint motion for exoneration, with an affidavit by Teffinger attached under seal. There, Teffinger gave his professional opinion that Jori-Ray was innocent, based on Lance Rockwood's MO of kidnapping and ransom, including several documented cases where

Rockwood was subsequently tied to those other scenes with finger prints and/or DNA. In Teffinger's opinion, Lance Rockwood killed September Stone as part of a kidnapping and ransom plan, not Jori-Ray Rose. He also based his opinion on "other circumstances" that he wasn't at liberty to reveal, meaning the stolen files.

The judge granted the motion.

He also granted a second joint motion that Jori-Ray would not be prosecuted by the district attorney's office for escape.

Jori-Ray was finally exonerated.

Teffinger ended up on the cover of Rolling Stone Magazine with his hands covering the breasts of pop star Likki Lix and the Caribbean waters sparkling behind them. So far, no one had figured out who he was, which was kind of cool.

Sophia Cruz had turned down the heat now that Teffinger had brought Kimona over from Haiti and had moved her in with him. Sophia made it clear though that she was still waiting in the wings if he ever changed his mind. In the meantime, she was dating a guy on the Colorado Rockies.

Teffinger looked at Kimona.

For a brief moment he flashed back to that horrible night on Haiti when he cut her down from the poles, not knowing if she was alive or dead.

He flashed it off.

"When we get to Moab, remind me to buy some beer."

She slapped his ass.

"As if that's something you'd forget."

98

It was a beautiful September night in Paris.

Jori-Ray and Alabama strolled hand-in-hand on the cobblestone walkway next to the Seine. Neither one of them cared if anyone saw them. Minds were a lot more liberal here than in the United States. Life was a lot easier here. It gave Jori-Ray peace of mind to be out of the country, even though she was technically and legally free. She was still afraid deep down inside that the truth might be somehow be discovered and everything would somehow come crumbling down.

"Do you think he'll ever figure it out?"

Alabama chuckled.

"Teffinger?"

"Yeah."

"No. Not in a hundred years. You need to stop worrying about it. Even if he did, there's nothing he could do about it. It's called double-jeopardy."

"You're sure?"

Alabama squeezed her hand.

"Positive, relax."

As always, the topic tightened Alabama up inside. She quickly replayed everything, now for the hundredth time, just to be sure, once again, that she hadn't missed anything.

She recalled meeting Jori-Ray for the first time after the

woman was charged with murder. She recalled Jori-Ray telling her, "Let's get this out of the way straight off. I did it. I
killed her. If that's going to be a problem with you, let me
know now."

Then the woman kissed her on the lips.

She recalled how she and Jori-Ray had fallen in love with
each other, how they concealed it so well, and how they'd
secretly touch under the defense table, ever so lightly and
fleetingly, during all those horrific days of the jury trial.

She recalled finally coming up with a plan for Jori-Ray to
escape.

Then she came up with a plan to exonerate her.

She knew a voodoo woman in Haiti named Janjak.

Teffinger, the detective in charge, also knew this same
woman.

She contacted Janjak to see if she'd participate in a little
harmless scheme if Jori-Ray agreed to do a ritual.

The woman agreed.

They lured Teffinger to Haiti, deposited him on an island
with Janjak's help, and made him listen to their repeated pro-
tests of innocence. The plan, at first, was to point Teffinger at
John Stone as the culprit.

Then something wonderful happened.

Alabama got a call from Grace Springfield, a former friend
from law school, who told her in confidence about receiv-
ing detailed information from a client who called himself
Pierce Locke, which was a fake name, not that that mattered.
The man was providing her with all kinds of incriminating
evidence about kidnappings he was performing. Grace was
worried that he was eventually going to kill her. She wanted
him caught and in jail if possible. Or, alternatively, she wanted him dead.

Alabama came up with a win-win scenario.

Grace would add a new false file to her collection, one that implicated her client in the murder of September Stone. They'd entice Teffinger to steal the files under the guise of finding information on the Mary-Ann White case.

Teffinger would go after the client.

He'd believe that the he'd actually and finally caught the real killer.

Eventually he'd catch him.

There was a danger that the guy might have souvenirs or admissions or documents regarding the other crimes but not the fake September Stone crime. That might cause Teffinger to have second thoughts. It all worked out though when the guy ended up destroying all his files, which, as far as Teffinger knew, also included the September Stone file, which never existed.

What didn't work out is that Teffinger didn't actually catch the man and get him off the streets. Luckily, he'd made an attempt on Grace's life and she was ready for him.

So that ended okay.

Luckily, Teffinger never expressly talked about September Stone when he finally met Pierce Locke, aka Lance Rockwood. Everything could have crashed right there and then.

And equally lucky, Teffinger found a way to exonerate Jori-Ray even though he really never had any admissible evidence. Ironically, he even got the father, John Stone, to help him.

Brilliant, really.

The whole thing.

Absolutely brilliant.

99

A Batobus came down the Seine River and meandered past, filled with gawking lookie-loos all excited about checking off something from the old bucket list.

Jori-Ray squeezed Alabama's hand.

"So you don't think he'll ever figure it out?"

"No. No way. He'll never figure it out." She smiled and added, "Just don't kill anyone else. I don't think we could repeat this a second time. You want to get some wine?"

"Sure," Jori-Ray said. "You know, when I think about it though, there is one loose end that keeps bothering me."

"Like what?"

Jori-Ray hesitated.

Then she looked at the woman and said, "You."

Alabama chuckled.

"Me?"

Jori-Ray nodded.

"I love you with all my heart and that's the honest-to-God truth. But you had to have known this day would come sooner or later."

She pulled a gun from her purse, stuck it in the woman's side, and pulled the trigger. Alabama dropped to the cobblestone and stared at Jori-Ray in disbelief.

"I'm sorry," Jori-Ray said. "I truly am."

Then she kissed the woman on the lips, rolled her into the

river and walked away.

"Now you're free," she told herself.

And it was true, too.

It was there, all of a sudden, in every fiber of her being.

Freedom.

Absolute, one hundred percent, freedom.

At last.

THE NEXT MORNING

100

There was a little café on Champs-Elysees that had great strawberry croissants and wonderful sidewalk seating. It was one of Jori-Ray's favorite places in the world to people-watch, wake up and stare at all the hustle and bustle, which she wasn't a part of and hopefully never would be.

Luckily, her favorite table, by the far end, was unoccupied.

This was the last time she'd ever sit there.

By evening tonight, she'd be in Bangkok. The ticket was in her purse. She'd made the reservations four days ago, party of one, one way.

She ordered blueberry-cheese pastries and chocolate coffee and freshened up her makeup while she waited.

The day was beautiful.

There wasn't a cloud in the sky.

The flight wouldn't even have a bump.

She was already packed.

After a quick stop here, she'd check out and grab a cab.

Then, poof!

Gone, baby.

Gone.

Her clothes were comfortable—loose jeans, a T-shirt and sandals; perfect for a long flight and a new life.

Two teenagers meandered up the boulevard with their

arms around each other. The boy let his hand slip down to the girl's ass as they passed by. She didn't move it away. Why should she? That's where it went when they had privacy. Why be a hypocrite about it?

A man sat down at the table next to hers, alone.

He was big.

He looked intense.

He looked like a cop.

He looked as if he was concentrating on not looking directly at her, but always looking in her general direction, as if keeping her in his peripheral vision.

She finished her breakfast at normal pace, then paid and walked off without looking at the guy. Three blocks later, at the entrance to her hotel, she used the reflection of the glass to look behind her.

He was there.

Thirty steps behind.

About the Author

Jim Hansen, a trial attorney and a novelist, also writes as R.J. Jagger. He is the author of the Nick Teffinger thrillers, the Bryson Wilde thrillers and the Nicole Stone thrillers. In addition to his own books, he also ghostwrites for a popular bestselling author. He is a member of the International Thriller Writers and Mystery Writers of America.

All of his novels are independent of one another and complete within their own four corners. Read them in any order.